MW00577618

Olive
Days

Olive
Days

a novel

Jessica Elisheva Emerson

COUNTERPOINT | CALIFORNIA

OLIVE DAYS

This is a work of fiction. All of the characters, organizations, and events portrayed in this novel are either products of the author's imagination or are used fictitiously.

First Counterpoint edition: 2024

Library of Congress Cataloging-in-Publication Data
Names: Emerson, Jessica Elisheva, author.
Title: Olive days : a novel / Jessica Elisheva Emerson.
Description: First Counterpoint edition. | Berkeley, California :
    Counterpoint, 2024.
Identifiers: LCCN 2024010042 | ISBN 9781640096530 (hardcover) | ISBN
    9781640096547 (ebook)
Subjects: LCGFT: Novels.
Classification: LCC PS3605.M474 O45 2024 | DDC 813/.6—dc23/eng/20240304
LC record available at https://lccn.loc.gov/2024010042

Jacket design by Nicole Caputo
Jacket images © iStock / Mariia Bondarenko
Book design by Laura Berry
Watercolor strip © Adobe Stock / Alex

COUNTERPOINT
Los Angeles and San Francisco, California
www.counterpointpress.com

Printed in the United States of America

10 9 8 7 6 5 4 3 2 1

For my Oklahoma love

Contents

PART II

PART III

Olive Days

I am forbidden to be alone in a room with a woman; God has mandated.

Rina said something—what he didn't know—but there was an edge to her voice. She was holding something out to him, a gift, and he could smell not perfume or sweat but *her* and it was so different from—so much more liberating than—the scent of his wife.

No, a person mandated. I only let myself believe it was God.

PART I

1.

Yoni had just turned three, but Rina's thighs and stomach were still lumpy; nothing had reverted to curves, not like after Shosh was born. She was examining the pucker of a thigh when David proposed adultery, although he refused to use the word. "A wife swap?" Rina said. It was the deviant bit of budding summer when observant Jews, unencumbered by holidays, have long stretches of time in which to practice something other than devotion to god. The purple jacaranda superbloom of May was waning, but wildflowers stretched from cracks in the concrete sidewalks, searching for a sun that would shroud itself until July. David didn't like the word *swap*, either. Her thigh rebuked him with a quiver; she did not look up. "Temporary," he said. "A trade. A spouse trade." He emphasized the word *spouse*, as if parity made it okay.

She looked up at David—already his prematurely silver hair pomaded into peaks and skullcapped at 5:00 a.m., his cheeks slick with the oil he used to calm his old pockmarks—and then back down at her thigh, ran her fingertips over the divots. So tedium came on this fast. They'd been going to the gym. He knew she was trying, he went with her each morning, after she dropped the kids at her mother's, before he went to the office, just to make sure she went, maybe.

Haredim didn't work out at mixed-gender gyms, of course, but many modern Orthodox like Rina were devotees, especially of a particular mega gym in her Pico-Robertson neighborhood of Los Angeles. She wore a knee-length skirt over her spandex, just like the rest of them, but didn't cover her hair. The wig hair never moved as it should, and headwraps yellowed with sweat. The unmarried girls pushed the boundaries of cultural modesty with tight shirts and sheer skirts, flaunting their hair, which they didn't have to think about hiding until marriage. Skirt hems caught in pedals at spin classes; men's ritual fringes bounced and twisted beneath T-shirts. David and his friend Brandon jogged side by side every morning, fringes swinging in tandem, and Rina—on an elliptical in the row behind listening to podcasts—had not imagined that the men were talking about tiring of their wives, about swapping them.

"You're bored?" she said. She was bored, god she was bored, but she never let herself think about it. She rubbed lotion onto her leg.

"It's a thing that people do. It helps marriages last," David said.

"You sound like a child," she said. "'It's a thing that people do.' I've heard all about their parties. The neighborhood's muddy secret."

Shavuot was weeks earlier and they were fine then. She looked at his reflection in the mirror—his smile always looked uncertain, not just in uncertainty—and smelled her hands, wishing Shavuot was still on them. It was one of David's favorite holidays because it celebrated Ruth, the first Jewish convert. He wasn't a convert, but ba'al teshuvah, a Jew who grew up nonobservant and initiated strict observance in his own life. A choice she once cherished.

Rina also was fond of Shavuot. As a child she loved standing on a stool in the open-windowed kitchen and helping her mother form tray after tray of savory bureka pastries, and the woody smell and spicy sap of her hands after she spent the morning hanging eucalyptus branches in shul. Still, now, when she bit into a bureka, she relished the crackling brine of the farmer's cheese with a leafy, astringent undertone, the remembered taste of eating them by the handful with unwashed hands. With guilt she would sometimes exhale after a bite; her ever-sanitized children would never know the taste of branches and sap.

At its core, Shavuot wasn't a religious holiday, and she was discovering that, at her core, she wasn't a religious person. Rina's father, and also her husband, stayed out all night on Shavuot learning Torah, but it was just sacerdotal buffer between the bookish and the world beyond. Shavuot was about the grain harvest in ancient Canaan, a celebration of nature and effort and bounty. In Israel, kibbutzniks filled their tractor bucket loaders with grain and showered the harvest down on revelers. In America, there wasn't what for wives to do other than make burekas and cheesecake and wait for their husbands to trudge home in the early morning, weary from study.

Until the gloomy Tisha B'Av in late summer—which came with all sorts of prohibitions against bathing, swimming, traveling, eating, drinking, or fucking—Rina and David were bound by nothing more than weekly Shabbos observance and, nearly as Jewy, regular Dodgers games. The weeks hadn't been great, but they'd been fine. The same.

"We don't think—I don't think—that Leviticus forbids it," David said. Rina moved her hands from her nose to cover her eyes. "There are rules; Brandon and Anat have already done this. There are rules not to do these things with people who live within three blocks. So it shouldn't be your neighbor."

"You can't make it halachicly sound. 'Thou shalt not commit adultery,'" Rina said.

"Well," David said. "What is adultery? If it's consensual, does it count?"

✴

It happened a month later, just after her thirtieth birthday. Rina could not remember giving her consent, but she hadn't mounted any particular dissent. She knew what Jewish law said—knew the source material, the rabbinic code, the commentaries—and he was wrong. She didn't care about the law, was unconcerned with sin, but it galled her that David tried to justify instead of saying *I want.* They'd talked about it every night, so much that a week out there was nothing left to say. David could not see that once his excitement ruptured in a rabid five-minute breach, his conscience would suffer and she would be punished.

Shabbos goes out late in the summer, so the couples, four total, gathered a little after nine on Saturday night. They met in Brandon's living room, a half mile from Rina and David's townhome, past the neighborhood's small circular park with its dry fountain and Mexican fan palms. Only half a mile away, but the townhomes and dingbat apartments on stilts gave way quickly to Spanish-style homes with archways and red tiled roofs, here and there a 1920s Tudor with small brown turrets, star jasmine vining up brick mailboxes. They went to Brandon's because he had one of those Spanish-style homes, four bedrooms built around a courtyard, plus a guesthouse. His four children were at their grandparents' for the night. Music played from surround-sound speakers, guitar and accordion, the nameless music of nameless bistros, and Brandon's wife, Anat, served red wine. Rina squinted at the little charms on the stem of each glass, at her own pewter flamingo; whether or not wineglasses were confused at the outset seemed beside the point.

There were bowls of nuts on the coffee table and a bottle of Scotch with tumblers, though no one had reached for it yet. The men talked about what the shul might do with the empty lot it just acquired (playground, event hall, parking lot) and the women, Rina included, talked about their children. It was the type of night where pints of ice cream and a board game might materialize.

Brandon cleared his throat and smiled at the floor.

She and David were the only first-time swingers in the room. Brandon and Anat went over the ground rules, and it sounded as if they were talking about a recipe cut from a newspaper and variations on how one might prepare it.

The apple bread is sublime, but don't use a jelly roll pan as the recipe suggests; put it in a loaf pan. If you and your evening partner decide to practice sodomy, a fresh condom must be put on prior to beginning and another fresh one after. You will find an ample supply next to the bed in each room, along with a trash bag.

The thing about sexual anomaly, Rina learned from a college boyfriend who liked her to shock his balls with a homemade device, and from David the first time he put a household object in her ass, is that in the moment it doesn't feel like an anomaly at all.

After the rules were delineated—god she hoped not to invoke most of them—partners were chosen by drawing names out of a hat, which had been a subject of debate between Rina

and David in their negotiations. David seemed not to care
which wife he drew. Rina didn't care who he drew, either, every choice an equal cheat, but she would rather have known
in advance who she'd be letting inside her. They'd received a
list of potential invitees two weeks earlier and part of the deal
was being willing to switch partners within any of the couples on the list. It went unspoken that this was a good-looking,
good-smelling sort of club. No one was too zaftig, no adult
acne, untended teeth, halitosis—none of the lumpish features
that sometimes came with limited gene pools. Probably everyone would vote for Obama again. They were young, even
though they all had children. They were living in a time of
the young; there was a feeling among them that they could
do anything they wanted. Elect a Black president, carry tiny
computers in their pockets, adopt nuanced views about Israel/
Palestine, serve quinoa for Shabbos, paint pottery instead of
going to medical school, commit adultery with good-looking
friends and call it kosher. She'd agreed to anyone but, please
god, not Russ Mordka, not Danny Farber and his cartoonish
mouth.

The women's names were typed on index cards, each
folded down the middle and placed in one of Brandon's upturned black fedoras. The men would choose after the women
left the room. Rina reached for the whisky, although no one
offered. Maybe it was there to ease her and David, newcomers, into the night, or maybe they'd all be drinking it later to
forget, but Rina drank a triple in one swallow. Anat gave a
small cough, as if she'd downed it herself, and Rina saw that
her drink had commanded the attention of the men. After all,
why were they there? She poured another.

Each wife was assigned a bedroom by matching index cards taped to the bedroom doors, and it did not seem

happenstance that Anat was assigned the private guesthouse. Rina followed the others down the hall, each with a charmed wineglass, until she came to the door that said RINA KIRSCH. She entered without a word to the others and closed the door of her room almost all the way to wait for a man. The men coming to the women like this, as if a question; like the Haredi custom of a husband laying his kippah on the pillow of his wife's single bed on the evenings he wanted sex.

She'd been assigned a guest bedroom—bed-in-a-bag linens and museum-shop art prints—instead of one of the children's rooms, thank god, but as she looked at the column of dim, brown light in the crack of the door, she felt like a child who'd been tucked in and left to wrestle with her own imaginings. Oh, to put on a nightgown, curl up under the comforter, and hope. Was this how her own children felt at night, glad to be left alone with their thoughts, yet hopeful that someone would come redeem them?

She sat on the edge of the bed and put her hand under her skirt. She'd shaved her legs just hours before—a rarity these days, although David made it known he preferred her groomed—but already they were stubbled. Would he care? She'd also used plenty of deodorant and the dregs of a bottle of white gardenia body spray from under her bathroom sink. Would she taste bitter? She flushed in spite of herself and her own primal scent mingled with the gardenia.

The pile of condoms on the nightstand loomed. Also, a trash bag and a tube of K-Y Jelly; it was brand-new, thank god. She looked away from the nightstand and its threats. She was the prettiest wife in the house, and David must have known it. He was an ass man, though, always said he preferred a runner's ass, a thing Rina did not possess. Would the wife he drew be surprised at his proclivities? Would he be brave enough to break into the lube? She looked back at the table. Anat had put a single daisy in a bud vase next to the lamp, and this small act of hospitality and suggestion of romance baffled her more than anything. She picked it up and was staring at its bruised and drooping petals when Brandon walked in the room and closed the door behind him with a click of the button lock. Oh god, she should have peed first.

Already tipsy, she finished her wine in one long pull and smiled. Brandon was a little younger and shorter than David. He didn't have the kinky, sallow hair or under-trimmed goatees of the other husbands in the hat. He wasn't as handsome as David, but charismatic and muscled, with a frat-boy, devilmouth smile that put people, including Rina, at ease.

"I've never had a blonde. Does the rug match?" he said. She pulled down her skirt waistband to show him, no reason to draw it out. He gave a low whistle. "You're going to remember this," he said.

The rest of his words—he talked a lot, sweet and filthy— were lost in the breathy, hour-long tangle. She came twice, something that hadn't happened in all her years with David. The first was immediate, as if her body was spiteful. She was naked, but Brandon's pants weren't off yet. She was trying to focus on his arrowed hip muscles, trying to figure out if she was supposed to take his cock out for him, when he put two fingers inside her and it just happened. She wasn't expecting it so she couldn't silence it, and her cheeks burned when Brandon laughed.

The second time was more like giving up. She was exhausted from all the times Brandon had stopped and started, tired of the taste of herself on him. She suspected he wouldn't let go of himself until she came again. She closed her eyes and imagined her virile college anthropology professor on top of her, a frequent strategy; imagined her favorite NPR host even though she only knew his voice; imagined another woman on top of her, tits flattened against hers; imagined David sitting in the corner of the room watching and touching himself, wanting in.

Fuck him. How could he think this would help anything? How could she let herself be traded?

Finally she held Brandon's hips in place until she accomplished it, then he did, too, then it was time to go home.

2.

From sundown to sundown on Yom Kippur—a weak day from fasting—Rina was at war. The holy day began, as always, with the early evening absolving of all promises and obligations; "Our vows shall not be vows" repeated three times. She wrenched her wedding band around and around, unable to focus on the Hebrew letters in her machzor, and pulled her overlarge hat lower and lower over her face in the hopes that the others crowded into the women's section of the temple would assume she was gripped by a spasm of righteous devotion.

Each time the congregation uttered *Avinu malkeinu*—our Father, our King—Rina thought not of god but of her husband, of their marriage, of what he might owe her for his conduct. They never argued about whether to swap again because, just as she suspected, David grew jealous immediately, jealous and full of regret that had nothing to do with Rina, or what he'd asked of her. Intellectually she knew he owed her amends, but she couldn't dislodge the stone in her heart; it thudded that she had it backward. David had given her a choice. She had failed by saying yes. She needed to ask forgiveness if the marriage was to survive.

But the marriage felt unrecoverable to her. It wasn't that she wanted to love another man, ever, it's that she wanted to feel loved by another man; Brandon's need for her had been so great that even though she loathed him and what they had done, she had remembered what it was to be needed for something other than the practical. Blot out our transgressions, the liturgy begged. But whose transgressions?

Sometimes she wished David would have an affair, an actual affair, just to free her of this partisan guilt. And sometimes she thought he was having an affair, with Brandon's sister, Aliza. David had known Aliza through Brandon for years but had gotten to know her better through their yoga classes and a book club. Aliza was tall, with knobby features and a genuine face. Rina knew her through occasional proximity in the women's section at shul and a handful of holiday meals. After David joined the book club, he'd asked Rina to set Aliza up on a number of blind dates; an unwed woman of Aliza's age in the community began to take on a patina. That ended after the club read some sappy love story, and David spoke of Aliza increasingly and then, abruptly, not at all. Rina didn't think they were having an affair, didn't think he would ever have an affair, but god that would make her choices easier.

Rina couldn't imagine David ever perceiving her as an eshet chayil again, a woman of valor, or how she could come to see herself as such, even though he kept giving her the blessing each Shabbos, kept saying she was adorned with strength and dignity, wisdom and righteousness. And even now, he looked unburdened in the men's section; she could see him through the mechitzah, shuckling as always, nodding to friends. He hadn't asked her for forgiveness in the lead-up to Yom Kippur. Had not, in fact, said anything about the swap other than express his jealousy, asking several times if she'd liked getting fucked. The swap hadn't been her idea, but she was the one left with no path toward atonement.

⚹

The holy days—the apex of Jewish absolution—came and went and still she was consumed by the idea that it was her fault, that she'd brought it on herself. One autumn morning, with a tinge of woodsmoke in the air from the recent wildfires and Halloween decorations in the stores taunting those who didn't celebrate, she dropped the kids at school, then went to David's office to seduce him. Maybe a blow job against her husband's leather books would provide some relief. Maybe it's what he'd needed all these years while she was nursing babies. He was shocked and pleased, but he couldn't get hard. Other than the rote Shabbos sex and sometimes in the morning when it was least convenient or appealing to her, David had little appetite since the swap. She liked to think his unexpressed guilt over the swap is what made him limp; it would have been almost a relief if the other wife was so good for David that he was daydreaming about her all this time later, no longer interested in Rina. But she suspected it was Aliza who was haunting his libido, because he woke up early to go to yoga every day and, Rina assumed, was rubbing one out in the shower.

He also did yoga in the living room Shabbos afternoons. He called it his practice, which made it sound like a job. He'd been doing it for years and recently rededicated himself to yoga, but he didn't seem to like it: after sessions he was always impatient, and whenever he talked about his practice it was to criticize Rina for not allowing him enough space for it.

After he gave up, zipped his pants, and slumped into his office chair, Rina—flailing—suggested she try yoga with him.

Maybe it wasn't a weekday blow job their marriage needed but vinyasa. He rebuffed her.

"Go back to painting," he said. "Yoga is mine."

He'd been bugging her about taking up a creative habit for months, and now he homed in on painting, although she hadn't painted since college, not really. She gasped a little, dizzied by his meanness. She loathed herself for no longer painting, for ever allowing herself to have painted.

David would grant her a divorce if she asked. He'd have to. His involvement with a community campaign to fix the plight of agunot, women whose husbands wouldn't grant them a Jewish divorce, would compel him. He had railed against their neighbor Seth Hartman for chaining his wife to a dead marriage, and even led the boycott against Seth's plumbing business. But Rina would never ask. A divorce for what? The humiliation of having once been traded? She wasn't raised to divorce; she didn't know anyone who divorced. Besides, she could not imagine sending her children off every other Shabbos, Yoni still practically a baby. Whose soft heads would she brush in the last moments before candle lighting?

She thought, as she often did when overcome with guilt, about the weeks after Shosh came into the world. Glorious, sleepless weeks full of love and magic, the only time in her married life that she'd been afraid to be apart from David, days that faded into nights that faded back into days, eating French fries every afternoon for two weeks with an irrational fervor, nursing her baby as she sat on the toilet and tried and failed to take her first postpartum poop. Crying and crying. Kissing Shosh's dry little lips. When she held her newborn, Rina would get hopeful flashes, intense bursts of feeling that perhaps her life could still be everything she'd dreamed while pressing down on her eyelids as a child: full of color

and electricity and the unknown. Full of god, maybe. But she
knew it was her body and not god that made Shosh's immaculate ears and eyes and toes. Knew that women's bodies were
more divine than any starring character in the old stories.
She stayed up late into the night gazing at her baby, holding
her tiny hand, and thinking, If I made this, there is nothing I
cannot conjure. She would be filled, for brief moments, with
a godliness that brought a completely foreign thrill. Maybe
that's why people kept having babies, to chase the thrill. She
would sit and nurse Shosh and be infinite. There must be
other ways to manifest this feeling, she would think.

She kissed David goodbye on the cheek, lips numb, the
same way she also kissed his secretary on her way to the elevator. Shabbos was coming and she had her weekly volunteer
shift at a community center, then plenty to prepare.

Tomorrow would begin the eighteenth Shabbos since the
swap, the eighteenth pummeling of her soul, or whatever it
was that formed the nameless parts of her. The sweetest day
of the week, the deepest joy of the Jews, a time for families to
revel in each other for twenty-five hours, a respite from work,
the day when she was doubly commanded to let her husband
put his pulpy hands all over her. To procreate. To give him
the third baby he wanted, and then the fourth. Rina did not
feel commanded, but oh, she felt the weight of the commandments, the leaded burden of the doubling.

It was hard to remember what had been so charming about
David. He'd always had a knack for fumbling certain social
situations, a hint of meanness in his humor, an acidic edge.
Had she found all that exotic after the soft, circumspect the-
ology students and expressive, compulsive artists of college?

Whether because she was pretty or amenable when she
chose to be or a little scary for the alacrity with which she

spoke her mind, men in college put up with almost anything from her. It was a game she used to practice by playing devil's advocate, being petulant, requiring high maintenance from a man, and telling white lies. Until she got tired of all the attention, the lack of being challenged no matter what ridiculous thing came out of her mouth.

But from the beginning, David argued back. About politics. About science. About books she read, the movies they saw on dates, the way she balanced her checkbook, which brand of toilet paper she bought. And especially religion.

He was already ba'al teshuvah when she met him in a friend's backyard sukkah the October of her senior year. He was keeping Shabbos and holidays but not yet wearing a kippah and tzitzit daily. She was years away from her first spark of atheism, but her views had started a shift toward believing things were unknowable. He was only a year older than her, in his first year of law school. It was a wonder that someone who was questioning could have fallen in love with someone who was deciding, but it was that they were both in flux, both enraptured by motion and change. They adored each other for what they were not yet, and it was beyond their early-twenties imaginations that they would feel differently when it came to pass.

Back then he was fascinating in his straightforward zeal for all he'd never experienced, which was plenty. They'd gone to Paris together for a wedding of one of David's distant cousins. His relatives put them up in separate cheap hotel rooms in the Marais, grumbling over the cost of two rooms. They were sleeping together already, but David, on his journey toward a Juris Doctor degree and piety, was adamant. She'd been to Paris twice—once with her family as a stopover on the way to Israel and once on a college trip with friends—and wanted to show him all her favorites: the Orangerie, the Kandinsky Library at the Pompidou Centre just down the way from their hotel, Bar Hemingway at the Ritz, Angelina, Shakespeare and Company. Though he'd never been to any of these, he was more entranced by the small things. The café au lait in the hotel atrium at breakfast. The way the hot and cold water came out separate spigots in the tub. The morning after they arrived, he walked to a soap shop to buy bubble bath and blue, moon-shaped bath beads and then drew her a bath in the freestanding tub in her room each night, making a science out of balancing the hot and cold. She didn't like baths, and the oil-filled beads made her feel like a little girl, but it was impossible to say no to his washing and shampooing, to the unexpected revelation of tenderness. On the last night, he climbed in the tub with her, produced a razor, shaved her clean, then carried her to the humble bed to service the fruits of his efforts before going to sleep in his own hotel room. She remembered thinking then that he was a generous lover, benevolent, even if she hated a shaved cunt, hadn't given her consent to the grooming.

Still, the days of that trip were some of the best they ever had, and she was nostalgic for it before it ended. She sketched the visual intricacies of the shoulder-high rows of flowers in Monet's garden on their excursion to Giverny, the mesmerizing taffy-pulling machines at the Bastille Day festival, and the line of men pissing into the gutters on a rainy day. David read American newspapers at the museums and marveled at the sheer quantity of pigeons and the metal tubes of mayonnaise at the kosher café near the Arc de Triomphe. She met his extended family and ignored his goofy Francophilia—after the first night out he encouraged her to pronounce *champagne* "correctly" even though they couldn't afford the kosher

Laurent-Perrier and drank only beer—and the long silences that tended to happen at lunch after their orders were taken. Her family cautiously ate dairy food at non-kosher establishments while traveling, but he wouldn't even buy a pain aux raisins from a street stand, so they took their meals at the handful of kosher restaurants in the Pletzl and dotted throughout the Right Bank.

When they boarded their homebound flight, she had a raging urinary tract infection from all the sudsy baths, and the also frequent and somewhat prickly feeling that David would someday be her husband. Less than a year later he was, but by then the David who washed and dried her in Paris had reduced to an amalgam of quirks she guessed she could live with, including the burden of personal grooming. He paid for the waxing sessions. After all, he paid for everything.

She, too, was reduced. To the creature that she was bred to be, the creature she'd aspired to as a child. Her life was altogether linear. It would be twenty-two years of becoming followed by maybe seventy years of being. Nothing ever happened that didn't fit into the template; her life in no way resembled art. This happened, then that happened, then the other thing happened. A child who delighted in her family and the divine, a teenager who performed without flaw in school, a young woman who went to college for a degree she knew she'd barely use, a bride who got married at the same wedding hall as all her friends, a hall that turned over every six hours, a hall that recycled flowers between weddings and served pats of margarine wrapped in golden squares of foil and had a chicken soup–stained satin chaise in the bridal suite but still charged four hundred dollars per person. She packed her novels into plastic bins beneath her bed, produced children, collected recipes, vacuumed the baseboards. And then, and then, and then. No wonder she was a champion list maker. Her life was a tally that only came into focus in the semicolons, the only mystery—and it wasn't much of one—what happened in the brief betweens.

Sometimes the softness returned to David's voice, or tenderness to his gestures, but it was not often directed at her. These days, it was often directed at Aliza. Rina was never self-conscious until the wife swap, until she sat waiting for a man and sweating and wondering about the stubble on her legs, the stretch marks like snail trails down her thighs. Now she hated passing the full-length mirror. The shape made by her stomach and ass in profile reminded her of a grandmother's body, of her grandmother's body. Made up of curves, sure, but stodgy, flattened in strange places, full in others. Utterly tradable.

The eighteenth Shabbos.

Like every Friday, she woke well before the family to do the dusting and wash the hard floors. Yoni always woke by five, a leftover habit from nursing until he was nearly three. Shosh liked to sleep later, but on Fridays Rina woke her at six and together they made the challah dough. This is why Rina did the shopping on Thursday—most of the women in the community shopped on Friday morning—so she would have fresh eggs for the children to crack open for the dough early Friday morning. Shosh was already an expert at fishing bits of eggshell out with other, larger pieces of shell. She sat Yoni on the counter, held him with one hand, and let him crack an egg and smash the yolk in his little hand, which she then promptly washed and sanitized. Rina loved to watch them together like that, Shosh on a step stool and Yoni wobbling on the counter. Shosh broke the eggs one at a time into a small bowl used only for that purpose, checked for any spots of blood, then slid each clean egg into the large wooden mixing bowl, the only treasure Rina had claimed when her grandmother died.

"Here you go, mummi," Rina said, using her favorite nickname, the one she used for both children when no one else could hear.

She handed them each a piece of dough. Yoni squished and poked his, but Shosh—not yet five—slapped it down expertly and started folding it over itself.

Preschool ended early on Fridays for Shabbos, and Rina always waited to braid and bake the challot until Shosh got home. Weeks that she made large batches for company—most weeks—she let Shosh take the small piece of dough for the burnt offering and place it carefully in the back of the toaster oven to smolder. While the loaves baked, she let them mash old bananas to make quick bread for Shabbos breakfast, let them eat more chocolate chips than they stirred into the batter, mopped the floor again after Shosh sprayed the pans with nonstick spray and inevitably missed. These were her favorite moments of Shabbos, her only true moments of peace, the moments before Shabbos even started and she had her children and their smiles all to herself.

The rest was shrill and strenuous. From the frenzy to be ready in the moments before sunset—David rushing home and foul, the children bathed and dressed, being ready for company to arrive or ready to walk to someone's house, leaving time for the men to daven at shul, being sure the food was done and tomorrow's lunch put up to warm overnight, carefully choosing which soda bottles to open so that you didn't break a commandment by twisting off a top that had been stamped in such a way that opening it would break letters apart in an act that could, who knew?, be like writing, thus forbidden on Shabbos—to the spilled juice, piles of dishes, and crumbs in every corner of the house that she'd just spent the day emptying so it could be filled again with the detritus of a day of rest.

The sweeter Shabboses of her childhood had been a pretense, all intense fondness from her parents during the blessing of the children, the best food of the week, games, books, napping next to her grandfather on the old couch in the den. Oh, the unscheduled hours—while the adults were at prayer—when her unfettered mind could burst free, free and full of electric colors and unnamable cracklings, like when she would press down hard on her eyelids, let them go, and then watch her nerves firing like it was a show. When they were guests in other homes, it was a wild freedom, reckless almost, to explore foreign rooms and foreign yards, marveling at the bookshelves and toys of others, pirating through the citrus trees that lined the tiny backyards, hiding behind pleated paper window coverings with a crayon and daring herself to break Shabbos by making a mark.

At sleepaway camp, her friends thought Shabbos afternoon was boring. They played cards and ate cold cuts and complained, but Rina exalted in the unstructured hours, often spent in the orchard. A counselor had shown her both how to reach up through the bird netting to pluck the ripe apricots that had already detached, and how to smash the downy green husks of the fallen almonds so that the drupes could be peeled out whole. You couldn't pick fruit on Shabbos, but the orchard offered its gifts to her just the same. Mostly she gathered olives. There were only two olive trees, but they were old and fruited madly in the early summer, and the campers were all taught how to cure olives as part of a Torah study on purity. On Shabbos afternoons, alone in the grove, she would gather the fallen ones, rolling them onto a flat path between tree furrows, and then lay on them in her Shabbos whites. She napped on the yielding olives and hot earth, with mulch in her hair, the small brown ants and garden spiders crawling over her apricot-sticky hands, waking to drowsily consider the light filtering through the trees, the ripeness. She rolled around a bit before she stood, the olives like beads in a massage chair, and then went back to her tent to strip off her shirt and examine the patterns of their purple juice. She always wanted her mother to ask how it happened, those landscapes of stains, but her mother never did. They would head straight to the laundromat when she and her brother re-turned from camp—her mother didn't want that much dirt in the machine at home—and her mother would cluck her tongue and say, "Well, they wouldn't fit next year anyway," wash her Shabbos whites with the color load, and fold them neatly. Later they would be torn into rags. Six summers Rina created masterpieces on her Shabbos whites—in the later years, she was worried her mother would be able to perceive the lust in the striations—until their rag bag was only strips of purplish white cotton. Her last summer in the orchard, the summer she thought her body might actually implode and shrivel to a pit if someone else didn't get inside it, she was so taken with her olive bed that she pressed a large, round one into her mouth and bit through it. A lasting bitterness.

At college, out in the California high desert, there was a large grove of olive trees that gnarled along the paths of the original quad. They were never smashed along the pathways because the landscape crew gathered them as quickly as they fell. Sophomore year she worked up the nerve to ask a gardener what they did with the olives and had to translate her question into her academically perfect but clunkily spoken Spanish. "¿Las usan?" she tried, after the gardener said they weren't for him to keep. No, he told her, they went to the county green waste facility. So she started a sort of club—although they had no charter or official designation—and Thursday evenings in April and October she and a growing number of students would harvest the olives. Eventually she had textile wonks from the art department weave baskets that they could leave fastened to the trees, and the landscaping department was so fond of her that they donated two old wooden ladders. She painted aceitunas down one side of each ladder and zeteem— the Hebrew word—down the other, and they left them in the grove year-round, like a shrine.

The club members weren't her friends, exactly, because she didn't exactly have friends in college. No one who understood her actual life, how it was constructed around ancient laws, how it was predetermined even though Jews believe in free will, how who she married would decide who she would be. They thought her skirts were bohemian and her Yiddishisms—despite her masterful code-switching, certain speech constructions just broke through—some sort of an East Coast accent.

Rina trained them in how to cure the olives. Late on harvest evenings they would sort the olives by size and color, tossing aside any shriveled fruit, any with beige olive fly scabs. Without washing, the olives went into a salt-and-vinegar brine, and wouldn't come back out again until it was almost time for the next harvest. The brine needed to be changed as the olives fermented. She often charmed some boy into doing it for her, dangling her legs off the edge of a kiln while he dumped the old brine into the paint drains behind the visual arts building.

At the beginning of her senior year, an engineering student

named Peter suggested they try making oil. The whole club gathered to blend and press the harvest, but Peter only took Rina into the lab where they ran it, bit by bit, through a centrifuge.

"How did you think of it, gathering the olives?" Peter asked. His hair wasn't long, not like the boys from the art department, but it was shaggy around his ears, unkempt like his fingernails. He was a person who didn't have enough time to braid and bun and style. His vanity was tied to his braininess. To be that free, Rina thought.

"It broke my heart to see the trees but not the fruit," she said.

"Do you go through all of life looking for what's absent?" he asked and moved closer to her. He didn't smell like cigarettes or weed. He smelled only of olives, acrid and thick.

"Negative space, sure," she said. "But mostly I'm just a noticer."

"And worth noticing," Peter said, then leaned in to kiss her. Their fingers were slippery, and his hands left oil smudges on her cheek and in her hair as they kissed.

"At camp I used to make myself beds of overripe olives," she said, with her hands wrapped around the back of his neck. "I would roll in them and watch the light change in the sky . . ."

"I don't care," Peter said, pressing into her. He said it in a gentle voice, a voice heavy with fondness, but to Rina it was like erasure. On the one hand, at least he said it, said what he meant, didn't pretend he cared about what she thought or how she was formed. On the other hand, it was her fucking olive club. She didn't go back to his apartment with him even though, figuring she'd never be as sovereign as in college, she almost always went back to their apartments. She never tasted the finished olive oil. And she never told anyone else about the camp orchard.

Even in childhood, Shabbos had been lonely. At home she trained in the kitchen alongside her mother, learning to shape gefilte fish loaves and braid bread and salt soup. Of course, her brother had no such training. All those hours in the orchard considering the sun, all those moments hiding behind the curtains at neighbors' homes and the tangerine trees in their yards, all those hours pretending to be asleep in the den and wishing someone would notice she wasn't. Once, at a nearby home for Shabbos lunch, the children had been playing hide-and-seek and no one could find her. The adults got involved with the search, then her parents became worried, then they began searching homes and yards up and down the street. Shabbos was nearly out by the time the host found her, found her because he heard Rina sobbing. She'd climbed up to the very top shelf in a utility closet and stayed up there four hours, with her arms wrapped around her knees, dedicated to the premise of the game and her sureness that if anyone really knew her, they'd know just where to look; if anyone really knew her, she'd deserve to be found.

She supposed being busy and exhausted was better than being lonesome and bitter. This is what she told herself as she swept crumbs on her hands and knees on the eighteenth Shabbos after her husband traded her.

There was a thing people said: Do the Jews keep Shabbos or does Shabbos keep the Jews?

A foolish expression. It was she who kept Shabbos, kept it for all the Jews, kept it despite the bait and switch that happened once she was in charge of keeping it. The wives kept Shabbos and the wives kept the Jews. The doughy, tradable wives up to their elbows in cold, gray sink basins, the waxed and stretch-marked wives. In this way, it was said, this way of keeping the Jews, women earned a holiness men could never possess. So instead the men possessed the women themselves, kept them. Let them, like lumps, smolder into ash.

3.

MARCH 2012

Thursday afternoons Rina's mother picked the children up from preschool while Rina finished her long-standing weekly volunteer shift at the Jewish Family Services Center under the guidance of Anshel, the director, a Haredi rabbi, ultra-Orthodox, with a tufted beard the color of peanut shells and altruistic blue eyes. For years she'd been doing this with only a few words exchanged between Anshel and her, although they were often personal conversations, transcendental even. Maybe in a different life she married someone like Anshel, cerebral and unselfish. Maybe in this life they could work around the traditions and the prohibitions and be actual friends, outside of a volunteer shift. These maybes, for years there had been maybes; there was always a question with Anshel.

The affair began on Purim; she wasn't there to volunteer but to deliver mishloach manot, and the staff, who typically worked on Thursdays, had the holiday off. Perhaps it was delirium: she'd been up until 3:00 a.m. two nights in a row, preparing gifts for family and friends. This year's theme was s'mores, and she put together ninety-seven packages of kosher graham crackers, kosher marshmallows, and chocolate, tied up in yellow and orange cellophane to look like flames, each hot glued to a pile of sticks she'd scavenged on four straight morning outings to Griffith Park, each with a personal, hand-written note. She'd let Yoni play with extra cellophane and Shosh tie up two dozen packages, only to redo her work later, untying and retying raffia until her fingers were covered in tiny, bleeding paper cuts. After the mishloach manot were complete she slept for three hours, woke early to take the kids to school, then began cooking an elaborate Purim feast of lentil-and-tomato soup, stuffed turkey breast, butternut-squash-and-mushroom pot pie, green beans with pistachios and date syrup, and three varieties of triangle-shaped haman-taschen pastries.

The margarine was folded into cookie dough and left in the fridge for hours while she fixed the meal. Then she made the fillings, two on the stove and one in the mixer. The dough had to be rolled out over and over again, and for this she used an unopened Coke can—more precise than a roll-ing pin. She cut three-inch circles from the dough, dolloped in the filling, pinched the edges together to form identical triangles. It was muscle memory, folding the hamantaschen, and after she brushed them each with egg wash, successive batches of perfect cookies went into the oven: lemon filled for David, peanut butter for Shosh, and cherry for Yoni. She preferred apricot, but there was not time. She had to clean the house, finish sewing costumes, print the delivery lists, then strain the plum brandy she put up after last year's Purim, so David could pass it around at shul; her slivovitz was famous.

On Purim morning, David and the children took the mini-van and half of the mishloach manot, and she took David's car and the other half. While they were out, dozens and doz-ens of families—children costumed and sometimes adults, too—delivered their own themed baskets to Rina's doorstep, wives weary from the strain of remaining jubilant on this, the most joyous festival. Less than a month later all remnants of these gift baskets would be junked in order to prepare the homes for Pesach, a process that made the Purim preparation seem as easy as cold pizza for breakfast.

If one resents a mitzvah, has one still fulfilled it?

She circled the block three times before finding a place to park near Anshel's office. She brought in the gift basket and then collapsed onto his shoulder, something strictly forbidden. They'd never even brushed against each other accidentally in all these years. He took a step backward and a sharp breath before circling his arms around her. They stood for a moment in the embrace, the voltage of years of unacknowledged tension flowing between them. Then they were on the floor. Just like that. The very reason the rabbis forbade contact: they became degenerates in the time it took him to undo the buttons of his shirt, a cautionary tale.

What did either of us do?

After the first time—flat against the industrial, low-nap carpet behind his desk, Rina on top, something Anshel had never experienced before—she cried, thinking of the night with Brandon nine months earlier, and Anshel, alarmed, pulled at his beard and said, "What did I do, what did I do?"

At first it was an emotional emancipation, all of Anshel's attentions.

She developed a habit of showering at noon on Thursdays, washing her hair and putting on a pair of underwear that she otherwise only wore on Shabbos. Most weeks she arrived to Anshel smelling of olive oil soap and drugstore crème rinse, departed smelling of undone laundry and an office supply store. The sex took no more than twenty minutes, usually in his office, sometimes in a car in the lowest level of the garage. She spent the balance of the hours at busywork: slipping papers into the complex filing system she'd devised, entering new clients into electronic spreadsheets, photocopying flyers for the lobby, and doing small bits of bookkeeping. If they were short-staffed she helped in the adjacent soup kitchen, mixing barley, canned beans, carrots, and ketchup into the giant vats of cholent for the community's sick, for their hungry. There wasn't always brisket, so she melted a little chicken fat in a pan and poured it into the vat. Her neighbors shouldn't feel like no one cared how their food tasted. She would often pack up bags of discarded eggshells for her compost pile at home and the little mouse that raided it daily. She turned the compost pile fervently, although she had no garden to fertilize.

She itched to tell Anshel about the night with Brandon, tell him because he'd listen, because it would free her, a little at least. She couldn't stand the loneliness of no one knowing that her body had betrayed her, her husband had betrayed her, her marriage would never again be fine, never be the godly repose promised by the liturgy, by the rabbis, by the children's books, by her own parents grasping hands at the Shabbos table as her father chanted that because of his wife, he lacked no gains. And what was Rina in the wake of this betrayal? She couldn't trust her husband, couldn't trust the tradition, couldn't—in particular—trust her body. She wanted so much to tell Anshel how her husband insisted someone else slip inside her, and then became angry over the slippage. But he could only take sin in measured doses.

Three months into the affair, Anshel asked if she'd ever cheated before.

"I'd have told you," she said. David still insisted that night hadn't been adultery, perpetual betrayal.

"Was it me or circumstances?" he said.

They were sitting on the floor, clothed but still sweaty, with their hands clasped and their backs against his desk. He put his black hat back on, but she took it off again, set it on his seat.

"I could ask you the same."

"You," he said. "It never crossed my mind before to . . . you know . . ."

"Say *fuck*. It's just a word. It's the right word."

"I'd never thought of being with someone other than Nechama."

"Bullshit."

"You don't have to impress me with your language."

"Before you were married? Before Nechama was picked for you? You must have thought of fucking women then?"

"I was trained not to think of specific women."

"What did you think of when you jacked off?" She saw revulsion in Anshel's face.

"Do people talk to each other like this?" Anshel asked.

Was it possible that he had never talked about masturbation with anyone? His father, even?

"They do."

"I don't with Nechama."

"I know," Rina said, and she tried to pull her hand away. He held on. "I'm sorry."

"Can you tell me I'll be the only one?" he asked. "Even if it's not true? We could go on like this forever."

Already the affair was simulating marriage. She'd broken the commandment, sinned wildly, but was still stuck with monotony, bickering, routines, emotional work.

Rina thought of a piece she painted her first year out of college, a self-portrait looking into a mirror, reflected dozens of times, reflected until she was just a dot of paint, with one small detail changed in each shrinking portrait, down to the final blue speck, the only blue on the canvas.

"We could not," Rina said, and she kissed his hand in order to withdraw her own. This would not be her redemption.

4.

AUGUST 2012

The community college class was David's idea. In the weeks after the wife swap—at the first real beacon of distress between them—David began calling their problems *her* problems, and decided it was about her lack of a creative outlet.

"You need something like my yoga practice," he said. "To bring peace into your life. So we can keep growing our family." He started saving the junk mail, circling listings for weeknight weaving and stained-glass classes at places that didn't sound real, like the West L.A. College for Adults and Los Angeles Academy of Figurative Art.

"These are craft classes, not art," she said.

"What's the difference? It will bring you back to what's important."

Rina tried to make the problems disappear, but she could not take a stained-glass class in a park. Anyway, she balked at the thought of being out of the house one night every week. She hated leaving the children with a babysitter; how could she go without putting them to bed once a week? And she could not imagine losing one night of work each week. When would she clean, launder, cook, prepare for Shabbos?

But also, she remembered the thrill of college, the freedom of hunching over an easel in a studio.

At eighteen she'd left Los Angeles to attend the University of Redlands, less than a hundred miles away and for only three and a half years; after the intensity of Jewish day school, it would have been difficult not to graduate early. While her high school classmates were busy at yeshiva, studying in Israel, or attending schools like Brandeis and the University of Pennsylvania, Rina earned her double major in art history and comparative religion at a sleepy desert liberal arts college alongside students who went on to seminary, and not the Jewish kind. Although in a technical sense she kept Shabbos throughout her undergraduate days, she spent most of those Saturdays—slow, dark, and full of expensive kosher cold cuts because she couldn't cook, spend money, drive, or turn on lights—in her extra-long single bed, in the grips of psychedelic mushrooms and gentile boys with names like Blaine and Kyle.

She had studied alongside students who now showed in large galleries. Alongside a woman whose video exhibit took over all of Union Station for a month. Another who painted portraits of celebrities for an important magazine. One of her professors was a famous Los Angeles guerrilla artist who excoriated politicians in portraiture. One night after she'd graduated and returned to L.A., she'd gone out cementing with his crew, bucket slung over her torso, hitting all the electrical boxes on north La Brea. It was almost midnight and the galleries, furniture stores, and cafés were long closed, but a handful of people filtered to their cars from a comedy club with eighties sitcom stars on the bill.

"Why are you here?" one of the professor's regulars, a woman with a very long pink ponytail, asked Rina. They were in front of a half-block-long antique and junk store, full of old movie props and marquees. A cage full of live birds wouldn't stop squawking.

"He was my teacher. I just . . ."

"You an artist?"

The caged birds weren't parrots, but Rina felt mimicry in their endless cries. *Are you an artist? Are you an artist? Are you an artist?*

Rina didn't know how to answer, and instead pulled a small painting from her backpack. It was a thumbprint, vivid with fluorescent paints, the pattern of the ridges forming an anatomical heart.

"Cute," the ponytail said, shoving it in her own back pocket. Stung, Rina went to hang posters across the street—where at least the birds were muted by the rush of occasional traffic going god knew where—and thought about all the paintings within her, how much she hated and loved the thumbprint, how she wished she could have showed the ponytail the unfinished piece in her bedroom, a painting of last summer's foothill wildfires with the burned-out husks of horse stables whose occupants could not all be liberated. She was stunned to receive a call from the woman a few days later.

The ponytail made a few introductions, and Rina paid her own room and board—until she and David were married—by selling paintings, some large like the wildfire piece and some in the tiny slots of the art-o-mats in Hollywood bars, made from old cigarette machines. She hadn't reached out to the ponytail since before her wedding. Somehow, she'd lost touch with all of them, could barely summon the smell—browning bananas, Chinese takeout, and wet newspaper—of the dive bar at Hollywood and Highland where they used to gather. She left all that behind, trading it for a closet full of old sketchbooks and oil paintings that she hadn't let David frame.

(He'd wanted to when they first moved in together.) Later she resented the negative space that could have been occupied on their walls, all plaster, finger smudges, old bits of tape, the colorless manifestation of her meekness.

In the months after the swap—after the failed blow job and before she ever collapsed into Anshel and devolved into sin—she started fixing David a strong old-fashioned when he returned from work each day. She bit her tongue, sometimes literally, when he forgot to wipe the kitchen counters, snapped at her in front of the children, or put them in front of a cartoon and tossed her on the bed to attempt morning sex on days when she was already running late for car pool.

A little more than a year after the swap, one broiling night in August not long before the kids went back to school, he brought home a thick catalog for a community college near the beach and went through it page by page with her. "My treat," he said, as if he didn't pay for everything anyway. There were painting classes, real ones. She relented.

When she told Anshel she'd registered for an art class, he had little to say other than his broken-record stream of "I love you" and the unhelpful "I wonder, do you think Nechama would like to take an art class?"

The oil painting class she wanted to take was offered on Thursday evenings and conflicted with her volunteer work at Jewish Family Services. Quitting would create more headaches than she was prepared to deal with, so she settled for a Wednesday-evening watercolor class, a medium she found imprecise and dainty.

On the first night of the course, she fixed fruit compote and cucumber salad, cooked chicken schnitzel and roasted sweet potatoes, then arranged three covered plates and left them with warming instructions. She was too uneasy to eat and left as soon as David returned from work, unsure how long the drive would take. Even though she grew up in Los Angeles and knew the way, she turned on her GPS to navigate to campus. She circled it twice before she found where to park, and then sat in her car for ten minutes because she was far too early. This much time to herself made her nervous, and so had the unaccustomed evening driving; she wasn't able to clear her thoughts. Would the other students know she was Jewish? Did she still know how to paint? It said all materials supplied, and she had paid the materials fee, but what if she was supposed to bring something anyway? Would there be an icebreaker? Her stomach churned. The walk from her car to the building was balmy and she stopped to check several map kiosks along the way. Would she show Anshel the paintings? Would she show the children? How would they fall asleep without her there to do the right things in the right order? What would the house look like when she returned? She bought a Skor bar and a Diet Coke from a vending machine and slipped them in her purse in case there was a break. She and Anshel never texted—she was grateful for it—but sitting in class waiting for the professor she wished she had someone to chat with. Anyone. What should she do with her hands?

She was the youngest by far in the room and was relieved when a man walked in who was near her age. He wasn't particularly tall but walked like a tall man, long strides and straight torso. His hair wasn't short but it wasn't shaggy, either, very black, and thick and textured like her son's hair, with errant licks. His large eyes made him look gentle, and she moved her purse off the stool next to her on impulse, watched him cross the room.

He came to the easel next to her and smiled; he was older than she'd thought, much older than she was, that or the years hadn't been easy. But his skin was smooth under dark stubble and actually the years looked like they had been easy. He took a framed painting of a grapefruit tree out of his large briefcase, set it on the easel, then dragged the easel to the front of the room, leaving his bags beside her.

"This is not a watercolor," he said, pointing to the grapefruit tree, which sat between two stucco houses along a driveway. His voice was deep and even, without salt. "But I thought I should show you that at least I know how to paint a little." The students laughed. "You are in the right place. Welcome to watercolor. If I could ask you each to take off one of your shoes, we'll get started."

The professor went to a supply closet and an older woman at the other end of the classroom jumped up to help him distribute heavyweight paper and pencils. Rina took off a shoe. The classroom was warm, but the concrete floor was cold when she put her foot down.

"Tonight we're going to sketch for about an hour, take a short break, paint for about an hour, and then come together to talk a little about the class. Some nights we'll do two paintings, but tonight we'll start with just one. Of your shoe. Sketch it however you'd like, and I'll come around and work with you. That's how this will go each week."

The cauldron of thoughts that occupied her before class dissipated, but the nervousness remained. She had to nervous pee, but it seemed like a rude choice in a first class, so she held her pencil mute over the page and sketched with her legs crossed, determined to last until break. By the time the profressor made it to her desk she was sweating, but she'd produced a sketch and it was alright.

"You're trained?" he said and moved his hand along her pencil contour on the page.

"I'm rusty," she said. It came out in a murmur, and he smiled. The lines around his mouth stretched from his nose to his chin. His teeth were very white, but not particularly straight.

"You are trained." He said it to himself, looked her up and down, then looked her right in the eye. She wanted to think he held her gaze for an extra moment, but then he was at the next easel, leaving behind a heavy, laundered scent.

She peed at the break, ate the Skor bar while she called home to see if the kids were down, noticed that the professor made a call at the far end of the quad. Probably to his wife; he wore a thick, gold ring with a blue stone set in the middle.

After the break they painted more and then they reviewed the semester plans for the course. His bags were still sitting next to her, and when he was ready to hand out the syllabus, he called on her.

"Ms . . . ?" he said, pointing at her.

"Kirsch," she said. "Rina Kirsch."

"Like the liqueur. Ms. Kirsch, would you take the stack of syllabi from my bag there and hand them to your classmates?"

She did, then sat back at her easel and looked at her own copy. His name was Will Ochoa. He'd forgotten to introduce himself to the class, but it was there at the top of the page, typed out, and again at the bottom, his signature. A community college teacher signing a syllabus, she laughed a little, under her breath, then looked back up at him. He was goofy and self-important and scattered and so utterly resplendent.

How could she even feel such things? Maybe it was because of David or Brandon. Maybe after four months the thing with Anshel wasn't a rebellion, not anymore. Maybe it was too much to hold, and each new thing looked lovely compared to the last. Maybe she was letting an unattainable handsome man—a man in authority, a man she never would have met at any other time or place—carry her imagination away from adultery and ungrateful morning sex and sin and drudgery. If the men in her life defined her, then, oh, god, why couldn't it be a man who spoke like this, smiled like this, made things no one had ever made before?

She knew he would take the place of college professors and NPR hosts in her closed-eye fantasies, take their place against her volition.

She hadn't been looking for a daydream; she hadn't even been looking for a practice. The class was David's idea.

5.

AUGUST 2012

Rina arrived a few minutes early the second week, but not so early that it would seem presumptuous. She tried to sit casually in front of an easel, changing positions several times. She couldn't stop thinking there was lipstick on her teeth.

When Will arrived, he went to set down his satchel on the desk, but he glanced at her. Or she thought he did. He spent a few moments arranging items, smiled to himself, then came right over to her. Or was it a smile?

"So," he said. "Welcome back."

"Hi," she said, in a quiet voice.

"Are you from here?" he asked.

"Yeah, my whole life. Near Pico and Robertson," she said. "You?"

"Orange County, but I've been in Topanga for a while."

"Oh," she said. All the possibilities she'd considered for the evening were throttled by her inability to think of anything interesting to say.

"If there's time at the break, I'll tell you about the time I lived in New York for a year. But fair warning, it's not a very nice story."

"I love New York."

"Oh, I did, too," he said.

The evening's assignment was to paint a plant. A small succulent sat in a cardboard tube at each easel, but Rina was full of anticipation for the break and couldn't devise a pleasing composition or focus on the cotton paper hanging from her clip.

They stood behind a large concrete planter during the class break. The garlicky scent of Los Angeles weeds mingled with star jasmine in the air. He smoked a cigarette and although the smell made her nostalgic for college, she worried the smoke on her clothes would work its way into her children's lungs when she tucked them in later.

He told her about his time in Brooklyn, about the cash-only French bistro two doors down from his brownstone near Fort Greene, the tiny yard where he could smoke and set up an easel in the mornings, the sooty and mangled view of telephone lines that somehow connected in the right places, how he'd just settled into seasonal dark and checking weather reports when his wife insisted they move back to California.

"You have kids?" he asked. "I think you're . . . you're Jewish, right? I figured you probably have kids."

"Two," she said. "Littles."

"Well, I got married when she got pregnant the first time," Will said. "Not long after the wedding she had a miscarriage and sort of blamed me for it. But then, in New York, she had another miscarriage and hid it from me. She was making me go to Alcoholics Anonymous meetings because I was drinking a bottle of Cab Franc at night, and meanwhile she hid a miscarriage from me. And then she said we had to move back to California. So we did."

She couldn't understand why he was saying these things

to her. She wanted it to be because they were the same; she wanted it to be that he perceived something in her, some kinship. Or maybe he had some woman in every class, some woman he charmed, reeled in with sadness and amber eyes and compliments. He finished talking, but she didn't know what to say. A little bit she wanted to match him story for story. Tell him about being traded. The silence went on a beat too long, and she could only process the last thing he'd said.

"An entire bottle of wine every night?" she said. David got drunk in the shul basement on Shabbos, drunk off a few shots of vodka. She couldn't imagine a bottle of wine every night. "Did you . . . it's not my business, but did the meetings help?"

"I went to them, that's all," he said, waving the hand that held the cigarette, but there wasn't any defense in his voice, no hard edge. "I did it because my wife asked me to do it. It was a tough time." He took a deep breath and Rina knew he was about to tell her something important; he had a way of stopping to breathe that she had already learned. "It felt like my heart stopped when she told me about the second miscarriage. She kept it a secret four months. The air went the color of ash when she told me. Do you know?" he said to Rina. "It's determined at conception, male or female? But I don't know if I lost a son or a daughter. With the first miscarriage I could grieve piecemeal. When the cramps started. When the bleeding started, garnet over the alabaster bathroom. At the doctor's office holding Holly's hand. Tending to her in bed. Sobbing by myself in the bathroom after she went to sleep . . ."

He drifted off as if he'd lost the place in his story. Rina reached out to touch his arm, but withdrew her hand before it reached him.

"Did you ever have a miscarriage?" he asked.

"I literally don't know what to say," she said. So strange,

the way she was at ease with him in some ways, yet her nerves stood all at attention when he was near.

"No, I'm sorry," he said. "I shouldn't have."

And then it was time to return to the classroom.

During the second half of class, as Rina worked on diminutive emerald rosettes, she considered that maybe he wanted stories in return. So after class, she told him a story about Israel—he knew nothing of Israel, of the gold-pink glow of Jerusalem stone at sunset or the smell of bread and mint in Tzfat—about the night she slept in a sand pit carved out of the dunes at S'dot Yam. That night on the beach, between her sophomore and junior year of college, she'd been so consumed with heartache over a boy that she hoped the waves would take her in the night, but instead she woke up next to a young soldier—the sun coming up behind them—and they sent postcards to each other for a year before he was paralyzed in a freak training accident and she stopped writing because she didn't know what to say.

"I'm sorry I didn't know what to say to you before." She got brave enough to brush the cuff of his flannel shirt in apology, just for a moment. Then not knowing what to do with her arms, she crossed them. "This class is better than postcards."

"Not better than a night in the sand dunes, though," he said, and for the first time there was an edge in his voice. She checked her watch; she could stay for maybe ten more minutes before it would be suspicious. Maybe.

"I was married once before, actually," Will said.

"Oh yeah?" His candor was bizarre, but her sense of growing power was thrilling.

"I was practically a kid. I married a girl from my brother Frank's Raza Unida circle. Until she took off for Arizona, to be with the other husband I didn't know she had. We annulled."

Rina had never heard stories like this and felt a sort of crazed drive to keep up.

"I tried cocaine once in college," she said. "I snorted it right off the thumb of a boy who wanted to be a priest. It felt so good that I never spoke to the boy again. Because I wanted so much more."

Will looked at her a long moment, right in her eyes.

Their wild flow was terrifying, but she kept talking and asking, almost against her own will. She wanted to say every thought she hadn't said out loud for eight years, the thoughts she feared she would take to her grave, the dumb frustrations that every other dumb housewife suffered. The raptures of motherhood, the dread.

She told Will about Shosh and Yoni. She wanted to tell him that she was a god, but of course she would never tell anyone about that. The exhilaration of creation was barbing at her consciousness, though. She was ready for the chase.

Ten minutes passed, then twenty, then thirty. She sent a quick text home: *Class ran late.*

He told her about his Dylan, two and a half and maybe on the spectrum, how Will thought he was therapy-bullied, how his little boy had brought poetry back to Will with his first, yelping gulps. Poetry had been important to him as a young person, he said, but years before Dylan's birth it had disappeared. Not by choice or design, it just no longer narrated his thoughts as it had for so long.

Rina didn't want to stop listening but kept checking the time on her phone.

"I have to go," she said. "Please remember to tell me about the poetry next week? I'll be a little early."

"Remind me," he said.

The week was a blur to Rina, a cliché from a dumb book,

nothing remembered and no goal other than getting to the third class. The last steps into the quad were unbearable, the agonizing fear that he wouldn't be there, the uncertainty of what to say and how to be if he was. He'd arrived before her and pressed a piece of paper into her hand. They picked up where they left off, as if the week had never happened.

"The first poem I ever memorized," he said. "Corky Gonzales."

She read it quickly, something about excommunication and blood.

He always had the ability to memorize things easily, he told her, and his brother took advantage of it in many ways when they were young.

"When Frank became active in MEChA in high school, when I was still in middle school, he had me memorize songs of revolution"—Will rattled off poets with names Rina had never heard—"writing about mestizo liberation. Frank put me on a pedestal, literally. People clapped and cheered and pounded on the Formica tables. In high school, in college, then after, I was always trying to get laid by reciting poems to women."

Rina flinched, and he saw it.

"I'm not telling you to get a rise," Will said.

"I know," Rina said. The truth was, she wasn't focused on the women he'd tried to fuck, just dejected that he'd pressed a piece of paper into her hand instead of reciting a poem.

"I'm telling you because no one else knows. I was a lonely, scrawny kid with an underbite. Girls didn't notice me. But then I tell them a poem and I get a blow job. I told them stories about how I did it, lied. Like, my parents didn't let me read after lights out, so I had to memorize stuff and recite it to myself. Like, I was in love with my high school English teacher sophomore year and did it to impress her. Like, I was dyslexic and memorizing saved me from embarrassment. My stories got more nuanced with time. They garnered sympathy."

"And whatever else," Rina said.

"Sometimes I told them it was synesthesia, but it wasn't that, either. I told them and they didn't know what the hell I was talking about, but I think you do."

"Colors come to life?"

"I can't help it. I could see syllables and line breaks like colors."

"Still?" Rina said.

"Your voice, like it's written in grass."

Rina looked down; they hadn't complimented each other like that. Was it a compliment, even?

"Anyway, I learned the European masters to piss off my brother. Early American poets. Contemporary writers of love and sex and other apolitical subjects. My mind had no limit and I memorized huge quantities of poetry. It became my guiding voice. My own thoughts, staccato. Everything in my world was someone else's metaphor. And then sometime in my thirties it stopped," he said. "The words were all still there, filed neatly in my brain, but they no longer surfaced. I had no one to whisper them to until Dylan's birth brought it all back."

This is how it went. While he set up the class, during the snippets at the break when other students were drinking their Diet Cokes and coconut waters, the redefinition she was desperate for took shape in small moments and coy glances. Other students glared at her on the quad, and she reveled in it. Sometimes he took a small packet from his pocket, ripped it open, and sprinkled powder onto his tongue. Sal de uvas, he said, antacid. Such an intimate thing to do, letting it dissolve on his tongue, right there in front of her. After class she told him about the olive grove; as long as he was showing his tongue, she might as well tell him the memories to which no one else would listen, the lonely purple stains of her soul.

"I wish I had known you then," he said, just before they parted for the evening. "In your olive days. I wish you could remember everything about the shifting light." Her olive days. It was as if a plate broke inside her then, in her solar plexus, a beautiful breakage, like her body had no end to the amount of wreckage it could hold. Like the breaking itself was her creating something.

The time went so fast. Another week a blur. The children, yes, yes. The dishes and the minivan. A whole week consumed with one thought: maybe if she said the right thing, he would whisper poetry to her.

For the fourth class he assigned a still life. He brought a bouquet of olive branches, drooping in a little vase of water, three twigs with shriveled fruit weighing them down. Rina hadn't worked so hard on a piece of art in a long time. There was so much on the line, her remembered creative self, the feel of a brush in her hand, Will, a certain liberty. She stayed in during the break, shading the leaves with a tiny brush. She wanted to be with him, outside there behind the planter, but even more she needed to impress him. She glanced out the window and seethed at the student he was speaking to in her absence, then let her jealous fuel spill onto the paper.

At the end of class she packed up slowly, just like every other week.

"Rina?" Will said. "Would you do me a favor if I asked?"

"Literally anything," she said, then tried to laugh off the immediacy of her reply. She shifted her weight, looked from him to the ground. Back to him.

He sucked in his breath but didn't speak and she thought, Oh my god, I read it wrong. I've been so foolish. There was an inner flash that said, You're out of control, and she almost turned and walked away, but then he spoke.

"It feels like we've known each other forever, right?" he said. "Sorry if that sounds stupid."

It did, it sounded stupid. It had been only a few weeks.

"I hate watercolor," she blurted. Anything to correct course.

He laughed and one kind of tension started to deflate.

"I hate it, too. I'm teaching it this quarter because the woman who's been doing it for years is off in Peru for six months."

"What do you usually teach?"

"Figure painting. And advanced oil."

She looked off into a corner of the ceiling.

"So if my husband hadn't signed me up just when he did . . ."

"David signed you up?" His hand twitched. She saw it.

"Thank god," she said.

"Thank god?"

"I don't mean it, about god, it's one of those things you can't stop saying."

"Thank goodness your husband made you sign up for a class you hate?"

"I don't hate the class," she said. "Obviously."

She felt his gaze locked on her face, and it was unbearable. These weeks of trading confidences casually, almost obsessively, and now she could hardly speak a sentence, could hardly look at him for even a moment.

"I told you I used to paint with oil in college," she said. "I'd like to take your other course."

"I don't know how much I'd teach you. You have loads of talent."

She tried his eyes but couldn't hold them long. He must've been at least a decade older; a decade felt like a lot.

"You don't have to say that," she said, but she felt pleased with herself, her olive branches, her shading.

"Oh, I'm never wrong about students. Or about how much salt to add or the distance I can get away with once the gas light comes on in my car," he said.

"Walk me to mine?" They hadn't ventured past the quad together yet, and when he hesitated, she quickly recanted. "Never mind." She hoisted her purse onto her shoulder, started walking. An idiot, an idiot spinning out of control.

"Hey, no," he said, catching up in two long strides. "I was just standing here trying to figure out if it was appropriate to ask you this favor. Please, let me walk you to your car."

"What's the favor?"

"I'm involved with this art show for the city. It's not related to the college. Every quarter we have to find four panelists. They can be anybody related to the arts. An artist, an administrator, a benefactor. Just someone who understands the principles and is willing to donate an afternoon and show up downtown. You're not judging them; you just look at their portfolios and then have a conversation with them. Offer feedback. I think you'd be perfect. Good for you, good for them."

"Will you be there?" she said.

"I will, but it won't be like class. We won't have time to talk."

"I'll do it," she said.

"The thing is, it's tomorrow. Someone dropped out yesterday and they asked me to fill it, and I wasn't brave enough to ask you until just now and I feel it's too late."

"I'll be there," she said. "Would you be able to give me a ride?" she said, then added quickly, "I get nervous parking downtown. David says I'm a terrible parker."

"Text me your address," he said. "Will David care that you're doing this?"

"As long as the children get picked up and dinner is on the table, he doesn't really seem to care what I do with my days. He assumes I'm busy because he's always busy, always working. And anyway, I am always busy."

"But not too busy for this."

They exchanged numbers in the middle of the garage.

A moment later, in front of her minivan, keys in hand, she turned to him, the fluorescent garage lights glossing his eyes so she couldn't be sure what he was thinking.

"Do you invite a student every term?" she said.

"Don't do that. Just. Be there tomorrow."

"Don't avoid my questions and then tell me what to do."

"Okay, I'm sorry. I'll be there tomorrow. At ten. I hope you'll come to the curb."

She climbed into her car, closed it, and buckled herself in. Will gave a limp wave as she pulled out of the spot and dread ascended; even her inner voice was too ashamed to pipe up.

David, this class had been David's idea. He couldn't just leave her be?

6.

She loved her little shtetl of a neighborhood, with the beige dingbat buildings over open carports, sundials affixed to apartment facades, waist-high hedges, and the sun-battered minivans lining the narrow streets. The jacarandas were bare by now, craggy and dry. In anticipation of Will's arrival, she saw with fresh eyes the old glass brick panels and the slatted metal blinds, the peeling sunset-colored paint on dozens of front walkways, and she was embarrassed. He would hate the faux-rock building sidings and the junk piled on stucco balconies. At the same time, she was proud. My people, she thought. Their roses and porch gardens; their upright pianos in the windows; their open windows behind white-painted bars wafting out the smell of fresh couscous, chopped peppers, fried onions, dill, the sour yeasty promise of dough rising, a smell like Rina's earliest memories, ingrained, sweet, barely remembered.

He was driving a black Land Rover and the first thing he said after she climbed in was "This is my wife's car, more comfortable," and that made for such an awkward opening that Rina didn't know where to go from there. She'd imagined saying, "Well finally, here we are," or "Brilliant" in a bad British accent, or "Now, where were we?" seductively. Instead she buckled up and settled into the smell of car wash spray and wet Cheerios.

All the words that flowed so freely in the evenings, they all dried up. Maybe this had been a mistake.

At the gallery, Will and an older woman gave the panelists swift instructions, a page of notes, a tour of the facility. Rina would meet with six artists for twenty minutes each, after spending ten minutes with each of their portfolios. Three before lunch, three after lunch, and the other panelists would all meet with the same folks. There was no outcome, just three hours spent in the pursuit of art.

All her advice felt phony, but she delivered it as if she'd done it a hundred times before. After all, she had a degree. After all, Will chose her despite her lack of experience. He'd seen—he saw—something in her. Rina liked one artist in particular, a very young woman whose abstract landscapes were painted on glass.

"Can you define what you're trying to evoke?" she asked the young painter, and then leaned in with a serious face, serious but she hoped kind, determined not to show she was an imposter.

The woman looked terrified. "The wildness of a new frontier," she said, like a question.

For lunch the gallery brought in sandwiches full of salami and cheese, nothing she could eat.

"Not even a bag of chips?" Will said.

"It's not that I can't," Rina said.

"Wanna take a walk?"

"Don't you need to eat?" she said.

"I'd rather hear about your olive days."

They walked outside. He went left; she followed.

"There's nothing left to tell," she said. "I rolled around in olives and ruined my clothes."

"Did you ever make a painting about it?"

"No," she said.

They arrived at a narrow lane, with two-story buildings painted brightly, all chalets and balconies and flower boxes. It made her dizzy, the contrast with the twenty-story buildings that lined downtown, the dingy oatmeal color of the surrounding blocks, the folding metal gates and graffitied windows that reminded visitors that these streets were home to many, and that the many were restless.

"A movie set?" she said.

"The loading dock for an old department store. And a college before that. And now, it's like fake Florence. Cappuccino?" he asked, and she nodded. They sat at a sidewalk table of a café, in the shadow of skyscrapers.

She didn't order anything. His drink came out quickly.

"Okay," she said and leaned in. "I'll tell you something about olives, but it's not true and it's not about me."

"The opposite of what I was hoping for," he said and smiled broadly.

"Have you heard of Mount Sapo?"

He nodded.

"Oh, well then never mind. It's a good story though, right?"

He scrunched up his face.

"No, tell me."

"Not if you know."

"I don't, actually," he said. "I hate not knowing things. Nine times out of ten you don't get caught, nodding along. Saying you've heard of an artist or an album or some stupid wine someone is drinking. I would learn way more by saying, 'No, I haven't heard of that.' But I'm habitually unable. And

I've never said that out loud before. So save me from this humiliation and tell me about Mount Sapo."

She'd been in a confessional in a church once, in Pisa, on a family trip, not so far from a street that looked something like this one. She imagined being in the booth with him, his long legs bent under the bench.

"It's where the word *soap* comes from. Sapo. The ancient Greeks did animal sacrifice on Mount Sapo. Wood ash from the altars would mingle with the animal fat and wash down the mountain. And the women who laundered their clothes at the bottom of the river noticed everything got much cleaner. That's how soap was invented, but the story is totally false," Rina said. "There's no such Mount Sapo. The Greeks didn't sacrifice whole animals, only what was left after the meat was eaten and the fat rendered. Some people say, actually, it was the runoff from the olive oil production, that's what mixed with ash and flowed down the river. That ancient olive oil production gave us the first soap. From something greasy came something totally pure."

"Where did you learn so much about olives?" he said.

"But that's false, too," she said. "Soap was probably invented in Babylonia, way before the Greeks. And the word comes from the German, where soap was used heavily before the Dark Ages. But in Aleppo they have been making soap from olive oil for millennia. So yeah, olives."

Will had been smiling into his undrunk cappuccino, and now he stirred the foam with his index finger and held it out to her. She licked the foam off without thinking, and then felt the blood rise in her face.

"We're late," he said. "And just so you know, I'm going to tell everyone that story exactly as you told it to me."

The second session went quickly, and every time Rina was

deep in conversation, she remembered the taste of milk on his finger, the salt underneath, and lost her focus. Soon it was time to go, time to climb back into the Land Rover.

She'd already been such a fool, staying late after class, telling her dumb trivia facts, riding in his wife's car with her purple sunglasses sitting on the dash, taking his finger into her mouth. She might as well find out what she wanted to know, what she'd been too afraid to ask all these weeks.

"How long have you been married?"

"Why does it matter?"

"You haven't talked about it other than when you told me about New York."

"Well, it's embarrassing. It's not going exactly as planned."

"Like?"

"Like I fix Holly's favorite tea every morning and I do all the laundry and leave little drawings in her purse and she throws them away without saying anything to me. And I just keep trying."

"Does she try?"

"She doesn't like to hang my art in our home," he said. "It's hard to get past that. But yeah, I guess she tries."

Maybe all this should've made Rina feel good, but her stomach was sour from the milk foam and speaking bitterly about his wife was still speaking about his wife. Rina wanted to know the secret depths of his paintings, not that his wife wouldn't hang them.

"I'm sorry," Rina said, as he pulled up in front of her house.

Will put the car in park.

"She sleeps curled in the corner of our bed, her body pressed against the wall, like a brush of my leg will bruise her. Is this what you wanted to know?"

"I only asked how long you've been married."

"Long enough for all that shit," he said.

"It sounds like my marriage. Only, completely different. Failing, anyway."

She was nearly going to tell him about the wife swap, but his spine straightened in his seat. "I didn't say failing."

She straightened up, too.

"Sorry," she said again and opened the car door. "I guess I'll see you Wednesday."

He stayed at the curb a moment and she didn't know whether to go inside or go back and say something else, then her downstairs neighbor wheeled a stroller around the corner and rattled open the front door of the building.

It wasn't until she locked the door of her townhouse behind her that she realized next week would be Yom Kippur and she wouldn't see him at all.

7.

SEPTEMBER 2012

If people made resolutions for the Jewish New Year as they do for the secular one, Rina knew what hers would be. As she performed the choreography of the Yom Kippur prayers—stand, sit, stand, three steps forward and back, sway, rock, cover the eyes, thump the chest in ersatz flagellation—she resolved to stop living as she had been; she resolved to figure out who she was again.

So these were the perils of a year.

Last year's confessionals were the prayers of a different woman. Now she thought only of the class she was missing because this year's holiday fell on a Wednesday; of Will Ochoa and the last, fraught words she'd spoken to him; of whether he'd feel her absence or have any inkling that his absence in her week hung gray on her with the drip-drip-drip of wet laundry on a line. That in his absence, she lost her spark of divinity. For the first time since before her marriage, maybe since ever, she had a peculiar sense that life could be different, larger. It wasn't ambition blooming in her empty gut as she struck at her own heart alongside the other women in shul, but it was related.

It was almost four thirty in the afternoon, and Chana,

who sat next to her, nudged Rina from her reverie of molten bronze eyes, paint-stained cuticles, and frown that on anyone else would be an indulgent grin. Imaginings of the paintings she would bring forth under the freedom of his mentorship, guided by his careful, stained fingers and splattered jeans.

"I'm going home to get ready for the break-fast," Chana said. "Walk with me."

Rina nodded, closed her machzor, and followed Chana around the rear of the lattice mechitzah that divided the women's third of the sanctuary from the men's side. She motioned to David and he came to the back of the room.

"I'm going home to set up the food," she said. "Bring the kids home with you after services."

"At least take Yoni with you," he said.

Yoni was still in the four-year-olds' babysitting room and if she took him now, she might as well not go home at all for the work she'd get done.

"Then I'll need the stroller and it will take forever to walk home. I'll take Shosh, bring her to me. You bring Yoni after shul."

Shosh had been sitting with her father on the men's side and stomped her foot twice upon being summoned.

"I want to stay with Abba."

Chana, who had reappeared with all three of her children, said, "Shosh, walk home with us. You and Rivka can run ahead," and the girl uncrossed her arms and slogged out into the heat behind her friend.

As usual, Yom Kippur fell on the hottest day of autumn and the women walking home to prepare the break-the-fast meal wilted under their heavy tights, their covered extremities, the hats and wigs that concealed their hair. On any other Jewish holiday the Pico-Robertson neighborhood—the chud, as the less religious Jews called it—was full of the fertile smell of slow-baking breads and noodle puddings, of heavy cholent stews braising since before the previous sundown, of cinnamoned cakes keeping warm under foil in a low oven. But because of the fast, few women put up hot food before Yom Kippur and the smells instead were cut grass, sweltering trash, and the women themselves, who needed—but would not get—showers before company arrived.

"Remember how in Israel the children love Yom Kippur because there are no cars and they ride their bikes down the middle of the big streets?" Chana said.

Rina frowned at her.

"I haven't been for Yom Kippur and neither have you."

Chana's head was tilted up, toward the light streaming through the trees. She looked confused, as if she didn't know what the word *remember* meant, or which story she'd been telling. Rina looked up, too; she knew what it was to be nostalgic for something you'd never had. The sun itself wasn't visible, but its light fought against the muggy cloud cover, streaming in a vertical spectrum of filmy rays to the horizon. When Rina was little, and even not so little, she liked to think of this kind of sunlight as god's giant eyelashes, of a benevolent eye watching her from under the clouds.

"The children do ride their bikes in the empty streets, though?"

"Of course," Rina said.

Chana nodded. "I thought so."

There was a moment without speaking. Rina never spoke to her friends like this, never spoke about anything other than recipes and their children, and the children they didn't have yet, and how long a commute took, and which warehouse grocery carried more kosher items. They used to speak differently, when they were girls. They used to talk about ideas. Rina used to have a friend in the community who painted, another who did community theater. Just when Rina was about to share with Chana about the sunlight, god's eyelashes, Chana said, "Nu, how many people will be by you tonight?"

"Maybe thirty," Rina said, immediately regaining the logistical rhythm of their friendship.

Soon enough it was time to turn into a paved and shrub-lined back alley that ran behind Rina's building. She wished Chana gut yontef and Shosh said goodbye to Rivka and walked ahead of her mother the final block and up the half flight of alleyway stairs to their townhouse.

Inside she fixed a glass of ice water for Shosh and also one for herself.

"Hashem says you can't drink today," Shosh said. "You're a grown-up. Don't do it."

Rina forgot Shosh was old enough to catch this transgression. It was one of the first things Rina had given up as her beliefs started to shift. She still abstained from food, of course, but may as well have been eating a pudding cup as drinking water on Yom Kippur. The first holiday she nursed a baby she'd been shocked to find out the rabbis, usually tolerant of infirmity, said a nursing mother had no right to water on the day. Her own smug rabbi assured her that his wife had nursed four babies through many a proper fast. Horseshit.

"Most people believe that, mummi," she said.

"I believe it."

"As soon as you're bas mitzvah you should stop drinking water on fast days."

"Abba believes it, too. I'm going to tell him."

"Abbas and imas can disagree about things and still love each other."

Rina listened to her own words, wondering if they sounded true.

Three hours later she was putting a new pan of cheese blintzes into the oven and getting ready to replenish the bagels when David came up behind her.

"The Haredim have arrived," he whispered in her ear, and she knew he meant Anshel's family. "Three of them anyway. Let's see if they eat a single thing at our house. I'll bet we're not kosher enough."

She stood up and turned, face glazed from the oven heat.

"If the Rebbe himself rose from the dead, he'd eat at our house. To you everyone's a heathen or a zealot." She clucked her tongue. "A BT should have more compassion."

Unlike Rina, who was raised in a modern Orthodox home (no wigs, regular street clothes, strictly kosher, keepers of Shabbos), David was raised in a barely Jewish home with an annual Hanukkah bush.

"Next thing I know you'll want to go back to observing niddah," he said and fingered her left ear lobe. She reached to rehang the oven mitts and he let go.

"Did you at least say hello?" she said.

"As a matter of fact, yes," he said. "But Anshel's not here yet. It's just his wife—"

"Nechama . . ."

"—and two of the girls. Do they have a son?"

"You know they don't. Five girls. Where's Anshel?"

"I would imagine still walking, but be sure to give his wife the third degree, too."

Rina exited the kitchen into the tangle of people that didn't fit comfortably in her tiny living and dining rooms, each of them balancing a paper plate of food. By the time she had refilled the buffet, Anshel had arrived with his other three daughters. She saw him near the front door and their eyes met over the crowd, but the toothy, unshaven image of Will came to her, and it was as if Will was standing there, close enough for her to smell his detergent, which was clean, unfamiliar, and a little sweet. Rina blinked and looked down and before she could look up again and maybe try to motion Anshel to the back, Nechama was by her side, baby Devorah on her hip.

"Could I nurse in your bedroom?"

Rina took Nechama by the elbow, led her down the crowded hallway past Anshel and David, who both gave looks that required something specific of her, up the set of carpeted stairs and into the master bedroom. Nechama and Anshel slept on separate twin beds, and Rina was embarrassed for her king bed, full of shame for all she'd taught Nechama's husband not in a bed but on an office floor.

As Nechama got situated, Rina busied herself, folding and putting away clothes David had tossed on the bed, picking up a pile of books the children had left on the floor. Small and pointless tasks to avoid returning to the crowd. From outside the door the women could hear the muffled conversations of guests on the stairwell, one name, Seth Hartman, rising above the din over and over again.

Nechama, baby at her chest, clicked her tongue and adjusted her wig with her left hand. She was a freckled beauty, svelte, with a round, clear face, big eyes, and ginger hair peeking out at the base of her wig, which was almost the same color.

"So much lashon hara so soon after the book of life has closed," Nechama said.

Rina nodded. Lashon hara, evil tongue. Many stores in the chud had hand-lettered signs above the cash registers that said לשון הרע, "No lashon hara here." Despite that, like anywhere, an awful lot of gossiping occurred.

"Do you believe there's an actual book where names are inscribed for a good or bad year on Yom Kippur?" Rina said to Nechama.

"Now you sound like my husband," Nechama said, and Rina turned to put a shirt in a drawer and hide her blush. "Where would such a book be kept? Do I think God has a magical pen? Who can say these things? The rabbis use metaphors so that we may understand how to live a life pleasing to God."

"You believe it's ordained at Yom Kippur who shall live and who shall die?"

"I believe I should live as if it's ordained."

"Do you believe it's ordained how life will go, for the ones who will live?"

Nechama made a face of noncomprehension, and Rina sat down on the bed next to her.

"So then, which does god think is worse? Speaking lashon hara against Seth Hartman, or what Seth Hartman is doing to his wife by refusing to give a *get*?"

Nechama's patient knowingness returned, as if nothing gave her more pleasure than answering the theological questions of the less learned.

"Instead of thinking about how God weights sins, we should think about how he weights mitzvot," she said.

"My goodness balances out the bad of others?" Rina said, wanting to know what Nechama thought with a sudden pull. "If I plant a tree or light Shabbos candles will god weigh that against someone else's business fraud?"

Nechama leaned a little closer to Rina, so close that Rina almost took it as an act of knowing.

"What a person can forgive, so can God."

"I'd better get back out there," Rina said, standing. She hoped, if Nechama ever found out about her affair with Anshel, that Nechama would never forgive her. "I'll shut the door behind me."

In the hall she passed and greeted, passed and greeted, kisses for the women, smiles for the men, and found herself face-to-face with Anshel at the doorway to her children's room.

"The girls are having so much fun playing," he said. "So many toys we don't have."

"There's lox and everything on the table," she said, pointing to his plain bagel.

"Around you I don't want to smell like fish and onions."

She tucked a strand of hair behind her ear.

"There's no chance of even one moment tonight, so—"

"I know," he said. "But we're talking, aren't we? When you fall asleep tonight you can think how I was the only one at your party with sweet breath."

They were standing far enough from each other and close enough to a room full of children to not cause suspicion, but if anyone had been paying attention, they would not have been able to ignore the way Anshel was looking at her, looking right into her eyes like a gentile.

"You don't always have to say such things to me." Her body had already gone static. "You're here. I invited you. Leave it."

"I love you."

"I know you do." She turned and made her way to the kitchen.

David was there, refilling an ice bucket, speaking about Seth Hartman to Brandon and Aliza.

"Every time a handful of brave women try to change the

laws and every time they are lambasted. I'll tell you how this looks to the greater Jewish community. Unthinkable," David said, looking at Aliza, and she nodded with fervor. Brandon fidgeted with his orange juice. He smiled at Rina and there was nothing private in it, no hint that he'd once buried his face in her cunt while his own wife got laid in the guesthouse. Meanwhile David and Aliza, who had probably never even hugged hello, were all bedroom eyes. "It's draconian," David said. "And what do we do? Boycott his business, that's all. He's treating his wife like a trinket, and we won't buy plumbing fixtures from him. For shame. I don't even need plumbing fixtures."

"So much lashon hara so soon after the book of life was closed," Rina said, interrupting and eliciting an air kiss and a lacquered blush from Aliza.

"I am not gossiping. This is about civil liberties," David said. "You just disagree with me."

"I do not disagree. I support the boycott, for one. I just have a certain amount of faith in the rabbis to solve the problem where it belongs, which is not in our kitchen."

Brandon started to say something, but David cut him off.

"I guess I should be pleased to hear you have faith at all," David said.

Rina dumped an armful of used paper plates into the trash and wondered, in a flash, what Will Ochoa would think of the Seth Hartman controversy or nursing women taking part in a fast or this dinner party or the book of life. Then—her heart rate surged—she wondered if he would even know why she wasn't in class. Would he think last week's walk to the car tainted something between them?

"No part of my faith or lack of it is constructed to please you," she said to David and stood planted in the kitchen, letting the three of them stare at their hands and suffer in the discomfort for a moment before escaping to other, less hostile pockets of conversation.

She pulled out her phone and checked the time; she'd already missed the class break. She thought of him there, beside the birds-of-paradise, smoking a cigarette, which he'd told her he never did at home.

She waited to call until she was sure class would be over. He picked up on the first ring.

"It's me," she said, right away. "I'm sorry," she went on, after a quiet moment, though there was plenty of background noise on her end. "I shouldn't have called. It's just. I'd forgotten to tell you I'd be—"

"Yom Kippur," he said.

"I didn't know if . . ." she said, but she didn't know how to finish.

"You knew."

"You made me feel dumb last week," she said.

"I know. I've gone over it a hundred times in my head. All the things I meant to say instead."

"So invite me for another coffee and say them." From where the boldness came, she didn't know.

"Does it have to be a kosher place?"

"No," she said. "We can have coffee anywhere and I'll tell you all about the cultish ways I do and do not eat. The why, we won't have time."

"Tomorrow?"

"I can't," she said. "Friday morning? I can come to campus."

"Until then," he said.

Much later, when she found out he didn't even teach on Fridays, she knew they'd both been out of control.

8.

She was at the butcher counter Thursday morning waiting for soup bones when the preschool called.

"How are you, Mrs. Kirsch?" the receptionist said.

"Thank god," Rina said, shifting her purse to her right shoulder to hold the phone against her left ear while she accepted the butcher's package.

"Thank God," the receptionist said. "I have Yoni here and he's vomiting."

Little Yoni, always with everything that comes around.

"I'm checking out of Glatt Mart," Rina said. "I'll be by you within thirty minutes to get him. Does he want to talk to me?"

"Poor guy is at the toilet," the receptionist said. "See you soon."

Already she had to prepare Shabbos today if she was going to meet Will the next day. Now with a sick baby. Should she make a dairy meal for Friday night? Too conspicuous after a dairy break-fast, besides company was coming, besides the eight-day festival of Sukkot would start Sunday night so this Friday would be extra festive in anticipation. She already had two whole chickens and bones in her cart, the frozen gefilte fish, and brisket for Saturday's cholent. She parked her cart along an aisle and loaded her arms with sweet potatoes, garlic, onions, horseradish root, fresh tomatoes, spinach, and artichokes, then dumped them in her cart. Carrots, celery, fruit she already had. The Friedmans and Katzes were coming for Shabbos and David wanted her to make her popular apple strudel, but a puking kid would be a fine excuse. So almond cookies instead, and strudel at the end of Sukkot. She grabbed almonds, plus mixed nuts and a box of chocolates to put out, grape juice and wine. Then prunes, hearts of palm, schmaltz, coffee, barley, cholent beans. Tea and canned tomatoes she had. They were going out for the first several meals of Sukkot—to her parents' and some friends'—but she'd have to bring something to each. She grabbed basmati rice, sultanas, foil pans, more hearts of palm. The spices she already had. Her items were almost all rung up when she thought to grab a bottle of Lysol and a tub of sanitizing wipes, and a clerk bagged while she ran to get the cleaning supplies.

She paid with a check. When filing the home accounting recently she'd found a dozen old checkbooks and it seemed simpler to use them then to tear them up. She'd been writing checks all over the chud for months. She dated the check at Glatt Mart and thought, as she often did, it had been over a year since David swapped her for a different wife. A year full of funny time tricks that unraveled her; days so slow that by 3:00 p.m. she was weeping, almost prayerful for the setting sun; whole months that went by in such a flash she feared she would never catch up on all that went undone, bill paying, photo developing, bleaching her persistent facial hair. The stopped and speeded time evened out, and usually it seemed like only a few weeks since she let Brandon breach his wedding vows inside her. She'd almost told Anshel about that night several times now, but as soon as she met Will Ochoa she knew that someday she'd tell him.

Driving the seven blocks to the school was muscle memory. She took possession of Yoni and his two in-case-of-accident changes of clothes; he'd puked on both of them. She kissed his head, and it nearly scalded her mouth. So it was a stomach flu, likely to pass in twelve hours, a day at most; it'd be gone before she saw Will. At home she covered the couch with fresh sheets and made Yoni a bed there—closer to where she'd be in the kitchen—brought him a very small cup of Pedialyte, a bucket with a little water in the bottom, and his pillow and stuffed animals. She brushed his teeth with water and wiped his face with a cool washcloth, read books with him, and then rocked him for a while, let him suck his thumb, kissed his sweaty forehead over and over. She stayed with him too long—her work would never get done—but he was so weak and lovely and she couldn't stand to put down his hot little body. At last he fell asleep and she set to work cleaning and sanitizing the house, wiping each doorknob, trying to stave off the germs to protect Shosh.

Waiting for her Friday coffee with Will was what she imagined the other couples must have felt in anticipation of the night of swinging, only more sacred. She wasn't waiting to meet a name on a card, she was waiting to meet stubble-faced Will, who was benevolent in all things, from the way he held his brush over the page to the way he coached cranky, middle-aged students. She tried without success to push him out of her consciousness so she could go about her chores. He texted her, she texted him; the work was slower and she had to wash her hands each time she picked up her phone to text, but she also seemed to move faster. She couldn't stop wondering what he would think of every little thing she did, from the way she folded a shirt into a perfect horizontal rectangle, left over from a long-ago summer job in retail, to the way she chopped garlic for soup, dicing it into a uniform pile that left her hands so sticky and pungent she had to wash them with lemon juice. How did Will chop garlic? Did he, even? David made exactly two dishes—spicy fish chraime and cholent—and he sliced garlic into thick coins for each, never letting his hands touch it. She wanted so much to call Will, to reassure herself with his voice, but she'd placed the first and only phone call to him, and she was too scared to do it again.

Instead she called the Jewish Family Services office to let them know she wouldn't be in for her shift because her child was sick, avoiding calling Anshel directly. She called her mother and asked her to pick up Shosh, then set to prepping Shabbos dinner and lunch, checking on Yoni every twenty minutes by pushing a digital thermometer into his ear and running her fingers through his damp hair.

Her phone rang and she saw his name so beautiful on the screen, the *i* next to the double *l*s like an anomaly, a blessing.

"Can you talk for a moment?" he said.

"Of course."

"I was just worried about Yoni, when you texted. How is he?"

"I'm still good to come tomorrow," she said.

"But how is he?" Will said. "Any better? Fever gone?"

"Yes. His fever broke," Rina said, hoping it would soon.

"And how are you?" Will said.

She paused for a moment. How was she? Who ever asked that? Could all this just be because he was nice to her? Did she just get wet for anyone who was decent?

"A little stressed," she said. "A little covered in bodily fluids."

"Let me tell you a quick story, and then I'll let you get back to it," Will said. "A long time ago, after college, I took myself on a trip. Like a graduation present. I went to Vietnam alone, and it was great. I was there for ten days, and for seven days I was so careful. I didn't drink the water, didn't eat ice, brushed my teeth with bottled water, kept my mouth closed in the shower. Then, on the eighth day, I took a river boat. And the water was so beautiful and I was across the world on my own, totally untethered from any responsibilities, and I felt amazing and so I jumped in the river just to feel how it felt."

"And?" Rina said.

"And I'm an idiot. The next day, my last full day, I had this big foodie tour of Hanoi scheduled. The most expensive tourist thing on my itinerary, a real splurge. I didn't feel so good when I woke up in the morning, and after the first stop I asked the guide if I could use a restaurant bathroom. Sure, he told me, the next restaurant is only half a mile away. And Rina, I shit my pants right there on a street in Hanoi. I mean I really shit them. You couldn't even believe an adult could let something like this happen. And then I had to run into an alley and strip down out of my pants, and keep shitting in the alley."

Rina laughed. Quietly, to not bother Yoni, and then not so quietly.

"All those trips to Tijuana and Rocky Point with my brother, Frank, all those hangovers, and I was never sick. But one stupid swim."

"And then you were just naked? How did you get back to the hotel?"

"I'll tell you the rest someday."

The someday rang in Rina's ears.

"Have I cheered you?"

"Yes," she said, still giggling. "I have to go; my mother is bringing Shosh home."

The sound of his sister coming home woke Yoni and he

dry heaved but nothing came up, so it would soon be over. Rina's mother made the challah and cookie doughs so that Rina could bathe the boy; Shosh wanted an early bath, too, so Rina drained the tub, sprayed it with Clorox, and sat and read a chapter book with Shosh while it refilled, and then the little girl bathed. Shosh mostly took showers now, and Rina drew out the bath-time shampooing of her daughter's hair, washing twice and leaving the conditioner in too long, slowly pouring pitcher after pitcher of warm water, watching it cascade in sheets over Shosh's long blonde hair.

Rina's mother left, and Rina and Shosh set the formal dining table for twelve, eight children and four adults; the family would eat in the kitchen tonight, as they often did on Thursdays when company was coming for Shabbos. While Shosh set out the challah board and kiddush fountain, Rina polished the candlesticks and imagined Will watching her. She'd tried, before bed last night, to cause herself to find Will in her sleep, but remembered no dreams upon waking.

Anshel called to check on Yoni. Rina made the phone call quick, wishing him an early good Shabbos. Anshel was convenient, a well-timed enterprise. He might as well have been drawn out of a hat and assigned to her. Will—so implausible, so poorly timed in his arrival—existed as if he was summoned from charcoal and graphite to remind her of important things she'd long forgotten, as if he was drawn—with his sad half smiles, his strong arms like polished cherrywood, his doubting eyes that she could sketch from memory—just for her.

After the children went down for the night, Rina took three Benadryl and, for the first time in years, went to bed early.

7.

SEPTEMBER 2012

She arrived at the college the next morning sweating, nervous, wearing jeans and a tunic instead of a skirt. Somehow it felt like dressing up. She took ten minutes to compose herself in the visor mirror, even though she'd be late. Her hair was still damp and wavy from a shower and the sun through the window fractured it into dozens of variations of blonde in a way that pleased her. She'd put on copper lipstick and glamorous sunglasses, men's cologne like she used to in college. Would he think she was an imposter? She should call. She was late and he should call.

She tested a casual hello, then dialed.

He quoted a poem instead of saying hello. The poetry, a beautiful point being proved. She smiled to herself, but didn't know who the poet was, or what to say. "You're late," he said, after a moment.

"The babysitter was late."

"You had to get a babysitter?" he said.

"Because Yoni was sick. He can't go back to school yet."

"I'm sorry."

"Don't be."

"The campus coffee shop is not babysitter worthy," he said. "We'll go somewhere else."

"Where?" she said, and maybe he heard the word twice, layered on top of itself like an echo, because then she was standing over him, sliding her phone into her purse.

"How much time do you have?" he said.

"Enough. But after today . . ." she hesitated. "It might not even matter, but after today I'll have my phone off until Saturday night, then again Sunday night until Tuesday night. It's a holiday, a long one. But I'll be in class next week. I just . . . wanted you to know."

He stood up and wiped his hands on the back of his pants, a painter's habit. "There's a famous Mexican restaurant in La Habra. It's far, but it won't take long on the freeways. Do you like Mexican? Can you eat at a regular restaurant?"

"I can eat a little something almost anywhere," she said.

"It must be so different, always thinking about food," he said.

"I think there's a Jewish joke in there somewhere."

"I mean in terms of what you can and can't eat, always making choices. But hey, Mexicans are always thinking about food, too. Before I sit down to breakfast I'm thinking about what I'll have for lunch."

"Then we'll get along fine," Rina said.

"We already do," he said.

"Okay, so you drive. I have no idea where La Habra even is."

"I grew up not far from there, in Fountain Valley," he said, starting toward the faculty lot. She followed.

"I'd like to see where."

He shifted his messenger bag to his right shoulder, and it made a barrier between them. Did she say the wrong thing,

again? She didn't know how to be with him, how to read his
cues.

"Weekend plans?" he said, after a moment, and she just
looked at him. "Oh," he said. "The holiday."

"Who was the poet you quoted?"

"Neruda," he said, as if she should have known.

If she couldn't say anything right, she might as well say
what was true.

"We're both here and both married. You said your marriage isn't failing. Every day I think mine cannot be saved. My
husband thinks we should have another baby and then another. And every day I do nothing different. I'm doing something different today. Even though it's probably a mistake.
Why are you here?"

"I . . ." he said, drawing out the syllable. "I'm sorry I said
that, about my marriage. I've been wanting to correct myself
for a week."

"Correct or recalibrate?"

"What?" he said. She was staring at the ground while she
walked, concentrating.

"Don't you think the outcome of lunch depends on it?"

"You think faster than I do," he said. They reached his car,
a fifteen-year-old Honda with a manual shift that was badly in
need of paint. "How about we get some food into us and then
we'll talk?"

He unlocked her side first, a rusty act of chivalry. She
wasn't in the habit of having doors opened for her.

"Or we could talk about the weather," she said.

He started down the spiral of the faculty garage's exit
lane. Yesterday he'd texted her *Tomorrow is so far.* She'd let
herself believe they were thinking the same thing. Will drove

very fast in silence, and she wanted to scream, Either put your hand on my thigh or throw me out of the car, but do something. They passed the Goodyear Blimp and IKEA in Carson and that was the farthest south she ever drove unless it was for vacation. Old malls and new malls whipped by, and still he didn't speak. He exited the freeway and glanced at Rina. She sat cross-legged in his passenger seat.

"I'm sorry," he said.

"I'm thinking."

"Think out loud?"

"I like to call a spade a spade," she said.

He looked at her again, and she looked back, trying to figure out if she had misunderstood everything, everything since they met. They passed one-story apartment buildings, warehouse clubs, fountained medical buildings, signs in Spanish and Thai, quiet parks, and so many new-construction mid-level hotels without cars in the lots, it was as if the whole place was anticipating a future economy built on vasectomies and rotisserie chicken.

"And?" he said.

"You go." She brought a hand to her mouth and bit at the edge of one of her nails.

"We're attracted to each other and we're trying to pretend otherwise." The truth exploded like shrapnel in her heart, but she didn't want to give him the benefit of her relief. Not yet—not until she was certain.

"We're not much pretending," she said, finger still to her mouth. "Have you ever cheated on your wife?"

"Not this wife." She knew it wasn't logical, the sting of hearing him say it like that.

"I'm having an affair right now," she said. "I mean with someone else. A rabbi. No point in not telling you."

She didn't want to look at him, but she saw his body clench and she couldn't help it. His jaw contracted and his eyes narrowed. "And this is happening *right now* right now?" he said, voice crimson and rising.

"Not since last Thursday, if that's what you mean."

"For how long?"

"Six months."

Had he ever known a rabbi? He'd lived in Brooklyn, so he could probably picture a certain type.

"There were no other affairs," she said eventually. Will had turned into a neighborhood and now they passed stucco houses with narrow lawns that chased the curbs along the wide street, low palm trees spilling pink dates, and brick-bordered hedges.

"Six months could be love."

"He loves me," she said. She stopped biting at her fingers and crumpled down into the upholstery of his passenger seat.

"You're in it for kicks?"

"It sounds awful," she said. Her cheeks were flushed now, she felt it.

"You make me crazy," Will said. "I can't even get my head around competing with your husband."

"It's not a competition."

"Oh, Rina. Oh yes, it is. And I want to win it so much. How's that for calling a spade a spade?"

He pulled over to an empty curb, put the car into park just beneath a NO PARKING sign in front of a beige brick house. He turned on his hazards.

"Are we going to fight?" she said, her voice quiet.

"This is where I grew up."

She sat up a little, astonished that he'd been so literal. The house resembled the others on the street. It was a tidy, flat-roofed two-story house with a front-facing balcony and a wrought iron railing painted white. It looked as if it ought to be covered in pink stucco.

"You said you wanted to see it?" he said, sounding unsure.

"Of course. Which was your room?"

He bent toward her, moved his hand close. The boldest thing he'd done, apart from his texts. The genesis of sin. He tilted her chin northeast, pointed with his other hand.

"Top floor. Just to the left of the balcony."

There were windows on both sides of his old room, one facing the street and one overlooking the grassy driveway that led to the carport, a dwarf grapefruit tree, and the next-door neighbor's cedar fence. He told her he used to sit in front of those windows for hours. For whole days. He painted the view outside and thought about the women who might love him if they knew him.

"I never imagined a woman like you," he said. Her face must have betrayed her, because he added, "I'm desperate to understand you. Desperate."

"I recognize the tree from the painting," she said. "The first night of class. How long did you live here?"

"My whole life. Until I was almost twenty. We only sold it after my mother died."

She shrugged away, looked back at the house.

"I'm sorry about your mother," she said.

"Hey," he said, his voice soft.

"I can't look at you."

"Sure you can."

She shook her head. Moved her gaze to the floor mats.

"You know the assignment I gave the class, the self-portrait? Every other student turned in something typical.

Familiarity with the general proportions of a human head, you know."

Rina remembered the assignment. She had painted just her eye, huge on the page, brimming and about to overflow with a tear. Her eyebrow crested at the top. The concave skin under her eye sloped to the bottom border. She hadn't used the pastels or wine-bright primaries of watercolor, nor the blue scheme a tearful eye might bring to mind. She'd used a full palette of greens. Long, mossy eyelashes, kale-dark pupils, specks of kelly green animating the iris.

"It looks just like your eye, only so much sadder than you let show," he said. "It makes my eyes water to look at it, yet I look at it all the time." On the first day of class, Will announced that he'd hold on to student work throughout the semester, and return a finished portfolio at the end of the course. She hadn't imagined him spending much time with student work, but it bathed her body with warmth knowing that he revisited hers. "I keep it in my trunk. I know that sounds creepy, but I do. I stare at it until I can't see. It gives me a feeling. Something I never felt, but it reminds me of being a kid. It reminds me . . ." he stopped for a moment. "It reminds me of my mother serving me a turkey sandwich in the yard right there, and setting out a dish of mustard for dipping because I didn't like it spread on the bread."

"I remind you of your mother."

"I'm trying to tell you . . ."

"I know," she cut him off. "Thank you. It's just, now that we're here, I don't know what's real. I worry . . . I worry I'm just a person who wants to want. Sometimes it feels so good to want."

"Hey," he said again. He put his finger under her chin again, turned her face back toward him. "This doesn't have to be the same as what came before."

"It's inevitable," she said, as if she were arguing with herself. Or god. But she knew which way the argument would go.

She looked up at him.

"Just like the painting," he said.

Her arms moved to him on impulse.

He wrapped her in a hug. They were ear to ear. He inhaled her the way people inhale babies. She nuzzled again the sweat in the side hollow of his neck, her body blazing. After a moment he pressed the side of his face against the round, yielding part of her face, and for some reason at that moment he seemed very brave.

She pulled back, but not much, and looked at him.

"It is inevitable, right?" she said. As the words came out, she was already leaning into him and their mouths collapsed into each other. For a moment they were motionless. Open-mouthed and fused, the first wet, sucking bite into an apple. Then her eyelashes grazed his face and he came alive with urgency. Kissing her and kissing her and kissing her.

Finally she took a breath and said, in quick bursts, "I don't love him, you know."

"Which one?" he said, buried in her neck, her damp-again hair.

She put a hand on each side of his face. Lifted him to look at her. Stroked her thumbs along the soft part of his cheeks.

"Either of them."

She slid her hands around into his hair and he sank back into her. The next time they came up for air it was so late that there was no hope for lunch. They rode back to campus without talking. He kept his right hand on her left leg the whole way, including two interchanges.

"I want to tell you everything," she said at one point. "I
don't know how to start." She lapsed back into silence and
the quiet was happy, almost natal. It kept the guilt at bay. She
could ignore the nagging of her own failure as long as he was
next to her.

In the student garage, he pulled up to her car.

"Wednesday at class?" she said.

"You really can't until then?"

She shook her head, opened the door, and started to climb
out. Then leaned back in.

"We can't, cariño," he said. "Not here."

"I know. Tres-tres-ocho-cinco."

"Huh?"

"Tu dirección. Donde vivías. I speak a little Spanish, from
college."

"But I don't," he said. "I mean, I can count. But."

"Your address." She spoke fast and moved her hands in
apology, horrified by her own assumptions. "Where you were
a boy. I'll never forget it."

She got out, closed the door, and got into her van without turning again. Even though it wasn't even her memory,
she was taken with that warm-bath, turkey-sandwich, almost-
but-not-quite-melancholy feeling. That unnamable something
bobbing in her stomach, her chest, her solar plexus. As if she
had actually been there, next to the little grapefruit tree, dipping her turkey into mustard. He couldn't name the feeling,
but she knew it exactly.

It was the feeling of being known.

10.

OCTOBER 2012

Rina woke from a dream and reached for her glasses to look at the clock, hoping it was early, two or even three in the morning, and she had hours of sleep still in front of her. But it was almost five and there was no point in closing her eyes again. Sleeping past five was impossible on a weekday; her entire family would be up in less than an hour. Drowsy, she untangled herself from her damp sheets and her body pillow—the one she'd started using during her first pregnancy and never stopped, a final end to the waning phase of David and her holding each other as they fell asleep— and pulled on the yoga pants she always left at the foot of the bed. It was the end of four exhausting days, three of them chag: Shabbos, followed by a Sunday of intense work, then the first two days of Sukkot. Sometimes going out for meals was more exhausting than entertaining: balancing trays full of warm food on the stroller handlebars, chasing the children all through someone else's yard, keeping them awake on the long walks home so they'd sleep well at night. Her exhaustion was compounded by the ceaseless thoughts of Will. Fourteen hours left until she'd be with him.

In the bathroom she leaned over the sink and examined

the shallow parentheticals developing around her mouth. The dream that woke her was a nightmare, but she couldn't remember the details.

She climbed to the office, a small loft that was the entire third floor of the townhouse, to check her phone for texts. Will had been texting her good morning messages all week, so she'd moved her charger to the outlet in the loft to prevent David from seeing morning texts blink in. She had no idea how she'd explain not keeping the phone next to their bed, if he ever noticed. She settled in under a portrait of an old sea captain painted on wood with a scrim of thrift shop grit, a flea market find in her late teens. He smoked a pipe and had flushed cheeks and a glum expression: not like the day's catch had been meager, like the facts of existence on this earth, on these waters, was too much for one old man to bear. He was lonely, that was certain. David hated the painting and had tried to excise it from their home. He thought it was ugly, and disrespectful to more religious Jews who hung uncannily similar portraits of famous, white-bearded rabbis in their homes. Unlike her own paintings, which she willingly shoved in the back of a closet, she refused to part with the Captain, so she hid him in the loft.

At 5:07 a.m. there was not yet a message from Will. Even though he told her she could text anytime, it didn't seem right to message him while night's tarry dark still hung over the city. Did it get lighter at his home first, up high in a mountain canyon? She slipped the phone into her pocket, sat in an upholstered rolling chair—another relic of her college days—and woke up the computer. She read somewhere that it wasn't productive to deal with emails first thing in the morning, but it was the only time she had to respond to the perpetual hundreds of unread messages in her inbox. She hadn't had time to check them before Shabbos came in on Friday, and had only glanced at her inbox on her phone on Sunday as she prepped for Sukkot.

Can you send your recipe for broccoli kugel? *It only exists in my head.* Will you be serving dinner to the homeless at the shul's monthly shelter night? *Yes, but it's demoralizing that we serve full turkey dinners as if our cooking itself constituted a holiday.* Would you like to join the school's Green Committee? *No, but I bring my own mug to PTA meetings.* Your kids are overdue for dental checkups. *Not as overdue as I am.*

She intended to answer the emails, but instead she sat in front of the fingerprint-smudged screen letting replies run through her head before marking everything "read."

There was a Shabbos invitation in her inbox that put a pit in her stomach. Almost every Saturday they had people over or went to someone's house for lunch, and lately it was impossible to get through such an afternoon without embarrassment: bickering, most often, or David telling an unfunny joke. Or berating her.

Two months ago, in the middle of serving a lunch to ten adults and eleven children under the age of five, someone asked for salt, which she never kept on the table.

"A little salt from the kishke into the rice and she could have saved two dishes," David said. The adult table was all flatware clinking for a few moments, and then lunch continued as if nothing had been said. His comments became more frequent. Sometimes Rina told a little self-deprecatory joke to release the tension; sometimes she excused herself with a smile until her fury receded. She would pull dirty shirts out of the children's hamper and hold them against her face, their smells releasing oxytocin to drown out the loneliness of her life, the pointlessness of her wasted years of toil. Her reputation in the community was spotless and seemed to take on more luster as David got surlier, as if her under-salted kishke and docility were a form of piety.

They often had Shabbos lunch at Brandon's home if they had no other invitations, and she despised it. The invitation came from a gossipy host who would narrow her eyes at David's comments and then talk with sympathy about Rina with other women after Shabbos went out, but at least it wouldn't be another meal pretending like Brandon had never seen her naked, or like her own husband didn't wish to see Brandon's sister naked. *What can I bring?* she typed.

She opened a browser and scanned the headlines of the *Los Angeles Times* but could think only of Will; he was her anomaly. He had a way of making her feel that she had to herself the parts of him that mattered. So she didn't care that the world was full of beautiful women and that he might see these women, focus in on one of their lovely features, sometimes think about taking them to bed. How odd that she'd ever wanted other men to be blind to beauty; she hoped Will would be engulfed in it. She wanted him without condition and did not suffer the usual outside threats pushing up against that want, eating away at her confidence, making her feel like a child. Yet she wanted to possess Will's time. It was jealousy, but not in any form she previously recognized. She was envious only of his car, the supermarket, the paint shop, his classroom, his couch, all the places he spent his minutes.

Yoni began to cry downstairs. She checked her phone one more time, then wedged it into the waistband of her sweatpants. It would be meal, dress, drive, drive, bathe, meal, drive, drive, prepare a dinner she wouldn't eat. Then it would be time to go to class. David yelled to her from downstairs and she began a mental countdown.

She arrived at class almost forty-five minutes early and was angry that he wasn't there even though they had no plans to meet. Despite all their communications, they hadn't dared map a timeline for what came after their kiss. But it was imminent and unstoppable; she thought of little else. She was angry he wasn't there, and it was a particular magnetic anger—obsessive and mythical—and the strength of it scared Rina. The classroom was unlocked, so she set up at an easel and started a painting of an apple she'd brought along for a snack.

He arrived less than five minutes before class, but she was still the only student. He looked at her near-finished painting and in his eyes, she saw confusion ebb into apology, then panic.

"Come," he said, taking her by the wrist, and she followed him into a supply closet with a wet pink brush in her left hand. "I could be fired," he said, then kissed her twice, softly.

"How are you?" she said, hands at his face, but didn't wait for him to answer before falling back into him.

They kissed a little more and then he pulled back and put his lips to the tip of her nose and she knew they were done.

"Now I'm fine," he said.

"I have so many things to tell you."

"I'll end class early. They always want to leave anyway."

"They're going to see us coming out together."

"Grab an armful of something and pass it out."

"What?"

"Anything. I'll wait. I need a minute."

He taught more than usual: a whole segment on shading before the break, using her unfinished apple painting as an example, tacking it to his easel, putting the apple itself under a spotlight, and shading it left to right. In the glare she saw the fruit had a large, flat bruise just under the stem, and was embarrassed that she'd brought an imperfect apple into his world. She missed what he was saying, absorbed in her own thoughts, but she was content to think in the brawny, honeyed bath of his voice. When he finished the painting she'd started, it was more technically perfect but had less character.

While the students worked on their own pieces, he went easel to easel. She strained to listen to his advice, and flushed with pride at the succinct, soothing instruction he gave, the jokes he made. He took seriously the work of even the most amateur students and was careful to give specific feedback and broad praise. At some easels, he sat to the side of the student and guided a hand into the palette and along the paper. As he got closer, she didn't know whether he would talk to her like everyone else, or say different things in quieter tones. And she didn't know which she'd prefer, only that her pulse increased each time he got one stool closer.

"This is a good thing," he said, sitting down not to her left or right but directly behind her and taking her hand in his.

Her hands were rough from housework, dry from endless washing, covered in tiny scars from careless oven and soup burns. Her nails were yellow with the saffron and turmeric she'd used to make rice to take to her mother's sukkah. She wanted to pull them away, but she saw that his hands, although much smoother, were the same: cracked nail beds stained with paint, knuckles full of pencil dust. She knew about intricate details such as the triptych he'd painted for Dylan's first birthday and Will's irrational fear of becoming color-blind, but little of his day-to-day life. Does he also cook? How does he keep the underneath of his nails so clean? Does he, like her father, have a medicine-cabinet manicure set for men? Does he work at them with a Swiss Army knife each morning?

It was warm—so warm—to have him there, and while his left hand did tiny cross-hatching on her page, two of the fingers on his right hand rested on the top of her thigh. Her left hand shook, and he gripped it tighter, and his breath on her neck smelled of coffee and cinnamon. Nerves she thought had been lost to time fired all over her body.

He was still talking, and even though he was talking about watercolor the same way he had with every other student, she already recognized that with her he had a different voice, a private way of speaking, a gentle something crafted just for her.

At the break they each went outside to call home, walking as far across the quad from each other as possible. She looked only at the cement paving stones for the duration of her short conversation with David, then she and Will came back together in the room before the others returned. He cut the apple one slice at a time with a pocketknife, handing her a new piece each time she'd finished one. He cut around the bruise and she mumbled, "Sorry."

"For what?"

She shrugged. "I think about you all the time."

"I know."

"How?" she said. Should she be playing some sort of game?

"I meant, me too."

"I'm going to leave the rabbi."

"Yes. That's important."

She snapped the last slice of fruit in half and handed part to him.

"David keeps talking about having the next baby." It came out in a blurt. Not what she meant to bring up on a ten-minute break.

"Don't," he said. "I can't think beyond that."

"Obviously," she said.

The second half of class he set them all working on a sketch of their own hands, to be finished with paint the following week. He walked around the room once, then sat at his desk and started drawing. But he kept looking up at her. And each time she looked back until she couldn't hold his gaze anymore and he gave a half smile to show he'd won.

With ten minutes to go he made another tour of the room and stopped only at her station, said into her ear in almost a whisper, "God, your eyes."

She made a big production of cleaning up at the end of class and the moment the room was cleared he said, "Closet," and she said, "Car," and he shook his head, so she gathered an armful of the unused charcoal she'd handed out at the beginning—it was all she'd been able to find—and headed back to the supply closet. It didn't lock from the inside, so he locked the classroom, closed the closet door behind him, and without a word lifted her onto a shelf. He hitched up her leg and her knee sent a box of 4B pencils clonking down the shelves and rolling across the floor. She laughed, a little sputter of a laugh. He tried to get inside her, but he was too tall, so he moved her over onto a pile of sketchbooks, pulled her forward, bent his knees. "Do I need something?" he said. She shook her head, said, "I have an IUD," and pushed away thoughts of disease. She would think about it when it was too late. His first couple tries didn't work and she grabbed him and said, "Here," and they were both slippery and tasted of charcoal dust but then he was making love to her and it was sweaty and short and holy and when they finished there were small tears at the corners of each of their eyes, as if they'd been looking into the wind.

He stayed in that closet with her a long time, pressing her damp face into his chest. "Cariño," he said, "cariño," stroking the hair back from around her face, breathing long and slow.

He tipped her chin up to look at him. "Do *you* want another baby?" he said.

"I've been brought up to want countless babies."

"But do you want one?"

"Yes," she said. "In my lifetime, yes. Right now, no. With David, no."

"David," he said, as if he could taste the name and it wasn't as unpleasant as he expected.

"You?" she said.

"I don't know. I don't have the energy to think about it."

"Well, I have to," she said.

"Are you sure you don't want another with him?"

She pulled away and started to smooth her clothes back into place. It was not the kind of thing she could talk about and be close to someone at the same time.

"I've been sure a long time," she said. "Until recently, I was going to do it anyway."

"I don't mean to press you. I just wanted to correct myself from earlier. It wasn't for me to tell you not to."

"Except kind of it was," she said.

"I can't wait a week to see you, Rina."

"Let me handle Anshel first," she said.

"The rabbi?"

"The rabbi. I see him tomorrow. I'll end it, even though it's a holiday. I'll be better for you then."

"Please don't fuck him. Fuck your husband as much as you want. I can't stop that. But please just tell me you won't with the rabbi. Or if you do, don't tell me."

She laughed.

"What's funny?"

"You," she said. "After that." On impulse she grabbed him around the neck and squeezed tight. "First, I haven't been with him since before Yom Kippur. Second, I'd promise you anything."

"Be in touch tonight?" he said.

"And tomorrow," she said.

They opened the closet door and went their separate ways to their separate garages and Rina felt if she looked over her shoulder, she'd be sick to her stomach just to see him walk away from her.

She woke up well before dawn on Thursday and spent the morning cooking for the rest of Sukkot, Shemini Atzeret, and Simchat Torah, and spoke to Will twice on the phone, more times than David called her from work in a whole week. She made tabbouleh, cold sesame noodles, corn salad, kugel, squash soup, barley soup, zucchini fritters, tzimmes, fruit compote, a huge fillet of salmon salt-curing with dill in the fridge, a brisket in the slow cooker, a chicken bake covered in the freezer, a triple recipe of raisin challah rising next to the stove, plus a portion of spelt challah for the Davidoff children, who had endless allergies. She did not get to the broccoli pies or desserts, and the green salads would have to be made each night. The anticipation of leaving Anshel—he would not take it well—made her queasy. She didn't taste as she cooked. The recipes were from memory; they would taste the same as always, taste like Sukkot, like the dust on the Santa Ana winds that blew hot through the holiday. She'd no idea what to say to Anshel. Not the truth. She washed the stove, washed the counters, washed the floor, bleached the sink, lotioned the thick skin of her palms in the futility of staving off the calloused old-lady hands that had already come to pass.

Twelve families would come for the last five days of Sukkot. The previous year on one night alone she'd made thirty-seven trips up to the sukkah on the roof and back down again. Was thirty-seven a lot? It felt a lot. Later that night she'd kneeled to bathe the children, kneeled to read two stories, kneeled to sing "Tumbalalaika" seven times until the baby was asleep, then washed the dishes, washed the floors, bleached the sink, lotioned her hands. It was almost two in the morning by the same she'd gone to bed, and by then the lactic acid had built up so much in her calves that it hurt just to lie down.

Despite what she'd told Will, despite what she felt, she didn't know if she'd be able to find the right words to end it with Anshel. After the kitchen was clean, she got in the car without showering or putting on lingerie. A small act of defiance. What would fragile Anshel think? She was already late; he would already be panicked. She looked sideways at the digital clock on her dashboard at a red light. She was only five minutes away from his office but gave it less than two minutes until he called. She checked that her headset was connected to the phone, then pulled into the intersection when the light changed.

She heard the accident before she saw it. Like an earthquake. A long scream of brakes, enough time to see a sedan hurtle through a red light in her rearview, into the orange sports car behind her. A millisecond later a different sound, a volcano when it finally stops its warning belches and sends the earth's core skyward. The sports car spun and smoked in the center of the intersection, got smaller in her mirror as she kept driving. The truck in front of her already had its blinker on, and she followed it in a U-turn, then turned left near a gas station, pulled over, called 911, and reported the accident.

Two people were getting out of the sports car. On all

corners of Pico and La Cienega folks stopped what they were doing to watch. The Guatemalan fruit seller with his knife mid-stroke, pedestrians not quite in the crosswalk but not quite on the sidewalk, a homeless woman who'd been sweeping in front of her tent, workers and patrons from a café and a nail salon. If not for the tangle of traffic already trying to maneuver around the wreck—gracious, for these few moments while the shock was fresh, in the silence of their horns—the intersection would have looked like a paused video.

Rina had been in one fender bender—her fault—and seen three major accidents besides. She couldn't remember the details of the accidents she'd seen, only that they'd happened and she'd been there. Unlike almost-wrecks—brake slamming, sudden swerving, narrow misses—which opened her adrenal glands and made her hands shake for hours, observing an accident was a benign horror.

Also like an earthquake, it hasn't been experienced until talked about, and Rina picked up her phone again just as a call rang through from Anshel. She watched the number blink on the screen for a moment, then swiped *ignore*. She meant to dial David next, the person she called in emergencies, and was halfway surprised when Will picked up.

"It makes it hard not to think about what you're doing today when you call," he said, but there was a smile in his voice. "Tell me it's done."

"There was a big traffic accident."

His tone changed to one she'd not heard before. "Are you okay?"

"I wasn't in it. It happened behind me."

"Are you okay?"

Sirens thrust through the afternoon traffic. The sports car looked like something from a science fiction film, almost a

living thing, its metal infrastructure showing under its torn
skin. The intact metal grid of the car's frame was revealed
along the entire driver's side of the car, where the siding had
peeled away.

"There are better witnesses, I think. I saw it in my mirror.
But I'll stay until the police arrive."

"But are you okay? Where are you? Do you want me to
come to you?"

Would he?

"No," she said. "Yes. Yes, I'd like you to come to me. But
no, you can't."

"Go home after the cops arrive," he said. "Have a cup of
tea."

She turned off the engine. "You know I can't."

"Cancel with Anshel."

"I don't want to."

"I thought you were dreading it," he said.

"I'm going to end it."

"We already agreed."

"There's agreeing, then there's agreeing," she said, and at
that moment another call rang through on her other line. She
glanced to see that it was Anshel, felt no prick of guilt ignoring the call.

"Cariño, you have all the time you need. Is that the cops?"
The sirens had become louder, then cut off.

"Paramedics."

"People are hurt?"

She ran her hands over the steering wheel, which, now
that the car was off, was getting warm in the chalky noontime
sun pushing through the windshield. "It's the resolve of the
thing. Now I know I can do it. There's no time to waste. I'm
terribly calm. When can I see you?" she said.

"This afternoon, after you've done it?"

"It will have to be very brief, before I do early pickup." She pushed aside thoughts of her unshowered body, her oniony hair, her ratty clothes.

"Where?"

"My place," Rina said, not only because she knew how to get away with it but because she was eager to start erasing Anshel and his memories from the places in her life.

"No."

"Why not?"

"Just no. How about halfway? Palisades Park. The path above the beach in Santa Monica. Will you have time?"

"Not a lot. But I'll be there."

"I love you," he said.

She was quiet for a moment. It was so soon, so fast, so illogical, but she loved him. She hadn't let herself think it until this moment, but it was undeniable. Here she was, on the shoulder of La Cienega next to a gas station car wash, watching the strange calm that followed a traffic wreck, and in the first, gleaming moment of their cardinal love.

"So Palisades Park in ninety minutes?" he said.

"I love you, too," she said and restarted the engine.

"For the record, I love you whether or not you love me. And I loved you all through the quiet when you were deciding what to say. More, maybe."

"Now everything gets harder."

"And still I'll love you."

As soon as she hung up, she received a text from Will. It just said: *letters.*

Letters? she wrote back. Her phone rang right away.

"I don't think we can text 'I love you' to each other," Will said. "That can't be on our phones. Not yet, anyway, so when

I write you 'Letters,' you take all the letters you need from the alphabet and spell out 'Will loves Rina' in your mind."

"That's pretty saccharine," she said.

"You don't like it?" Will said.

"I like it."

"Good. I love you," he said.

"Letters," she said and hung up.

There was nothing to do but walk into Anshel's office and tell him. She hardly saw the crowd of women in the lobby signing a protest about Seth Hartman's refusal to divorce his wife, didn't hear a few of them call her name before she shut the door to the office suite behind her and, so he would know she meant it, looked Anshel right in the eye.

⚘

Thirty minutes later, she was standing on a sidewalked ridge above the Pacific Ocean in Palisades Park, the piecrust cliff beneath her. Behind her, with his arms stretched around her shoulders and down into the opposing pockets of her cheap sweater duster, pilled by many years of infrequent wear, stood Will. He had muscles in places where she had none, and they contracted against her back when he breathed, convulsed when he laughed.

It was autumn, and although early and sunny, there was the feeling of dusk ready to advance. To the left, on the Santa Monica Pier, the Ferris wheel turned slowly and the roller coaster whipped around its white track; to the right, the rolling mountains of Malibu sloped straight into the sea. There was no horizon, no meeting between the dimpled, melanoid sea and the violet sky; the world was like a domed snow globe, and nothing seemed to exist outside of her periphery, outside of the sea and the hills and Will. All around them was the scent of eucalyptus and the strong, leafy sap of horizontal-growing trees whose name she didn't know. The sea smelled like everything, like the sum total of evolution, irreducible to its parts (salt, kelp, fish, thunder, quantity). She said something and he laughed again.

She'd thought so many times for so many years about her own unhappiness, but it didn't occur to her to think, standing there along the bluff, about whether she was happy now, in this moment of betrayal and of love, in this moment with Will.

She was just there, with him, their orbits bent along the same ellipse, the two of them whipping along the rails.

11.

They only thought they were busy before they met each other.

Rina had the cooking and cleaning and driving and scheduling and volunteering and pickups and drop-offs and making baskets of food for people who were sick. Will had a double teaching load; the organizing of the details of his father's slow death in an Orange County assisted living facility, the same one in which his mother had been before she died in hospice a year earlier; the orchestrating of his entire homelife because Holly worked long hours as an administrator at the USC business school. The house was always a mess when he got home. Toys on the floor. Dylan's dinner on the table, usually half-eaten toast with cheese. The bathwater undrained. Will did the grocery shopping. The cooking. Most Wednesdays, even if he'd fixed a plate of leftovers before he went to teach class, Holly called him on his way home from class to have him pick up a ten o'clock dinner for her. Her job was in outreach, but at home they communicated in empty spaces, Will told Rina. The white blocks between stanzas. The gesso muddled by paint.

Where there had been no time, Will and Rina carved

out pockets to see and communicate with each other. Even though Will had limited cell service in his home and they lived far apart. The drive from his Topanga Canyon bungalow to the community college took only fifteen minutes if he left at the right time. Same as Rina's drive from Pico-Robertson to campus. But the joining of these two stretches of commute made it a traffic-heavy, hour-long drive in either direction.

At first they would see each other just Wednesday nights, meeting before class for a walk along Santa Monica's Palisades Park and a view of the ocean. Each of them requiring their spouses to get home earlier than usual, each with their own excuses. Then two other mornings besides. But life apart began to seem like a waste of time and, without talking about it, they started to see each other most weekdays. Even when the plans were specific (Dockweiler Beach at 11:00 a.m., the second lifeguard station, or Palisades Park, the bench under the giant eucalyptus) they were last-minute. Made in a flurry of texts the night before. A quick morning-of phone call after David and Holly had both left for work. Will was always promising that they would get work done while they were together. That he would write lesson plans or grade homework while she sat next to him in the back room of a coffee shop, stuffing envelopes for some charity event at her kids' school or sketching on a pad of newsprint. But it never went that way. It was difficult to look at anything other than the other's face. There was never enough time to talk. Every time he learned something about her, he left feeling robbed, a little panicked that there was still so much about her he didn't know. She was breathless with her own boldness and power, with her luck. How did she come to be sitting in secret across a table from this man—this man who looked into her eyes and saw to her mangled roots—her hand on his knee under a wobbly, coffee-stained table?

The worst were the days they expected to see each other but couldn't because of meetings, doctor's appointments, a sick child. Although that didn't always stop them. He brought Dylan to her house twice when the boy was home from day care with the sniffles. Met her children a handful of times when she brought them to the Santa Monica Pier after school. Dylan couldn't report accurately back to his mother, not really, and there were just so many children in the frum community that if Shosh and Yoni told a story about Dylan at the dinner table, David wouldn't catch it, not even with a name like Dylan. Dylan needed no explanation of the newcomers; Shosh and Yoni were just new friends. But Rina's kids, who spent time almost exclusively with Jews, needed a reason. In her experience, the truth went over well with children, who were sometimes gullible but more often shrewd. So she told them he was her art teacher, and they asked no further questions about the relationship, which was never affectionate in front of the children. After a while she took the same approach with David, told him her art professor had a kid near Yoni's age and they played sometimes at the pier. He just nodded from behind his laptop.

They grew sick of making love in the supply closet, the backseats of their cars, and once in a movie theater bathroom after a barely watched matinee, and they started risking their own homes. The day Obama was reelected, with TV news running in the background, they did it on his couch and he told her, "You know I've never even fucked in my own living room before?" Later Will told Rina how that night Holly came home early to watch the election returns, and he was on his knees sniffing the upholstery and couldn't think of any explanation.

"It smells," he said.

"So wash it," Holly said, tossing her keys on the coffee table, then turning to the cable news. He picked up her keys and put them on a hook. But, he told Rina, he would never wash the couch.

With each passing week they were more tolerant of less sleep. They stayed up late doing all the things they used to do during the time they now spent together. She looked at her calendar and saw only negative spaces, blanks between obligations. They grew to hate weekends.

Thanksgiving was the first time they couldn't sneak away for days. She texted him details that seemed to surprise him, how Jews ate turkey and jellied cranberry just like everyone else. He texted her a play-by-play of his tías once again not understanding that he didn't eat meat, of the second year without his mother not being any easier than the first, of the horror movies his nephews watched in the den, of the ivory smell of the capirotada, with its bread and cheese and almonds. He texted her poetry, which he started attributing after she hadn't known the Neruda. Thanksgiving was Edna St. Vincent Millay.

Cell phone bills had to be intercepted, but so far the affair didn't require big lies. They always threw away receipts from coffee shops, movie stubs, parking tickets from the garages in which they fucked in their backseats. They created email accounts to use only with each other. If one was curious, there were little details. The couch sniffing. The dearth of paint splatters on his weekday clothes. How Rina started fixing all David's favorite foods at home, trying to stave off any churlish curiosity that could upend her freedom, encouraged him to go daily to yoga, instead of her previous, studied neutrality on his practice. The way they were each listening to music from their youths, without being able to explain why.

He applied to teach the one and only Saturday extension class the art school offered, which was taught from 5:00 to 8:00 p.m. Much of the year that would fall during Shabbos, a time when Rina would never be available. Anyway, weekend nights were almost impossible. If the department chair let him teach it spring semester, he'd quit one weekday class and it would free up three additional hours of time for them to spend together.

One Sunday in early December, Will had to go down to Laguna Beach to sort out holiday plans for his father, to make sure the facility knew when his father would be coming and going. He invited Rina to drive down to Orange County with him. It was the first time they'd seen each other on a weekend. She parked her car in the lot of a bank a half mile from her house and he picked her up there. She had to tell a fancy lie at home. A lie that Chana's mother-in-law was coming unexpectedly on Monday night and there wasn't time for Chana alone to prepare. Their affair was burning blue.

"I wish you could come inside and meet him," he said, as they started down the 405. "He'd like you. Better than he likes Holly anyway."

"I told David I don't want another baby." Car rides made it easier for her to say the things she never wanted to in their precious moments of intimacy.

"How do you feel about that?" Will said, an edge in his voice. Why was he angry?

"I'm the one who decided I can't have another baby with him."

"But how did you feel after you told him?"

"Conflicted."

He stared at the road, jaw clenched.

Over the ocean to their right, the sun hit the dissipating marine layer like a paintbrush on the surface of water. Will gripped the steering wheel, veins bulging on his hands. A two-propeller military helicopter swooped low, a slow-moving hole cut from the taut fabric of the sky, revealing the soft gray mist of the universe outside the earth's atmosphere. The helicopter heaved closer, and Rina had a flash of reaching out the window and pulling it from the sky and flinging it into the water just to make Will talk. She'd expected him to be happy.

"When I was a little girl my grandfather, my mother's father, would offer me pinkie dips of his Scotch," she said. "I hated the taste of it, but I loved my grandfather and he loved having a secret. It took me years to tell him those tastes made me sick to my stomach. But god, Shabbos dinners improved once I told him. Even though I hurt him."

"But now you're a whisky drinker."

"That is the angle you would see."

"How did David take it?"

"Not as well as my grandfather."

"But you do want another baby," he said.

"Are you asking if I might want one with you?"

"I don't know," he said, looking at her, then back at the road. Her, then the road.

"I want a baby with you. With all my essence."

"You don't believe in essence," he said.

"Sure I do. Call it biology. As much as it's in your essence to put one in me."

"You're funny."

"David doesn't think so," she said.

"David doesn't love you like I do."

"No," she said. "But he does love me."

They arrived and Will parked underground. They took the elevator up together and Rina set off to walk along the bluffs behind the complex.

Minutes later he came running back out, catching up with her on the path. His eyes were wild; she almost couldn't recognize him. She took a step backward.

"Is it your dad?" she said.

He shook his head.

"Oh my god. Dylan?"

"An accident," he said. "Taxi home. I have to leave."

"No, I'll drive you."

He got in the passenger side of the car, and the smell of his anger and fear bludgeoned the air between them. He pulled at a tuft of hair over his ear, yanking it out from the root. Repeated the details Holly had told him, although it didn't sound like he was talking to Rina. Dylan playing outside, Holly in the kitchen, Dylan in the neighbor's driveway, the neighbor's car backing out over Will's baby.

"Why was she not outside with him?" he said, over and over again. "He lives half his life in his own head. When he gets like that, he can't hear a sonic boom. Certainly not a garage door. Not a car."

"Cariño—" Rina said.

"Don't call me that," Will said.

"Think only about getting to Dylan."

"Where was Holly?" he said.

"The point isn't what's happened. The point is he's alive and you are his father."

"How do you know he's alive? They airlifted him."

"They airlifted him because you live at the top of the canyon. Be grateful for it. Believe he'll be alive when you get there."

"If I hadn't been with you, my son would still be whole."

"I'm driving fast," she said, wiping at her eyes. He seemed satisfied with her tears.

It took almost two hours to get to the Children's Hospital in East Hollywood. By then he'd talked to Holly seven times; Dylan was alive but in surgery. Will directed Rina to valet park the car, grabbed the ticket from the attendant, and walked through the automatic doors without a glance over his shoulder.

She didn't sit down in the lobby with a plan to stay, she just didn't know what else to do. It was the first day of Hanukkah and she'd made a party the night before; there weren't big plans for the second night, thank god. She worked out a story before she called home. Chana's oil-burning hanukkiah had caught her drapes on fire, one kid had smoke inhalation, Rina had to stay and watch the other kids while they took the baby to urgent care. David didn't know Chana well enough to check, so she didn't feel guilty about lying, but the guilt over worrying about her relationship with Will while his child lay limp upstairs? That she wrestled with like lead. Sometimes, on nights when David came home late from work, Rina constructed gruesome and self-serving fantasies. She'd imagine him dead. A car accident, most likely, or an explosion of natural gas mushrooming in sulfuric waves through the vast garage underneath the law firm; his eyes would sear blind before he asphyxiated, before he burned. Did David ever fantasize about her death, imagine she would never come home? Was he hoping it right now? Open a path for him to explore Aliza, their shared practice, the chintzy fiction of their book club? God forbid, did Will hope she would disappear? Simplify his life?

At 10:00 p.m., more than nine hours after they'd arrived at the hospital, Will stepped off the elevator and into the lobby.

He saw her right away, and she saw he was confused, like he barely remembered the fact of her. But he came to her, collapsed near her feet.

"The doctors gave Dylan something to sleep," he said.

She unfolded herself from the chair, ungathered her skirts, sat next to him on the floor.

"He's alive," Will said.

She made a calming sound, like white noise. Offered him a sleeve. He wiped his eyes and nose on her sweatshirt, and she stroked his hair.

"When he was five months old, we took him up the coast. He was just able to sit by himself. I remember because he took his first swing ride on that trip. He could hold himself up in a bucket swing. We rented this house with a huge pinewood loft over the bedroom. Way more than we could afford. I spent a couple hours each afternoon up there drawing. We bought him this floppy orange koala bear in the town, the softest little animal. We named him OJ."

His breath steadied. There weren't many people in the lobby, and most ignored them with polite forward stares. An older woman watched them as she knit. Rina was anxious to know what was happening with Dylan right now, but she didn't interrupt.

"Dylan would lie like an island in the middle of the bed, and I'd toss OJ over the railing of the loft so it landed on him," Will said. "Holly would throw it back up and I'd toss it down on him. Over and over again. It was the first time I heard his real laugh. His stomach shook with it. He'd laugh so hard he could barely breathe and then it would trail off and I'd toss the bear again. I would recognize that sound anywhere. My son's laugh. Even in a crowd of laughing babies. But I can't hear it in my mind. It's like pain. You remember feeling it, but you can't remember how it felt. I want so badly to hear that laugh."

He stopped, maybe because he'd said what he meant, and for a moment their breathing was in sync.

"You should go home and be with your kids." His words were muffled. "They're alive and fine and everything is so fragile—"

"My kids are asleep now. I needed to be near you."

"But you have to go home."

"You going home to get clothes?" she asked.

"Out for food."

"Want me to ride with you?"

"Sure," he said. "Yes."

She drove his car and paid for the fast food. Dylan's body had been well-positioned under the car, Will told her; the tires only ran over his left foot. He was scraped all over and a piece of his scalp had to be sewn back down. Besides the broken foot, most of his ribs were cracked. He'd had a very short surgery, and Will had been with him all day; there were deep bruises under Dylan's eyes, and a tiny oxygen apparatus in his nose. Frankenstein stitching cut a wide arc from his crown down into his hairline, and as soon as the anesthetic wore off, Dylan had tried to scratch at the stitches and kept tangling the IV line. The nurse said it was a good sign, and Will hated her for it.

"Holly's too afraid to touch him," Will said. "But I held him all day, as lightly as an egg."

Rina parked his car back at the hospital and then called a cab for herself.

"I have to make doughnuts in the afternoon," she said. How trivial her life: donuts. "Or maybe I'll make them the next day. I'll come back in the morning for a little while."

"I can't see you," he said. "Holly can't know. Not now."

"She doesn't know what I look like," Rina said. "I'll just be sitting here, to be close to you. Anything you need."

"I wasn't angry with you, cariño."

"Yes," she said. "You were."

"And you waited anyway."

She touched his cheek with her thumb. He put his hand on top of hers, held it there.

The day after the accident she again sat for hours in the Children's Hospital lobby. She and David were going to a Hanukkah party that night, but her duties were unusually light until then. The previous Friday Rina had made and frozen two loaves of chocolate-orange challah to bring with them.

She sat in the lobby making happy Hanukkah calls to lonely old folks in a retirement home, until Holly went home in the afternoon to pack a bag and have a shower and Will called Rina on her cell and told her she could come up. He warned that Dylan looked worse than he was because his bruises had deepened and he was swollen from intravenous steroids. Even though Dylan had his mother's hair and coloring, in personality and facial expression he was all Will. His tiny body was purpled, bandaged, and tangled in a hospital bed, the smell of iodine and baby shampoo. Her extremities pulsed with fear, and she looked away.

"Can you pick him up?" She whispered because Dylan seemed to be sleeping.

"I held him all night."

"Can I pick him up?"

"No," he said.

Dylan opened his eyes and tried to sit up a little and his face tightened then went slack with pain and panic. She couldn't hold air; a strangled sound came from her throat. Dylan tried to say her name, and she looked at the ceiling and blinked hard. From this feeling a person could die.

On Dylan's third day in the hospital, Will went home for a few hours, to bathe and rest on a real bed. Rina spent the early morning setting up an after-school Hanukkah project for Shosh and Yoni; putting up the yeasted sufganiyot dough to rise—she'd promised David some for the fourth night—while defrosting a jar of her homemade strawberry preserves for the filling; loading onions, garlic, prunes, carrots, tomatoes, raisins, and a dripping slab of raw brisket into the slow cooker for dinner that night, double the amount they would eat so she could take some to Chana's family (a kindness, yes, and a follow-up to her lie). Ordinarily she'd brown the beef first, but she wanted to get up to Topanga. She shredded potatoes to fry later and left them in the fridge with a few lemon slices to slow their graying. She cleaned the kitchen, bleached the sink, vacuumed the flour dust, rinsed herself in the shower, brushed her teeth, and pinched her cheeks. She lotioned her hands, but they still smelled of sulfur and blood.

Rina met him in the canyon. Fresh from her own shower, she climbed in a shower with him, washed his hair, knelt in front of him under the steaming waves of water, worked on him, worked a long time—until he could release his body from the anguish of caring for his son's body—in one way swallowing a little of his tension, drawing out a little of his ache. Then she pulled the shades and drew the blankets up to his neck and sat in his living room to read a book until it was time to wake him.

Even the architecture of Will's bungalow reflected quirky

Topanga, a small community of artsy folks, a tapered, Aspen-
filled canyon slashed by a stream high in the Santa Monica
Mountains halfway between the ocean and the San Fernando
Valley. The bones of the house, he'd told her, were over seventy
years old, but in 1972 most of it had been razed and rebuilt in
the arcology style of architect Paolo Soleri (when he'd told her
this, she'd nodded like she knew, then went home and looked
up Paolo Soleri). There was a kind of domed tower built at
one end of the living room—where a fireplace might otherwise
have been—that let in light from small windows well above the
height of the roof and was used by Will and Holly as a narrow
bookshelf. The living room was also domed, with diminutive
windows to match the tower, and Will had painted the dome
like a pansy, deep purple with huge raindrops of yellow coming from the middle. Bells hung from the dome, soundless and
spooky in their hulking stillness.

The air in his home tasted the way alchemists' studies look
in old oil paintings: linseed oil, loam, the carbonated richness
of something fermenting, motes of dust gone stale in the large
dome, wood and rust on the tongue, as if Will was molding his
surroundings until he manifested one day in the impasto of an
old master, all carob paint and spotlights shining down from
those clerestory windows. He'd picked every color of paint,
finished every piece of furniture with his own coarse hands,
hammered mismatched nails into the door of his bedroom to
form the shape of an aspen, turned the small family room into
an actual fort for Dylan by lining the walls with rough-hewn
logs (which he'd told her he split himself with an axe in the
backyard just to see if he could), and a hundred other details
that made her love him more in the noticing. Holly's influence
came only in her implied tolerance of Will's whimsy, a bouquet
of silk flowers on a credenza, and the absence of his paintings

on the walls ("They remind her of the year in New York," Will told Rina early on). But all the magic of Will's home made her feel that hers was deficient. Almost all the art in her town-home was Judaica and, even though she'd decorated the place, it didn't contain much other than framed photographs to iden-tify it as something of her making. The Captain was squirreled away in the loft. Even the books she displayed were the same as the books in all the other Jewish homes; she kept her fiction, poetry, and college textbooks in plastic bins under her bed.

Will's home was also full of houseplants. Growing out of baskets and old shoes, nested in globes and tin cans and empty bottles of wine, planted in a thumbful of soil in a hollowed-out cork and a spoonful of soil in a broken light bulb. They hung from the ceiling in pots, were stuffed between books on the shelves, and were placed like picture frames on sideboards. The only place there weren't plants was a brick enclosure by the front door that seemed to be meant for them but was in-stead piled with coats and shoes, toys and sippy cups. She touched the nascent, unfurling yellow leaf of a cutting taking root in a glass of water on a cart next to the armchair. It was soft as the flesh of her Yoni's small palms, damp, too, and she feared damaging it but could not stop running it between her thumb and forefinger. In the neighborhood no one had house-plants; they were bohemian and alien, a luxury of the gentile. One more thing that demanded attention, one more thing to die when the Cossacks returned. The goyim polished the marbled green leaves of their houseplants—she'd read about that in novels—and gave the dogs bones that could have been used for soup. The Jews instead had—Rina had—fresh flowers every Friday evening on the table, a fleeting pleasure, hauled out to the compost bin on Monday morning with the relief of another Shabbos lived in peace. Maybe Will's plants were

an act of rebellion against ancient colonizers; maybe he culti-
vated his home to prove he was there, to establish that which
is wild cannot be fully tamed, to prove that paradise could be
his. But then, maybe the plants were Holly's.

He'd instructed Rina to let him sleep no more than forty-
five minutes, but she let him go for an hour—as long as she
dared without risking being late for school pickup—and then
climbed under the covers with him, bundled herself her-back-
to-his-stomach in his feline curve, held his hands, and moved
them over her body until his own need woke him and he made
love to her quick, then held himself in her for a long time,
held her tight, cried a little into her neck, his sounds like the
whimper of her own son after a nightmare.

"I was dreaming about the Rose Bowl," he said.

"The football stadium?"

"There's a course you can walk, around the stadium. At
the base of the San Gabriel Mountains, so different from
where I grew up. My mother used to take me there." His voice
was muffled and slow, almost as if he was still in a dream.
"She would pack a lunch and take us to the art museum in
Pasadena, then we would have a picnic outside the Rose Bowl
and walk around the track. We never had dogs because my
dad didn't like them, but she taught us the names of all the
breeds people were walking. She gave us a quarter if we spot-
ted a Lady from *Lady and the Tramp*. Cocker spaniels were her
favorite, but we almost never saw them."

"Do you take Dylan there?" she said, holding her palm in
the divot of his chest so she could feel his heartbeat.

"Not yet," Will said. "I will when he's a little older. I go
there by myself. Or, I used to before us. On days when I didn't
teach. Days when I was supposed to be painting. I went to
look at mountains instead."

"You live in the mountains," Rina said.

"Different mountains."

She smiled. "Will you take me there?"

"Of course," he said. "Of course I will."

"We didn't have dogs, either," Rina said. In the neighborhood there were as few dogs as houseplants. He nodded, but she didn't think he felt this connection as strongly as he ought to.

After he left, she made the bed, cleared some rotting fruit from a pearlescent raku bowl on the kitchen counter, took out the trash, and locked up with the spare key under the mat. She drove ten above the speed limit when traffic allowed, picked up the children on time. At home Yoni and Shosh made hanukkiot out of Plasticine clay, rolling and swirling colors together while the townhouse filled with the smell of frying doughnuts. She put their little menorahs in the oven to bake, filled the sufganiyot with jelly, poured in more oil, salted and rubbed a second cast iron, and began to fry the latkes. Just enough for dinner tonight; she'd make more—traditional and ginger scallion—when they had three families over for the seventh candle and Shabbos. She bathed the children and fed them dinner. David came home around eight and he lit the candles and the oil lamps; they sang Hebrew verses about saving grace, let the children open a gift each. It was past bedtime, but David wouldn't let her put them to sleep until the candles were out.

"It's not work to read to my children," Rina said.

There was a rule that women could not work in the light of the Hanukkah candles, a law that prohibited them from doing anything utilitarian during that time, anything other than remembering the miracle. Like many men, David made a gift of long-burning candles to her each year. Called it a "vacation."

Like everything, it just made more work. She couldn't clear the table, gather up the crumpled wrapping paper, clean the kitchen, pick out the rainbow of plastic crumbs smashed into the carpet from their afternoon project. Instead of mopping the floors at ten, she'd be mopping them at eleven. Such a blessing she had never wished for.

"But you should sit down," David said. "Take a few minutes."

"Then you put them to bed," Rina said, and the children sent up a chorus of complaints. "School starts at the same time as always tomorrow morning. Did the rabbis think of that when they gifted us this time?"

The day before Dylan left the hospital Holly had to go to work before USC closed for the winter holidays, so Rina spent one more morning with Will and Dylan, her own children healthful and robust in their school nine miles to the west. She'd done some of the Shabbos prep the day before, but there was still plenty. She didn't have much time.

Christmas crafts were set up in the hospital playroom down the hall from Dylan's room, and while Will napped in the tiny hospital bed, Rina sat on a striped rug with the boy and helped him poke cloves into an orange, wondering if he could distinguish her from a doctor or nurse, and then—when he lost interest—read board books while he fidgeted in her lap. There were two children cutting snowflakes from paper and one young father gluing pom-poms onto a snowperson while his toddler, slack eyed, drooled on a beaded toy. These crafts must have seemed secular to the hospital volunteers who arranged them, inoffensive. It sent a jolt down Rina's spine, though, brought a flush to her face. What could snow mean—especially in southern California—other than Christmas? Jewish schools were free of references to Halloween and Valentine's Day, of course, but also to winter. Her freshman year of college, the Halloween and Christmas decorations in the dining hall stunned her with their presumption and their magnificence. She would never eat a can of SpaghettiOs—mythical SpaghettiOs, unkosher for no specific reason, taunting her in endless Sunday-morning cartoon commercials, not even looking so delicious, just so *regular*—but she could commit the minor mutiny of cutting out a snowflake, a Christmas snowflake. Did her children long for SpaghettiOs and snowflakes? What would David say if next Sukkot she let the children cut snowflakes from construction paper instead of pears and apples? What if they strung popcorn and cranberries, which also had to do with the harvest, instead of dried lemons and wood beads? Shosh was nimble with her hands; Rina would only have to show her once how to carefully thread a blossom of popcorn so as not to break it. But who would show Rina? Would popcorn and cranberries betray her peoplehood?

Rina hated the idea of prayer but was soothed by the practice, and she prayed for Dylan as they played. She envied less observant Jews who, not steeped in twelve years of formal Hebrew education, could chant the prayers in meditative bliss, ignoring the contemptible meaning of the words. "It is our duty to praise the Master of all"—*lateit gedulah l'yotzer b'reishit*—"who has not made us like the nations of the lands"—*v'lo samanu k'mishp'chot ha'admah*—"who has not made our portion like theirs"—*v'goralenu k'chol hamonam*—"for they worship vanity and emptiness." She, of course, did not believe a higher power could heal Dylan but couldn't help saying a refua shlema prayer for him as he sat in her lap thumbing board books—"May the lord answer you on the day of your distress"—over and over again, under her breath and in her head.

And she said it each night before bed as Dylan healed, too. She was muddied by saying it, incomplete if she abstained. As she mouthed the prayer in bed she focused with fervor on the little boy, but afterward added, *and dear god, who does not exist, please let him get well so I can have Will's mornings back.* Praying to a god she did not believe in to heal her lover's son so she could resume her affair without remorse. It was the kind of selfish thinking her husband believed earned the scorn of the almighty, but she could no more prevent this thought's coming than she could have prevented a car from backing over the child.

In the week leading up to Christmas, when Dylan was back home, she didn't see Will at all. Her only comfort in this was that, because she didn't have access to money that was fully her own, she hadn't yet thought of a way to buy Will a holiday gift. They kept in touch through text, and in this way, she knew that Will had taken up smoking again, that Dylan was sleeping well at night, that they planned to spend Christmas afternoon wheeling Will's father up and down the corridors of his Laguna living facility because it turned out he was too weak to come to the city, even under Frank's wife's fastidious care. She did not know if Will missed her, if he thought of her from across town, if he would remember that he loved her, but the sting was diminished by how thoroughly she'd internalized him: in his absence he was with her, paint-crusted cuticles, agate class ring, wine breath, and hot, yielding mouth. As sappy as all that. Sometimes she felt him with such force that she looked up and expected to see the steep cant of his face, the shadow of him moving toward her, "Cariño."

Rina was more aware of Christmas than she'd ever been in her life, and when David picked a fight with her on a Monday night, she knew it was Christmas Eve. While she'd been playing *Kosherland* and *Chutes and Ladders* with her children and the neighbor kids, Will was texting from his brother's in Pasadena, picking the meat out of tamales, avoiding the Jell-O salad, drinking beer, watching scratchy DVDs while the kids played in the other room and ran in to scream at the jump scares, listening to his brother complain about how *muy fresa* Will was, dreading the Christmas Day visit to his father. (She was too embarrassed to ask what *fresa* meant or even Google it, in case it was offensive. She knew it was offensive to Will; that was enough.) Will told her they were doing posadas this year, which Rina gathered was like Christmas caroling, but with plays about Jesus.

David came into the bedroom while she was sitting on the floor folding the laundry she'd run just after Shabbos went out on Saturday night. She slid her warm phone under the sock pile in her lap but didn't look up. David clapped his hands in front of her face.

"All day like this, all yesterday, all Shabbos, too," he said. "What is with you?"

She shook the static from a pair of his boxers with a sharp snap of the wrist. Her hair was unwashed, her unshaved legs splayed. She'd been picking at her skin, and she was wearing a fifteen-year-old cutoff T-shirt. Other than being unpresentable, she could think of nothing she'd done wrong. All Saturday afternoon she played with the kids so he could sleep off his drunk from the shots of vodka he and his friends took Shabbos morning in the basement of the shul. She took the children to the park twice on Sunday. Today he'd been at work, even though half the firm was gone for the holiday.

"So dramatic. Just tell me what I've done now."

"You tell me. Tell me anything," he said. Rina shook her head and shifted a pile of Yoni's laundry into a basket. "For three months you walk around like Snow White, whistling to yourself and being a June Cleaver of a mom—"

"June Cleaver?"

"—but now we're having chicken nuggets and scrambled eggs for dinner every night, you didn't make challah on Friday, you didn't come to shul, I couldn't get a single word out of you all Shabbos, much less anything else."

"I'm not having this fight with you."

"Everything is on your timetable," he said, his voice rising. "What are you doing with all that time anyway, that we should eat chicken nuggets? You can't be spending *all* your mornings volunteering—"

"I raise your children."

"Then there's time for a baby."

"I told you I don't want a baby right now." This shook David, she could see it. He softened for a moment.

"What happened to your art class? That was helping."

"With what?" she said, but then realized she had an opening, the lie coming to her all at once. "Anyway, I signed up for another one next quarter," she said. "Two nights a week. Hope you can be bothered to watch your children."

"This is what happens when you don't have anything to believe in," David said, his voice full of venom again. "You need something to fill your core. Maybe you need to be medicated."

Rina stood up and whipped an undershirt against a bedpost. A dumb but satisfying gesture.

"Two weeks out of eight years and I need an intervention? I do everything here, you workaholic fuck."

"I pay for it all. No more unilateral decisions from you if you want me to keep paying for it all." He was yelling.

"So this is all about another baby? Why would you want

another baby with a woman who you think needs to be medicated?"

"Maybe I don't."

She took a breath, thought of the children, tried to quiet her voice.

"Couples therapy," she said. "That's a unilateral ultimatum."

"I'm not going to sit in a room while you berate me."

The doorknob rattled.

"It's not a good time," David said.

"Are you lying on top of Ima?" Shosh said from the hall.

Rina shook her head and sat back down in front of the laundry. David pointed a finger at her. "You're unbelievable," he said. Then he opened the door and slammed it so hard behind him that it bounced in its frame and skimmed open again. "No," he said to Shosh, and he brushed by her in the hall. "I definitely am not."

Rina transferred the clean laundry to suitcases she pulled out from under her bed. Except for the year after Yoni was born, when he was sick with croup all winter, they always spent the week before the secular New Year with Rina's maternal grandparents in Palm Desert. Between Rina's parents, sister, brother, sister-in-law, uncles, aunts, cousins, and sometimes David's parents, they took up ten casitas at the resort where her grandparents owned a small vacation home behind the golf course. Most of the rest of the resort was also taken up with Jews from West L.A., and years when Hanukkah extended beyond December 25 there was collective candle lighting in the hotel arcade, the only one of the ornate common rooms not decorated with an elaborate Christmas tree.

The drive took three hours, but this year felt interminable because she couldn't check her phone, which had buzzed four times in her back pocket, the buzz-buzzzzzz-buzz pattern she had set for Will. Rina rode up with her parents, Shosh and Yoni, and a carful of kosher meat, cheese, wine, parve cakes, and frozen blueberry blintzes from Pico Kosher Deli. David drove with Rina's sister, and Rina spent most of the drive fantasizing the whole vacation would be without her husband, this placid. Her phone buzz-buzzzzzz-buzzed a fifth time, and her body contracted. She clutched the steering wheel to prevent herself from reaching for it, the urge to pull over so great it made her temples throb.

All week she tried to be nice to David, tried to get her childless siblings to take care of the kids, tried to avoid her parents, who suspected something was wrong but could not have guessed the immensity of the wrongness. For the most part she spent the week attached to her phone, though Will's texts became sparse.

He was angry with her, angry that she was on vacation with her husband, angry that she wasn't able to talk on the phone. But for four days he and Holly took Dylan to San Diego and he was equally occupied. She didn't understand what he didn't understand. He was haunted by the idea she might sleep with her husband, obsessed with it, and kept texting her *please don't* and *letters* over and over. She couldn't even think of him fucking Holly, she just couldn't let it enter her head. He texted her a photo of Dylan at a candy shop in Old Town San Diego, a selfie from an ice rink right on the beach. She could hardly look at the photos because she didn't want to think of him that happy with Holly. So she deleted them. But Will asked for photos and then obsessed over the details, interrogating her about the pepper trees, why the children were still so pale, why David was always on his phone in the background. The irony of demanding this information from her via a string of texts was lost on Will.

Most years she spent the bulk of vacation in the pool. Each set of eight casitas had a tiny private saltwater pool between them, and she reveled in the extra buoyancy even though it stung the children's eyes. She would float at the surface, eyes closed, imagining she was on a rooftop in Jerusalem or a luxury train in the Canadian Rockies or a forest shack in the barren Russian shtetl her family inhabited a century ago, or anywhere other than the same casita, year after year, the cost of which could easily finance a family trip abroad. She would spit and breathe into the children's goggles so they didn't fog, fastening them on their little heads and playing Marco Polo for hours, helping them imagine they were in a jungle stream, an icy cave pool, a great fountain in a European capital. *Marco, I will swim with the sockeye until I reach you. Polo, I'm in a beaver's den; you'll never find me.*

But she hardly swam at all this year because it separated her from her phone and the possibility that Will was trying to reach her. Also, the pool was where everyone else was and she didn't want company. Her brother played Marco Polo with the children; the children complained he didn't do it right.

"New Year's Day, cariño," Will said, the one time they were able to talk by phone. "Meet me at the corner of Barrington and Ohio. 3:00 p.m. Can you?"

She was on the fenced-in porch of their casita, sitting in a square of shade cast by the upstairs balcony. Ten feet away her husband, siblings, and children splashed. Her blood in the shallows, her choices overseeing them.

"An intersection?" she said, trying to visualize that particular corner. "Are you leaving me?" The woman on the porch next to her, whose brown legs looked as if they'd been brushed onto the chaise with one long stroke, turned toward Rina and looked at her over her huge sunglasses without reproach. Rina shrugged a dumb shrug.

"It's your gift," he said, with a soft voice. "Can you?"

"I'll figure it out."

"Don't call until then. It will be better."

"The intersection will be better?"

"Don't be glib. There are surprises left in life."

She looked at David, pink from the sun, lying face down on a fluorescent raft that took a quarter of the small pool. David had once said there were few surprises left in life; it was at the obstetrician's office before Shosh was born. But Rina overruled him and found out their first would be a girl. Looking at David's back like that—the hairy patches that didn't exist when she met him, the muscle tone that only appeared in the last two years, since he joined the gym right around the same time as Aliza—she wanted to feel something. Confused about why she ever loved him. A surge of love, maybe, forceful as the vulgar waterfall spilling into the south end of the pool. She heard a scratching and noticed a roadrunner, fierce and fronting, on the patio with her. She stared at the bird and it stared back at her, eyes mean. She looked away and shuddered, failing to feel anything at all about her husband.

"I don't have a gift for you," she said. The bird's claw scratched at the terra-cotta.

"Good," he said. "Don't get one."

"Letters."

"You'll love me even more on Tuesday."

There was a plan. She hung up and cautiously crept to the casita while the roadrunner hopped forward and back, puffing up its torso. She changed into her swimsuit and rummaged for the ring toss set for the children. When she peeked back through the blinds, the bird was gone.

She smiled her way through three days, listened (actually listened) to the things her children said to her, acquired a constellation of tiny ant bites from playing with them for hours in the grass, laughed at things that were funny, ate actual meals instead of the power bars and tinned holiday popcorn—David always brought home tubs of it, gifts from his clients—on which she'd been subsisting. She was almost happy for almost the rest of the vacation, until David said, "Nice to have you back," in front of her parents, and she retreated into her silent fantasy where only she and Will and the children existed. Where it was always early morning or setting dusk and she was well-rested and over-sexed and baking pies and never vacationed in Palm fucking Desert where the air tasted like dirt.

Each year the resort had a black-tie New Year's Eve ball and the Kirsch/Green family always left before sundown on New Year's Eve to beat the holiday traffic, earlier if New Year's Eve was on Shabbos. But on the 30th David came into their huge travertine bathroom, where she was plucking her eyebrows in the magnifying mirror, and said he'd been talking to the brothers and why didn't they all stay an extra day or two, go to the ball, now that the kids were old enough to be left in the room once they were asleep.

"You can use it as an excuse to buy a new dress if you can get to the shops before Shabbos," he said. He had a hard-on, small and ridiculous in his yellow ten-dollar swim trunks.

"I don't want a new dress," Rina said. She kept the panic from her voice but couldn't keep the flush from her cheeks.

"Every girl wants a new dress," David said, wrapping an arm around her from the side. She let him keep it there. "I already talked to everyone. It's meant to be a surprise. So, surprise."

"We're not staying."

"We are," he said, pulling her sideways and breathing onto her neck.

She turned and kissed him full-on. He stumbled backward and pulled her with him. She shrouded her face in his shoulder and stifled a gag.

"I have plans New Year's Day," she said. Half-truths seemed like the only option. "While you're at the Frisch's football party. You know I hate that party."

"What are you doing?" He pushed against her, a knot, in a way that would have dropped her to her knees if it was Will. Or maybe anyone else.

"Just. A picnic," she said and started kissing him to the bedroom. "With Jewish Family Services people. It's not babysitter worthy."

He didn't say anything else but locked the door.

"Are the kids with my folks?" she asked.

He nodded and pushed her down on the bed.

"Turn me over," she said.

"You mean?" David said. "Can I?"

"Whatever you want," Rina said. "But we are leaving today." She closed her eyes and thought of the picture she would paint Will as a gift. It would be a picture of her peach-fuzzed, olive-shaped navel, an extreme close-up, so close he wouldn't know if it was anatomical or, say, a seed from which a tree would grow. The sex was worth it to get home to Will, but she decided at the start she would never come again with her husband inside her; her faithful body complied.

✶

The intersection had four corners. After all these months the mass of her love for Will was still so intimidating—the current that shot from her in search of his nearness, seeking him like heat, so furious—that not knowing which corner he meant alarmed her. Compounded with the weeks it had been since she'd been with him, it made her second-guess the way she dressed, the way her hair fell, the way she talked and walked and looked up at the light, chewing her lip, waiting for it to change. She'd taken care of everything to get there, dropped Yoni at her mother's with his little bag, packed up books and markers and paper for Shosh to keep occupied at the football party, made two trays of her five-cheese heart attack kugel in foil pans for David to take with him, cut roses from the garden to send to the hostess, prepared egg salad and sliced fruit for David to eat in case he should be hungry when he got home, washed and dried the sink, ran the laundry, lotioned her hands. Her headwraps, too delicate for the machine, were soaking with detergent in a bucket.

She saw Will park, recognized him at once even though he was driving his wife's car, and for a moment fidgeted with her watch and couldn't decide whether to cross toward him or stay where she was. She pretended she hadn't seen him, let a piece of hair fall into her eyes, investigated a giant dandelion growing from a seam in the cement, considered taking a fabricated call on her cell phone.

He waved and grinned and she tried to look surprised but not too surprised. She pressed the button on the crosswalk; he motioned her to stay.

"Why'd you wear a skirt?" he said when he reached her side. "We're going to scale a fence."

"You might've told me."

"And ruin it?"

She leaned in, clumsy, to kiss him. She never understood the way, in movies, reunited lovers fling themselves together at airports, train stations, thresholds. Time made her shy.

"Not here," he said, then swerved. "Follow me."

They walked around the front of a huge high school, more like something you would see on the East Coast or in a movie, with its brick and sculpted cement, trimmed hedges and rows of dormant jacarandas. The place was a compound, but Will went right to a narrow gate marked SCHOOL DISTRICT RE-CEIVING, and even though it was some eight feet tall, the chain-link was easy to climb.

She straddled the top, looked at the ground. Getting down the other side was going to be more difficult. There was a view of the flat, Spanish-tiled roofs of the Westside; large, generic patches of green from the non-native trees; king palms leaning above everything, their fronds rustling not with wind but with tree rats. She squinted and the neighborhood reduced to a smeary map of colors. The hard lines of the homes disappeared, the rectangular grids formed by streets meeting each other at the ends of blocks turned to smudgy ashen creases, the oval turquoise pools to thumbprints. It was the way sixty-two degrees in January looked, as if California winter had scrawled its name along the lower right corner of her field of vision.

"Need help?" he said and swung one long leg over the top so that he was facing her.

Rina looked down and laughed.

"I might," she said.

He swung his other leg over and dropped to the ground, his buff cowboy boots thudding with a sound that made her ankles shudder.

"I'll catch you," he said, arms out, and he did, and then he pulled her, hand in hand, behind the brick wall of an outdoor cafeteria and kissed her twice, quickly; he smelled like cigarettes but not unpleasantly, and his warmth flooded her and she was suddenly famished—hungry for a steak, two steaks, even—as if she'd been starving for weeks. "One for hello and one for I missed you. Follow me."

He led her around a small maze of buildings, picnic tables, and trash cans and down a sloping rubber sidewalk.

"Did you know there are underground rivulets running all over the city?" he said. She shook her head. "There's one that runs under Wilshire. Comes from snowmelt in the Santa Monica Mountains. Makes a right turn under Barrington. And then, magic."

They walked up a hill toward a huge cypress tree until they reached a pond with a careless, gossamer waterfall dropping from a few feet above. They were overlooking a softball field in the middle of the city, but in the shade of the giant cypress, with the moil of the water, they might as well have been marooned on an island.

"Oh," she said. "Oh."

"That's not the best of it."

He knelt down next to the pond and motioned for her to join. He pointed to the bottom; it was maybe a foot deep, and she could see water percolating up from the sandy base, a constant stream of thick, halcyon bubbles. He dipped his hands in and brought a huge mouthful to her, tipping his fingers toward her as a mother bends a soft spoon into a baby's mouth. There was something almost religious about the look of his hands cupped like that, of the stinging water, its crisp lack of flavor, the metallic taste of Will's hands underneath it. In his pacific watering of her she could almost feel her neurotransmitters firing, serotonin washing through her like the secret springs, her very atoms realigning like the simmering sand.

She sat down, took off her winter boots, and placed her socks inside, dipped her feet in the water.

"You're not happy, cariño," he said, searching her face, below his. His skin was winter russet; his face looked many years younger, a decade younger than he was. When he was serious, like this, she couldn't even see the folds of his laugh lines.

"I wish I'd known you as a child," she said. "I weep at night for not having known you."

"I don't want you to weep at night or ever."

"Sure you do," she said, and he sat down in a bit of moss and dirt and slumped back as if he was leaning against something, though there was nothing there.

"I want to make a joke, but I don't have one," he said.

"We need to talk about the big stuff."

"I know. But this was supposed to be your gift."

"It's magical. This is a good place to talk about things."

Will started the volley, a back-and-forth on their chances at a life together. A who-leaves-whom-and-when, until they came to an impasse.

"I got that Saturday afternoon class," he said. "That's one more morning we can see each other. It's not nothing."

"It can't stay like this," she said. "You can't work like this. I can't run a house like this."

"Dylan is barely out of the hospital. He needs both of us. Holly says he cries for me when I'm gone," Will said. He looked west and she followed his gaze; the sun was moving lower.

"You won't be leaving him."

"You don't understand. You're the mother. You get to keep everything."

"You think I want to do that?" she said, her voice shifting. "To take my children away from their father? If you think that, we come from different worlds, you and me."

"I've just been waiting for you to say something like that."

"Glad I didn't disappoint," she said. She'd been scratching at the ant bites on her calves and now pulled her skirt back down, brushed her hands off on her knees.

"You always look down your nose at me silently. Is it because I don't come from old money? Or your community? Because I haven't been to Paris or Prague? Because my parents worked for a living?"

"Your dad's a surgeon."

"But his dad packed orange crates onto trains and my great-grandfather shoveled shit on some Spaniard's farm."

"Yeah, Will, that's how the generations go. My great-grandparents died in Treblinka and my grandfathers didn't go to college."

"You think my world is so small," he said, steamrolling ahead, "because where I come from fathers don't always get a tidy fifty percent split, right?"

"Right," she said. She stood up and brushed off the back of her skirt. "That's why I'm here."

She pulled on her boots and set off in the opposite direction from which they'd come, her ears ringing with an angry rush of blood. At first she hoped he wouldn't follow her because she'd only say something awful, then—at the bottom of the hill—she wished he would follow her because maybe he deserved to hear it. She got a little lost in some construction near the soccer field and was glad he hadn't followed as she stumbled. It was dark, but Will could probably see her from the top of the hill. Why didn't he follow? There were a few large, unused pieces of cement sewage piping on the field; she

used to play in lengths of brightly painted cement pipes like
this in the yard of her elementary school. She crawled into
one, leaned her back against the curve of the cold cement, put
her feet up opposite, and let the cry come, mourning for a life
she'd barely dared imagine.

Part of the reason she hadn't dared was the inescapable
fact of Will's goyishness. How could she say to Will that
however much he loved her was not enough? He must also
love the things she chose to nail to her door, the way she
chose to wash her hands, as well as the days she chose not to
eat? It was not enough to respect these things, but he should
make them his own? Where would she mine the courage to
tell him that loving these things was no different than loving
her, then waiting around to see—did he still love her? How
could he mine the courage to opt in to being hated by the
world, reviled, blamed; opt in to blood libel and *The Proto-
cols of the Elders of Zion* being a target on his back? Accept
and absorb the weight of six million dead, the anxiety over
the Israel/Palestine crisis that emerged from those murders?
How could she ever tell him that yes, of course what she
wanted was for him to become Jewish, to accept fully the
burden of the laws and the proud but grisly history? To do
that one thing for her, that huge thing, so they could start
doing what it was she knew they could do together, even if it
was just pouring a glass of wine for the other—and meaning
it—at the end of a long day? How could she hope to explain
the anomaly of her nonbelief versus the beliefs of her people? How could she say such things, such things to a person
she loved without any other condition? A person she chose?
A person she would go on choosing whether or not these
things were ever said? How could she have fallen in love with
him in the first place? With a person who did not sing her

songs, speak her language, know her food, share in the limited scope of her genetic pool?

The sobs begat more sobs.

"Calm down," he said. He was squatting in the bright circle at the far end of the tube. She hadn't heard his approach. "We're just scared."

This made her cry harder, but she nodded a little, wiped her nose on her sleeve, the snot and mascara. He climbed in and arranged himself next to her, curling his knees against his chest.

"I keep thinking of you with Dylan. In your lap in the hospital," he said. "The family life I'd like to have instead of the one I do. You holding my son was like pushing the last piece of a puzzle into place. One of the big ones. The borders are tricky. Sometimes you have to push and push."

She nodded and hiccupped, lying by omission over the dialogue she'd just had with herself.

"Everything is going to be okay," he said. "You'll see."

She sat up and looked at him, steadied her breath.

"Things do not just become okay; people make them okay," she said. "Maybe we should take a break. A break, maybe, from each other, to see if we can make things okay."

"If that's what you want," he said, so quietly that she at first wasn't sure what he said.

"I thought you would—"

"If you need a break, you take one. I'll be here when you're ready. But I don't want a break. I need you for this. I need to lean on you. I'm sorry I upset you. I'm sorry I said those things."

His mood swings were frightening. She was used to David's temper—erupting at the times it was expected—and the way her calm responses inflamed it. She understood what scared Will, but his responses were confusing just the same. She wanted to say, Fuck you; I can't be your rock while I'm leaving my own family, but what she said was, "Okay, love. It's okay."

He scoured the side of her face with his stubbled cheek and his tears slid down, hot. With his corduroy jacket behind her head, he laid her out, sunk into her neck, wove his fingers into hers, and raised their hands together, palm to palm, over her head.

All through high school, through the hormone-drenched years of college, even her marriage, her sex life existed on beds and couches. Now here she was, thirty-one, with children, fucking in offices, supply closets, backseats, construction sites. Her body surged thinking of herself that way, surged under Will's huge hands on her stomach, her calves, pushing up the long, cotton layers of her skirt. He breathed his shallow breaths onto her belly, her inner thighs; she pressed her hips into the sand and concrete; he sunk his mouth into her and she gasped, making all the humid, mewing noises she thought had left her long ago.

"Turn over," she said, her ears ringing again, louder than they had earlier in her anger.

Holding onto each other they turned inside the tube and she pulled at his pants, consumed with hunger for his body. They didn't share what was inborn, but in this way she could take him into her, be filled with him, internalize his own storied genetics, his grassy-sweet DNA.

Afterward he thanked her.

"For what?" she said.

"I thought . . ." He fidgeted with the buttons on his shirt. "Before you, I thought that was gone from my life forever."

"Your wife doesn't swallow?" she said, trying to make him laugh.

"Just. I didn't think I'd ever give or get again. And I keep meaning to tell you that. It sounds dumb, but it feels like a big deal to me."

She nudged him. "You should've married a Jewish girl the first time. Or the second." She tensed a little with her accidental mention of marriage, the very crux of their cultural dissonance, but he laughed. "Habits develop at sleepaway camp and all those youth retreats. We're taught not to get knocked up."

"I bet," he said, still laughing.

"Never tell my mother I'm perpetuating stereotypes," Rina said and smiled.

"I'll never tell anyone what we did here," he said, raising one eyebrow. He meant to be playful, but the truth that his comment underscored returned Rina to reality, to the immensity of what lay in front of them. Will must have seen it in her face; he closed his eyes.

"I need a cigarette," he said.

They reorganized themselves, shifted everything back into place. She had to pee and squatted behind one of the concrete tubes, then followed him into the thick darkness, across the field, up the rubber sidewalk, over the fence.

"How do you know about that place?" she asked.

"My brother," Will said. "That used to be a healing place for the Indigenous Gabrielinos. And for Frank, if the colonizer steals from one he steals from all. He and his friends used to break in here in high school and, I don't know, have political meetings by the spring. And drink beer. He was always dragging me to stuff like that."

They walked two blocks east to a convenience store, where Will bought a pack of Marlboro Reds.

"I'm going to quit next week."

"Sure," she said, and they headed back in the direction of her car, him tamping his box of cigarettes against his leg and walking close, but not too close.

Will stood with his back against an oily wooden telephone pole and tried to light a cigarette with the second to last match in his book. It flickered out before the flame caught and there was a flash of desperation in his eyes. Rina wished to return to a time when she believed in the universe spitting warning signs, because she knew his unconscious panic over an unlit cigarette was a sign of the hazards of a life with him. She had a brief split of sympathy for Holly.

"Should've gotten new matches," he said.

It was a January night specific to southern California. The day had been warm and the night was, too, but with an unrealized threat of a chill off the ocean, so that people might carry but not wear jackets, so that Rina shivered in the balmy air against a cold that didn't really exist. She leaned into Will, cupped her hands in front of his face so that he could light his last match and drag the cigarette to life. Then she stood on her toes and kissed him hard after he exhaled, her mouth filling with the earthy residual of the smoke and her own briny taste. He didn't glance at the passing cars or pull away and when they eventually came up for a breath she said, "I don't think we should see each other anymore," at which he dropped the cigarette, crushed it out on the sidewalk, and took her back in his arms and in his mouth as if she hadn't said anything at all.

It was preemptive; she didn't actually think she'd be able to leave, but she'd come to believe in the last weeks—the last hours, even—that despite all his protests and all those kisses, he was capable of leaving her. All his wife had to do was put together the correct words in the correct order and everything he'd ever said to Rina would be a pretty lie and he'd have only nostalgic sympathy for her in her brokenness and write her emails full of the same bullshit he'd be selling himself, *We were just being foolish* and *You'll be better off* and, worst, *I'll never forget the way you made me feel.*

"Take a trip with me," he said. "This month. The opposite of a break. Let me prove I'm not biding my time just because I need time."

That was the prettiest lie yet, and Rina fell back against his mouth, content right where they were, on a noisy side street in West L.A., sparkling Christmas lights in her periphery, the smells of too-early citrus blossoms and smoke, the cold that wasn't.

12.

Pico was lined with the shops of the community, everything packed tight, especially by Los Angeles standards, like the Jews were afraid of taking up too much space. Tiny produce stores. Bakeries. Dry cleaners full of black woolen caftans circling the neon-lit windows. Wig shops with the word *shaytl* painted on the windows, Styrofoam heads on display. Judaica stores with menorahs, upside-down hands, and gold-lettered books in Hebrew. Nail shops. Storefront shuls, not much different from the Pentecostal churches further east on Pico. Bigger, ornate synagogues with stained-glass windows and security guards at the door. Butchers, restaurants with hechshers in the windows, signs in Hebrew and Farsi, a kosher food bank, preschools, modest clothing outlets, ethnic markets. Here and there something out of place: a psychic, a smoke shop. Last week's Yiddish newspapers were always blowing out from overflowing trash bins; litter in the tree planters sat in limp contrast with the scrubbed thresholds of the shops, the standards of kosher law, Rina's own immaculate home. Will had been to Rina's many times—nervous, desperate trysts on the couch and even once on her bed; she always called David at work first, to confirm his whereabouts, but refused to put up the chain, damning as a scarlet *A*—and sometimes they ventured out on short walks afterward. They pretended not to know each other, just to be out in the world together.

Will wouldn't stop talking about taking a trip. Even paces ahead of her on the sidewalk along Pico, he was talking about brochures he picked up at Triple A. She ducked into a grocery store.

She wondered if walking into the cramped store behind her was like walking into a foreign country for Will. Rina said the place smelled like an Israeli shuk, and he told her it smelled like the urban alleys of Hanoi. The wet mint, the near rot of too much produce, the mineral affront of the meat. When would he share with her the promised details of that mythical trip? The store was too small for carts to push up and down rows, so Rina showed him how to jostle to park it along one of the narrow aisles. Rina grabbed an armful of groceries and made her way back to her cart on aisle two, dropping them off and going back for another load. She'd made a list, but never took it out of her purse at the store. The act of making it was enough for her. Hummus, pita, two dozen eggs, an economy bag of frozen peas, nondairy whipped topping, pomegranate molasses, spreadable white cheese, cucumbers. The cucumbers were no bigger than a hand's length and bright as spring grass. Old ladies elbowed for a place at the bin, labeled PERSIAN CUCUMBERS. They pawed through them, tossing aside dozens before bagging what looked like a month's worth. She looked at Will, tried to gauge what he thought of her people. He muscled between the old women and picked Rina a bag of the firmest little cucumbers. The most gleaming. He handed her the bag. "Because I can't kiss you in public," he said. She took the bag with a frown, looked into his eyes for a moment.

Then, without looking around, she leaned in and kissed him quickly. Right next to his nose. She kissed him in public, but she didn't commit to a trip, to the lies it would require.

The next day he called her from work. Told her that he'd sat in his car the previous night, sat in front of her townhome with his engine and lights off, looking into her lit windows and ignoring text messages from his wife. He took out a cucumber, rubbed it against his shirt, bit into it from the middle. Like a corn cob. The juice ran over his hands. The clean, sweet taste of it filled his mouth. Downy jade skin prickled against his chin and fingers. The bright smell of it mixed with the musky winter storm, with the wrapped fish he'd picked up at the store. It was like he was eating into Rina, sucking at her soft, yielding places. Letting her juices run down his face.

"Not since I was seventeen have I come in my pants," he said. "Fully clothed. It didn't take long, either."

"Alright," she'd said, with horror and with a rush of tenderness for him. "I'll go with you on a trip."

⚓

"I'm going to get caught," Rina said when he picked her up a block away from her house, two weeks later, in the afternoon. She spoke in a monotone, as if stating a fact. She'd told David she was going to a women's prayer retreat, one a little outside of their community, a little more religious, a type of thing that happened regularly and was verifiable, so long as David didn't speak to any of the other women that went. Will told Holly he was going to stay by his father for a few days, hired babysitters for the evenings, made a guilty visit to his father that very morning before coming back north to pick her up.

"I bullied you into this," he said. "I'm sorry. What do you want to do?"

"Just drive," she said. "Fast."

He did and for a long way, all the way out of the city and into Malibu, they drove without speaking. He'd never seen her in a dress before, and even in her anxiety over the trip she'd picked a special one, a beautiful, brown, ankle-length dress, and a gauzy white wrap. It was modest, but only just. When she sat cross-legged in the front seat, she knew he could see that she was wearing skin-colored nylons. He loved to touch her legs when she wore nylons. She tried to keep her mind on seduction, but it kept turning toward trouble. Near the end of Malibu proper, with a dilapidated motel to their left, expensive condominiums to their right, and no ocean visible, she said, "Yoni and Shosh never get splinters."

"That's great?"

"It's a sign," she said. "We're doomed."

"This is the beginning of our life," he said.

"It might be the end of mine."

"I'll take you back home," he said, and flipped on his turn signal.

"Worse by far," she said. "I've gone a long way to tell this lie already. Packed the kids off to my parents until Tuesday. Made four night's worth of dinners for him. Four nights of dinners, with soups! Packed fucking prayer books in my bag. Showed him fake emails. You know why he buys it? Because he wants to. Because I told him the retreat is about this issue he's all hot over. About women whose husbands won't give them a *get*."

"I agree with him on that."

"Fuck off."

"You still don't think he believes you?"

"Does Holly believe you?"

He considered for a moment, moved one hand from the wheel to her leg; she smiled to herself. Stockings looked old-fashioned, but he adored them; silk and fat, she made her legs an offering to him. Once when touching her legs, he'd told her, "You have no pity for my body." But now she shuddered, and he withdrew his hand.

"I'm not sure I care what Holly thinks," he said.

"You want to get caught?"

"I want you. I'd rather not get caught. I'd rather it happen civilly."

"How could it?" She looked away before he had time to register the tears splashing down her cheeks. "My mother was always burning matches and digging splinters out of my hands and feet," she said. "I can smell the sulfur and the flesh, still. I've never dug a single splinter out of my children. But I keep matches and Bactine and needles in the medicine cabinet. Their lives are so regulated. Where? Where would they ever get a splinter? How can a person withstand heartbreak if they've never had a splinter? Baby ducks swim, baby horses run, but our babies are protected from even the most benign hurts. We are all doomed."

"My baby was run over by a car," he said. Then, as if in apology, put his hand back on her leg. This time she didn't shudder. Nor did she put her hand on top of his, weave her fingers through his.

"Sorry," she said. "I wasn't thinking."

"I'm going to marry you," he said. "This particular heartbreak will come to an end."

"You think so," she said. "Wife number three."

"That's not fair."

"I can't ignore the past because I love you."

"You do still love me?" he asked.

Rina looked at him then. Couldn't he see it? Her eyes full for him to their conical roots?

"If you need to hear it—"

"I'm sorry, I didn't mean—"

"If you need to hear it, I'll spend all four days telling you how much I love you and why."

"Maybe just spend one of them that way," he said, and she laughed. Wiped snot from her nose. Everything else began to fade, and he put on some music. She wanted to stop and be with him right then. He'd reserved an expensive cabin in Big Sur all four nights, but the idea of opening a cheap motel room with an old alloy key, of following him into a dingy room the color of prairie dirt, she couldn't stop thinking about it. Anyway, she was in stockings. He'd be willing to bargain.

"Stop at the Madonna Inn," she said.

"What do you know about the Madonna Inn?"

"I used to come up with friends in high school. Sometimes college," she said.

"But your family didn't eat at normal places."

"We didn't eat *meat* at normal places," she said.

"Will I have to stop eating at certain restaurants when I'm Jewish?" he said.

"What?" she said, stern. They were quiet again, but this time she suppressed a grin. Even if he didn't mean it, he'd said it.

At the Madonna Inn they had grilled cheese and pie in the coffee shop. It was someone's floral American dream of Bavaria, a Disney-fied motor hotel. She led him by the hand around the dining rooms—where all the seating was booths and all the booths flamingo pleather—into the bar, with

outsize wingback chairs upholstered in bright pastels, gum-
balls the color of cheap lipstick, and rock candy laid out like
quartz at a gem show. There was a ballroom with a dance
floor, a white piano, and a spiral staircase.

Will told her he'd been to the Madonna Inn only once, as
a boy, for a great-uncle's wedding.

She grabbed him from behind and said, "I could come
down those stairs."

"Your dress would have to be pink, like everything else
here," he said. She could see herself walking down those
stairs, but her dress wasn't pink. It was the color of the soft
insides of challah, the part the children always dug out. Off
the shoulders, a train. Her hair pulled back and to one side, a
flower at her nape. A meringue flower she could picture but
not name. She described it to him, asked if he knew its name.

He said *edelweiss*, though she knew those were small and
fuzzy and starlike. He hummed the tune to "Edelweiss" and
she thought of waking up, greeting her new husband. Having
him, being had, finally secure in mutual having and knowingness. Blooming forever.

"That song makes me cry," she said quietly. She tickled
him a little, digging into a layer of his gut with her fingers.

"I'll bet they have an old guy who plays piano. Our first
dance, Sinatra."

She laughed.

"One of the towering cakes from the coffee shop?" he said.

"We'll have to eat it all ourselves. Naturally we can't invite
anyone," she said. "Do you think the management will think
it's strange? A wedding with no guests?"

"We don't care," he said.

"I'm glad you're not one of those people who want to dance

me around this ballroom to silent music. One of those men who pull women in and say, 'Dance with me.'"

"That doesn't happen in real life."

They began a slow sway. Probably imperceptible to the group of white-haired ladies playing bridge and clinking tea in a far corner of the room. She was still behind him. Her arms around him. Her fingers in the soft parts of his stomach.

"Come downstairs," she said. "I want to see you take a piss in the famous urinal."

"See me?" he said.

A blonde doll standing on a swing hanging from the ceiling moved back and forth with a motorized whirr.

On their way downstairs, they took a photo in front of a stone fireplace. They looked at the photo, arms around each other, then she erased it from her phone. There were silk flowers everywhere.

"Holly likes to put out silk flowers when she's sad," Will said. "But they give me the willies."

"Go pee."

He couldn't pee in the Madonna Inn's famous grotto, though. The bathroom was full of women with expensive purses and take-out bags of food. They snapped pictures of the rock wall and waved their hands in front of the motion detector to activate the waterfall that washed the piss into a tiled drain.

Rina and Will stepped back out of the bathroom, and he pulled her into a dark cave. They wedged themselves between a gumball machine and a penny press.

"How many boys have you taken in there?" he asked, pressing her body against the curved rock wall and his into hers.

"Dozens," she said, and she kissed him, their glasses

knocking. He was fully hard; she felt him thick and raging against his jeans.

They kissed and ground into each other as people in bolo ties and flip-flops shuffled by.

"They're going to tell us to get a room," he said.

"So let's."

They rifled through the postcards in the lobby that showed over sixty themed rooms. Their three favorites were Pioneer America, Antique Cars, and Old Mexico. Instead, they took the cheapest available room, which wasn't cheap at all. But it did have one of the famous rock showers.

They put the shower to good use and went to sleep with the windows open. The ocean was too far to see, but the breezy marine fog thickened the air. It was tangy in Will's hair.

"Tomorrow night we'll be so close the sea spray will glaze your face," he said, next to her in a bed for the first time after dark.

"Always so sappy," she said, then turned to face him.

She fell asleep that way, facing him. Her breath on his neck, one leg hooked around his hips, his body rising dough.

In the morning they were still tangled, and the room was cold and flinty. She did not want to wake when she felt him stir, but under the covers his long fingers went to work on her skin, running over her divots and scars. She came awake in his hands, in his mouth. It was the first yawning morning sex of their affair, and she said so.

"Let's give ourselves permission to stop counting the firsts of this trip," he said.

Overnight a spider had spun an exquisite web between his window and side-view mirror, dew-wet as they packed their bags back into the car. The spider, a striped and big-bellied species she did not recognize, was still at work. It moved along the upper edge of the web. Although she initially recoiled, Rina stood watching the spider and drinking her coffee for a long time.

They took the Pacific Coast Highway the rest of the way, and somewhere past San Simeon a traveling fair began to pass them in the right lane. A parade of twenty-five gleaming pickup trucks, each hauling part of a brightly painted ride. Large, magnetic signs that read LUCA BAUTISTA CARNIVALS and included a phone number with an unfamiliar area code. The trucks were driven by Chicano cowboy types. The men with large felt hats and button-down shirts, the women with smaller hats, long hair, sun-worn faces. Rina sighed as they passed half of a Ferris wheel.

"The kids?" he asked.

"Do you ever just want to stare so hard you forget how to blink because you'll never see this exact scene again in your life, even though this road, those weeds, those tire skids will probably still be there the next time you drive this way?"

"Whoa, I was thinking whether Dylan was old enough to like kiddie rides. Not the tire treads on the highway or the nature of change," he said. "Sometimes I think I'm not interesting enough for you. That you're going to wake up and see that I'm just an overgrown introvert, trying to make up for being the lanky, pimple-skinned chavalo who was too quick to fight. I'm going to run out of big thoughts and you're going to keep going forever."

"I know you. You know better."

"I want to build you something," he said.

She yawned. "You don't have to build me anything."

"A library," he said. "I'll build it myself. And fill it with beautiful books. All the ones you've read and I haven't. And plenty that you haven't read. So many that you haven't read. Poetry. And I'll build it just for you. With stacks and everything. And then you'll fill it with beautiful children to read the books with."

"Fill it?" she said, smiling. "Children, yes, if that's what's on your mind."

"I thought I was too tired for more."

"There are going to be three anyway."

"Four at least," he said. "And what a world our baby will come into. There's no going back after Obama. Can you imagine? We'll have a female president next, then maybe a Latino. Maybe a Jew."

"Never," Rina said, shaking her head. "There will be everything before a Jew."

A Luca Bautista truck went by with a baby saucer ride, poorly executed Mickey Mouses painted on each cup. She pointed and he looked.

"You'll see, cariño," Will said. "Everything will be different for Dylan and Shosh and Yoni and our baby. Different than it was for us. People don't hate each other the same as they used to."

"Are you nostalgic for your childhood?" Rina said. She waved at a passing toy train ride as if there were children in its cars.

"For what? Being pulled over a hundred times in high school for driving while brown? For my dad being talked to loud and slow like an idiot when he was always the smartest person in the room? For all the latchkey afternoons because my parents were working?"

"I didn't mean it so politically, but I guess," said Rina. "Are you nostalgic for that? Or the taste of your mom's food? Or the way it felt to ride bikes in the afternoon and not be tethered to a cell phone or padded down at every joint?"

"The taste of asado de boda, even though I stopped eating meat when I was twelve after we had a field trip to the Francisco packing plant, sure," Will said. "I remember certain colors. The way things felt. Watching my grapefruit tree and being lonely."

"I want our kids to be nostalgic for their childhoods," she said. "On their bad days. Crushingly nostalgic."

"I don't want them to have bad days," he said. "And I don't want them to have splinters."

"Yes you do," she said. "You want them to have their hearts broken, too."

"I'd do anything to prevent Dylan's heart from being broken."

"Poor Dylan," she said, then said nothing more. There was the whoosh of the highway and rattle of empty seltzer cans in the cup holders. She put her head in his lap and opened his fly. It seemed to shock him, at first. He tried to stay between the lines but could not, so he pulled over and watched for police cruisers. His fingers tangled in her hair, and her ears began to ring. She felt certain his were ringing, too.

It was two more hours to Big Sur. They belted classic rock songs, spun silly fantasies, snacked on vegan jerky and kosher cheese curls. They picked up the keys from a mailbox outside an office in a strip of a town, then found the cabin. It was more like a mansion, hewn of pine and glass and more than worth the money Will took secretly from savings. Took it stupidly, Rina had told him many times, but here she was.

The place was all wet redwood. Resin and rot, constant sea spray, constant damp like a blanket protecting them from everything they didn't wish to face. When Rina walked onto the back deck it felt like it was raining, but it was just the fog. Even though it was early afternoon it looked like evening, and in the shafts of light she could see moisture choking the daytime color from the air. It was cold in Big Sur, winter cold.

"Which fireplace should we use first?" Will said, and she followed him from the bedroom to the great room to the fire pit on the deck. He decided all three and started bringing firewood in from the stack in the garage while Rina unpacked.

"The brochure shows where there's a market," Rina said when he came to light the bedroom fire. She'd pulled the comforter off the bed. Laid a clean sheet on top of the blanket. She was smoothing a robe out on the bed. "I'll go get some groceries."

"I'll go with you," he said.

"It'll take less than an hour."

"Why did you do that with the sheet?" he said.

"Because the blankets don't get washed. Don't you do that at hotels?"

"Never thought about it."

She kissed him on the nose.

"Let me come. I'll miss you," he said.

She gathered her purse and a hoodie. "You keep saying we are starting our life together. In this life we will not always go shopping together. Tomorrow I'm going to take a long walk without you and I'm going to enjoy it. And we're going to take a nice, long walk together. That is the way to start a life."

"I like grocery shopping with you."

"If there's a fire in the hearth when I return, I couldn't complain," she said. And then she walked down the stairs from the bedroom loft and clicked the kitchen door closed behind her.

He called her once while she was gone to tell her to get cucumbers, tangerines, and fixings for s'mores. The service was terrible. "One more time?" she kept saying, over the static.

If one of their spouses called, they'd be ruined.

When she returned, she found five mason jars full of dried peach pits lined up on the mantel. Four years' worth, he told her.

Pits whose fruit he had consumed in unwitting anticipation of Rina's arrival in his life. When he ate a stone fruit he would work the fibrous flesh out from around the woody center carefully with his tongue, sometimes sucking on it for days. Then he washed the pit in water and lemon juice, a trick he knew from cleaning brushes. Soap would dilute the fruited scent that clung to the pit. The stones went on a piece of waxed paper on a shelf in his bell tower, where the light bleached them. In the summer they'd be dry in days.

After he'd tasted noyaux ice cream made from apricot kernels at an art gallery in Brooklyn, he became obsessed with the idea of what pits would smell like as they burned. There was cyanide in the pits, he told Rina, but he read that burning them wouldn't be dangerous. He began collecting them from June to August when peaches and nectarines were in season. Started to eat imported Chilean stone fruit, inferior in taste, from January to April. As he filled mason jars, he imagined building a brick hearth in the backyard. For woodfired pizzas and s'mores. A campfire on Dylan's first overnight in a tent, with the crickets fiddling. Veggie dogs on sticks and tomato soup bubbling. Slices of plastic-wrapped American cheese and a serape around the boy's shoulders. Things like that.

But now he gifted Rina all the jars. They shivered on the deck with the salt and the wet and the fog. She opened the first one slowly, the hollow pop of the aluminum lid, and was surprised at the thick smell of the pits, pale and wooden, a heady wine scent.

"Take them by the handful, and throw them on the fire," he said. "When I was a kid, my mom bought canisters of magnesium and copper chloride powder, and it changed the flames to blue and white, magic."

The pits didn't change the color of the fire, but as they burned they changed the smell of it. The almond layered with all the usual smells of smoke and burning wood. A light, sweet scent. A young forest. Early morning at the orchard of her summer camp. The pits made noises, too. A sustained hissing at first. Then each of them gave a loud snap, a giant popcorn kernel hitting the lid of a cast-iron skillet. He set two jars by the fire pit and one each by the indoor fireplaces. He'd eaten enough fruit over the years to fill the cabin.

"Will we have to extinguish them for you to keep Shabbos?"

"As long as I don't have to tend them, they can keep burning."

"And what do you want, cariño?"

"For them to burn."

She may have thought to bring a robe and a book, but he'd thought to bring four years' worth of dried peach pits, a gift to her.

❊

The fire in the bedroom burned low, and Rina stood up, groggy, to toss in another handful of peach pits. As they released their oil with soft cracks she lay back on the bed, which, two nights in, had sheets covered in wine stains, sweat, her. It smelled like almonds, smoke, and mildew, like the Los Angeles Zoo when she stood watching the children at the playground at the top of the hill and a breeze kicked up from the south.

Will was lying on his stomach.

"There's a midrash about Rebecca," he said. "Is that how you say it?"

Midrash was the Hebrew word for interpretation of Torah, and Rina was so warm and comfortable and drunk that it didn't register how odd it was for Will to be talking about rabbinic text. She'd spent many drunken nights of her life talking about midrash. She nodded at Will and arranged herself on a pillow.

Will told the story of Rebecca's pregnancy, how she'd long been barren, how she and Isaac had longed for a child but then, once pregnant, how Rebecca's pregnancy had been difficult and painful and she went to god in her anguish and asked, "If, so, why am I?" Rina knew the story, of course—though she called Rebecca by her Hebrew name, Rivka—but more than the words, she heard Will's voice, coarse and low, so close to her ear. Will was saying something about existentialism, Rebecca trying to understand her place in the world, god answering her not by removing her anguish but by contextualizing it, reminding her she was part of something larger, that she had purpose and so would her children.

"She was the first person, in the bible, to take the initiative to address god directly," Will said, and Rina traced circles onto his stomach with her finger. "It's amazing the way Hebrew verbs work. Rebecca went to *lidrosh*, to inquire of god. And that root became the root for *midrash*. I don't think English works the same way—I mean with paradigms written right in."

She sat up, wine-heavy.

"How do you know all this?"

Will had been joining email lists, he said. Receiving weekly

Torah portion teachings in his inbox. Her stomach seethed, maybe the wine, but maybe from the odd mix of pride and horror that struck her upon hearing this. She grimaced.

"I love you. You love this," he said.

"I was born into it."

"You don't know how to live without it."

Rina opened her mouth to protest but couldn't summon a retort. If there were bacon in the house, she'd fry it up at three in the morning and eat it, that's how much she wanted him to be wrong.

Will combed his fingers through her hair, which hurt against her sweaty tangles, but she put up no protest. She kept her eyes closed tight and tried to capture the memory because she knew she'd want to replay it for weeks. Even now, minutes after their last fuck, she replayed its choreography and began to get wet again.

"So you've been learning all this for me." She traced circles down his stomach.

"For me," he said. "I signed up for conversion classes, but I want to do them on my own. If I make this choice, it has to be for me."

"But it would be because of me," Rina said. Last month this would have been the answer to all her terror over the future, but now it shocked her: what if he did what she wanted and later he regretted it, the way she regretted the years she wasted being devout?

"Of course, because of you," Will said. "Now my whole life is because of you. But it's helping me understand parts of myself that I never did before. And I went from reading Tevye stories to Hebrew etymology in a week. You know why? Because I read that story about Rebecca and I had find out how to conjugate the verb 'to know.'"

Rina propped herself up, forgot about distracting Will with careless fingers.

"It's *l'da-at*. That's the infinitive."

"That's how you make me feel: known. I can't read the letters, but I looked it up," he said. "It's a three-letter root. I can figure out how to say 'I know, I knew, I will know.' But I can't figure out how to say 'I am known.'"

Her eyes were hot. For months she'd wanted to tell him exactly this—what the feeling was, that she felt known—and now Will, lavish with his hands but so frugal with his words, had said it. She was known, known so well they could sit without talking for hours and with a single, changed exhale Will would know that the fading light made her nostalgic. Known in that he refilled her wineglass when there was still half an inch left. Known all the way back to her lonely childhood, even though there were still so many stories to tell and Will was still listening to them all with keen intent. He knew without being told what to do with her body; he knew she liked broccoli on her baked potatoes; he knew she often needed to be alone with her own thoughts, yet still in his quiet company.

"I started a series of paintings," he said, his voice drowsy. "Called *yodea*. It's from the verb 'to know.' They're of trees and things. Cypresses. You remember the cypress. They're not worthy. Not yet. But I would make them a wedding gift to you. I would make them your ring."

He turned over and folded a pillow under his head. Rina stayed where she was, vertical and unmoving on the bed as her circuitry slowed.

She would marry him. She would let herself be known.

Early Monday morning, their last morning in Big Sur, Rina left Will in bed—his eyelids fluttering in REM—to take a walk along the shore while the tide was still high. About a half mile from the cabin, they'd discovered a place where they could get to a small gravel beach via a path trodden over the ice plant and the tiny pink wildflowers. The flowers were bright and the same shade all the way through, yet somehow more concentrated at the center, as if the spindly pistils were milking the pink from the petals. It was a long, steep walk down, slippery with orange sand. The smell reminded her of a salt-brined duck recipe she made for Shabbos, with kombu and plum stuffing. She got the recipe online and it was so cumbersome—three days of work, the refrigerator colonized by duck carcasses in salt water—that after the first time she fixed it, she swore she'd never make it again. But their guests thought it was wildly exotic and it reminded David of the flavor of the eel sushi he had loved as a teenager, before he kept kosher. At synagogue the next week a half dozen women asked her about it and for a spell, until David found out how much duck cost, she made it almost weekly; she toted rows of brined ducks in giant foil pans when they were invited somewhere. Until Will, this is how she had been known, for home-brewed liqueurs and hand-cured ducks. For the things she produced that were consumed and shit out. Nameless, just like the smell of the water and the kelp.

On the beach she picked her way over to a crop of breaker boulders, sleek with damp plant life and slime. Foothold after foothold, she walked along the rocks until she was as far into the ocean as she dared go, past where the tide pools had been alive with hermit crabs the previous evening, past where the sea lions lay at sunset. There were two sea lions nearby now, playing in the shallows on the calmer side of the rocks to her left, their heads bobbing with the roll of the waves. She was far on a peninsula of rock, almost surrounded by water, and the waves soaked the front of her parka each time they broke in fifteen-foot crests just a few feet in front of her. She stood there, immobile and cold, eyes on the brightening horizon. All the thoughts and fears that had for months been the overwhelming buzz of her mind seemed more manageable, if she kept her eyes on the rising water, the place where the sea stretched into the sky.

Oh, the fearful buzz.

David will notice my jacket is ruined; Jews don't get divorced; I can't marry a non-Jew; I'm not even sure I can marry a secular convert, a Chiloni; if Will converts, what will he even be? I will break my parents' hearts; I'm ruining my children's lives; I'm ruining his child's life; I'm ruining my own life and worse than that, Will's.

To these were added unrelated thoughts that took on sudden gravitas. Would her children also like this place? Would she be unselfish enough to someday bring them here? Why did her inner ears hurt near the sea? Did Will like peanut butter? If he died before she did, would she be able to go on being alive? Why did the Impressionists think they could master light? The water ebbed off the rocky sand in a dazzling patina of silver sparks; just to attempt such a thing on canvas was the height of ego. How could anyone—how could she—when faced with the barbaric muscle of the sea in its auroral glory, believe it had been formed and placed by a creator? How could anyone believe a creator existed at all in the face of things imperfect, things like oceans and the eyes through which they are viewed, and the series of chemical actions and reactions that are elevated when called love?

These thoughts didn't come as clearly when she was with Will. Yet she could never bear to be alone with her own thoughts again without the fact of his existence keeping her company. She was an island unto herself, and the marine sounds engulfed her. The din of the water against the rocks and under that the tinkling rush of undercurrents, the sound of her own coursing blood when she cupped a hand to her ear. Ceaseless scuttling of millions of tiny creatures taking and leaving shelter, only perceptible in the short moments between breaking waves. Further still, the faint buzzing of colonies of flying insects swarming black in vertical columns above the heaps of seaweed decaying on the beach. Now the sound was a cocoon. If Will was ever gone from her, these noises would deafen her.

"You're soaked," Will said when she came in the door. It was reckless, that early, in all the surf, alone. "You alright?"

"It's the most incredible thing," she said. "These flies. They're not shaped like regular flies; they're more slender, like an oval." She held her fingers together to show him; her words came rapidly. "There are so many that some of the rocks look black, but they're swarming. And when a particularly big wave breaks a bit farther out—it's amazing—they all rise at the same time, buzzing in the air above the rocks in formations. It's menacing. But they know the sound of a normal wave from the sound of a threatening wave and up they go, all at once. How do they know that?"

He took her around the shoulders and kissed her forehead hard. She could feel his lips pucker from the salt. "It seems like you're not alright?" he said.

"It's like Jews. We hear the coming *modim*, the coming *barchu*, and we bow. Or we're up on our toes. Or we're prostrated fully on the floor muttering the same words over and over again. Up we go, down we go."

"That's a bad metaphor, cariño. The flies learned to do

that because their ancestors who failed to heed the waves were drowned. It's basic evolution."

"The opposite of Jews."

Will raised his eyebrows.

"My ancestors died because they wouldn't abandon their ritual," she said.

"I don't think the Nazis discriminated between practicing and nonpracticing Jews," he said.

She nodded, kissed him, slogged off to take a shower and start packing, which is the thing she'd been dreading since the moment she started unpacking. With a towel wrapped around her she threw away the leftovers in the kitchen: half a pint of Ben & Jerry's, a few stray golden Oreos, the dregs of a bottle of wine. She ate a cucumber and packed an unopened bag of almonds into Will's duffel.

And then they were in the car heading south and she was driving. Near Hearst Castle, Highway 1 evened out and the hairpin turns made way for flat road, cattle ranches to their left and rocky beaches to their right. They stopped to eat at a Mexican place in Cambria, split the last bottle of kosher wine she'd brought, spoke little.

Will drove after that, cutting across Highway 46 through the wine country of Paso Robles to get to the 101. Rina, who preferred PCH and a view of the water, went to sleep. She dreamed that her children were in the backseat, flush-faced and napping. She dreamed that she was flatulent and Will was disgusted. She dreamed that the sheep country around them was full of safari animals: lions and hyenas prowling the green hills, antelope bending their slender necks to the grass. She dreamed that the car braked hard, accelerated again, swung in a broad arc to the left, then braked again.

She woke to the sound of Will's car door slamming shut. He was shouting and gesticulating and Rina turned to see a motorist pulled over behind them. Rina unbuckled her seat belt in an instant, sweat gathering in itchy pricks all over her body.

"Were we in an accident?"

"Get back in the car," Will said to her.

"What's the matter?" she said, but he had reached the motorist and didn't reply.

Will was shouting at an unkempt older woman, hair permanently windswept by the sea, who had started cleaving herself out of her car before changing her mind. She remained half in and half out and Rina couldn't tell if she was more frightened or enraged.

"Look, you," she was saying to Will. "I am calling the police." She held out a cell phone, put one leg back in the car.

"Are you out of your mind?" Will shouted. "I have a kid. You drive like that with kids on the road? You crazy asshole. You can't just cut in front of people. We could have been killed. They should take your license away. I should report you."

"You have a baby in the car?" The woman seemed uncertain. "Is there something wrong with the baby?"

"You're lucky I don't have my baby in the car. Where did you learn to drive?"

"Will," Rina said. He ignored her.

"Look, I didn't see you." She was lodged back into her driver's seat and was shouting out the door at Will. "I'm going now. I'll call the police."

"Will," Rina said again. But he just stood with his arms on his hips, nodding as the woman started her car, signaled, and pulled back onto the freeway. Rina got back in the car and buckled, shaking. A muscle spasmed in her right eye, the sharp behind-the-ear pain that meant the beginning of a migraine.

"Can you believe her?" he said when he got back to the car.

"No," she said.

"Imagine if we had the kids with us."

"Terrible," she said.

For two and a half hours she pretended to sleep, lost herself in the lyrics of the music Will played, and then, when he switched to the classical station once they could pick up L.A. radio again, lost herself in the frenzied witch's sabbath of *Night on Bald Mountain*. Will seemed calm in the driver's seat, but she could think of nothing but his outburst.

"You'll get yourself killed like that," she said, just past the junction of the 10 and the 405 freeways, half an hour from her home.

"Like what?"

"Yelling at that woman before. She could have been any-body. She could have had a gun." Will said nothing but his jaw contracted. "What did she even do so wrong? You're always telling me all the times you, your brother, your parents got pulled over. It's not bad enough just to be you out there? You have to make problems?"

Will was quiet for a slow mile.

"I'm sorry," he said.

"I don't want you to get a phone call from the police," she said. "I don't want them to make a mistake."

"I'll be fine. I'm sorry," he said again.

When he pulled up a block from her home she was crying. The whole trip, and then this.

"Hey," he said. "It's the beginning."

Rina nodded. He pulled her suitcase out of the trunk, then leaned into her.

"We can't," she said. "Not here."

"Letters," he said.

"Letters."

"*L'da'at*," he said. She nodded, wiped her nose and eyes, began rolling her luggage up the street. The grumble of Will's car thundered inside her chest, but she looked at the sky, blinked hard.

13.

"Is that you?" David called. Rina shut the door behind her. No Shosh and Yoni launching themselves down the hall. She didn't answer him. She would cry again if she spoke, and she was so tired of crying; her eyes were ready, but her willpower filled them with sand. She hung her purse on a standing hat rack in the small foyer. It had belonged to David's great-grandmother and David's parents gave it to them when—as empty nesters—they'd moved into a smaller house. David grew up with it; he told her stories about draping it with decorated sheets and putting it on the porch around Halloween. Rina didn't grow up with Halloween, and the idea of this porch ghost was romantic, foreign, and a little stressful. He told the story about trying to climb it, toppling backward, receiving three stitches in his chin at age six. (This after he suggested bolting it to the floor when Yoni started walking and Rina was offended he hadn't suggested bolts for Shosh and they'd had a two-day fight that ended without screwing the hat rack down.) Her purse, as it always did, caused the hat rack to lean on their uneven floor, then settle back into place with a familiar *clud*. *Clud*, the sound of her entire married life, of her family, her children, her cabinets full of wedding gifts, her solid silver candlesticks, the jewelry box closing shut on the emerald earrings David gave her on her first Mother's Day, David's voice, carrying over the burble of the sukkah on the night they'd met, the sound of his voice now calling "Rina?"

"It's me, I'm home."

"The kids are at your parents'," he said. "Why don't you come up to the study?"

They never called the loft the study; something was wrong. How long had David been sitting in front of the computer practicing "Why don't you come up to the study?"

"What is it?" she said, unmoving.

"About the affair."

There was a short moment of relief that it was nothing to do with the kids—not directly, anyway—followed by a grim panic and the quick onset of vertigo. She dropped the handle of her suitcase.

"I have to pee," she said. "I'll be up."

"I'll come down," he said.

It started while she was still in the bathroom. She'd closed the door, which she almost never did at home. He started by telling her not to bother denying the affair, which had been her gut instinct, even though it made no intellectual sense. He told her she had betrayed the children most of all. Told her she would be accountable to them most of all.

"It's convenient you don't believe in god," he said, over the sound of the faucet as she washed her hands. "Because next you'd be accountable to him. Your lover, I think, will suffer more on that count."

She emerged. David stepped forward into the threshold, blocked her exit from the bathroom by stretching his arms out against the doorframe. "Do the children know?" she said.

"You tell me."

"And so, other than suspicion, how do you know?"

"You didn't go far enough outside the community."

Topanga Canyon was pretty far. Who could have seen them together? Who might have committed lashon hara against her?

"Someone told you?"

"You're awfully calm," he said.

"But what should I be? You've told me not to deny it."

"Don't pretend like you're doing me a favor."

"I'm sorry," she said.

"Not good enough."

"No," she said, then ducked under his arm and went to sit on the edge of the bed. She wrung her hands together, astounded that an action so cliché could bring such comfort.

"What do you want me to say?" David asked.

"I have a feeling you've been practicing plenty. So? Go ahead."

"You are such a bitch," he said, then sat down next to her, shoulders slumped.

She thought about how to say it best, how much of the story to tell, but she would tell him she loved Will, she had to. She would leave. No point hurting David in phases. She'd have to go to her parents for a while. Why hadn't she thought this out before? Why, when there was no reception at the grocery store in Big Sur and she panicked, why then didn't she plan at least a cursory path out? How far back in time should she go? To the trip to Paris before they were married, should she tell him she never wanted a waxed baby cunt? All the times she asked him to go to therapy over the years? It seemed petty to mention Aliza when Rina herself had committed the actual sins, but it was a fact, David and Aliza were always off in corners together. Should she tell him that if he never made her take that art class, she never in her whole life would have encountered Will, beautiful, paint-stained Will Ochoa, her Will? Or would she be brave enough to tell him the one true fact, that she would have kept waxing and atrophying along-side him forever, kept shellacking ducks and constructing goody baskets and putting up fruit brandy, kept churning out babies and bottling up disbelief, kept being the invisible hero of the relentless Jewish calendar, kept being everything he needed her to be, so long as he'd never traded her over whisky and a daisy and a bowl full of condoms, never let Brandon ask her if the rug matched the drapes, never let someone else's husband foil her own conviction with his foreign hands and filthy words?

"Tell me, were you full of shame that his wife was there over the weekend?" David said, finally.

This she heard as if listening to a conversation in Yiddish. The sound was familiar and she knew the words, but the meaning remained alien. Why would Holly have been in Big Sur?

"What?" she said.

"Bonding over the same man? The same rat bastard? That wasn't on the conference agenda?" His voice was rising in anger; his words were practiced. They were coming to what he had rehearsed.

She opened her mouth to say, How did you even know he was married? when she realized David was talking about Anshel. Anshel! If her husband had been facing her instead of sitting next to her, the surprise in her face would have told the whole story, down to the peach stones.

"It's over," she said, her mind recalibrating.

"Even should that be true, it hardly matters."

"It's been over for months," she said. "How did you know?

Does Nechama know? Does everyone know? Who told you? How do they know?"

"It was a good guess that you confirmed," David said. "I've been thinking it for months. With your scrambled eggs and your extra shifts at Family Services, then no shifts at all. So I checked your email while you were at that conference." David looked her straight in the eye. "While you were there with his wife."

"Please don't tell anyone else. You'll ruin his life. Nechama's."

"Is that all you're worried about? What about me, Rina? I'm right here." He waved his arms, a dumb little wave.

"You checked my email?" she said. Thank god she and Will used secret accounts. Thank god.

"I always wished you lost fifteen pounds," David said. "Just so you know."

"That one I'm going to let you have, because you've been practicing and because it's no secret," she said. Anyway, she was full of self-reproach over how she'd used her body—her fifteen-pounds-too-heavy body—to exact vengeance on the Rina who had been too meek to refuse to be traded. "But think carefully about what you say next."

"I wish you were more adventurous in bed." He said it the way a person spits out a bite of gristle: awkward, with his hands in front of his mouth.

Her impulse was to laugh, but it was too sad. She never kissed him after he went down on her, didn't like him to tie her up, didn't consent to cause him pain when he asked, was not made giddy or lusty or really even jealous by being swapped for another woman. She never did with him what she did with the others—although she let him have his ass play; it was exhausting to decline—and he would never be able to grasp that his being capable of trading her neutered her spirit

and dampened her nerves, sterilized her spirit long before he
ever got up the courage to actually pursue the switch. She
stared ahead, said nothing, hating herself for not also admit-
ting to Will, hating the sanctimonious relief that came with
not being caught in both affairs.

"You ruined my life, you know?" he said.

He straightened up and then he let her have it, talking
and talking and talking. Chicken nuggets, again. The community, his business, their friends, the children, *the community*, scrambled eggs. He talked so much he had to stop and
get a glass of water from the bathroom, then he carried on.
She wanted to retort, to talk about being traded, to bring up
his emotional affair with his best friend's sister. She listened
without response; she had no high ground but would cede
nothing.

"Your parents are aware we are having marital difficul-
ties," he said, at last. "I told them that much. They're expecting you. I'll see the children Shabbos and every other Sunday
until you . . ." He took a moment, maybe to find his practiced
words. "Until you recover yourself."

The last days with Will had been so full but being without her children for five days had been difficult. The thought
of being without her children regularly seemed impossible.
How could she ever sleep in a house absent of their hypnotic
breath, their morning voices, their scent? A terrible mother—
only a terrible mother would allow such a thing to come to
pass.

But then.

The first, tingling moments of a freedom she'd never known
as an adult. Every other weekend without the children. Every
other weekend alone. No meals to cook. No crumbs to sweep.
No coffee tables in need of arranging after she tucked them.

No spilled toothpaste in the sink, no little-boy pee on the toilet, no tiny shoes to line up by the door.

She heaved a large, rolling duffel from beneath the bed and began to pack. She would grab the Big Sur suitcase, untouched, and would just need to grab more medicine for her Dopp kit along with clothes and pajamas that didn't smell like salt and sex.

"What are you doing?" David said.

"Going to my parents," she said.

"What are you taking?"

"Whatever I'd like."

He slumped down again; his voice became gentle, worried. "You don't need to take everything."

She'd been fidgeting with an old luggage lock on one of the giant zippers. There was still an airline tag that said DEN from their last real trip, to a friend's condo in Colorado over three years ago. She looked at him square.

"Are you kicking me out or not?"

David stalked out of the bedroom, slammed the door, opened it to say "You're really something, you know?" then slammed it again. Rina resumed the cry that had begun when she got out of Will's car.

She waited until after the children's bedtime to go to her parents'. David didn't come back into the bedroom and didn't say anything when she closed the front door behind her. Her parents were less than a mile away, down Beverly Drive and through a hilly thatch of bay trees. She pulled into the wide, bricked driveway. The lights were still on downstairs; they were waiting.

Rina dragged the duffel and the suitcase from Big Sur into the foyer and waited. No one came. She left them there and walked to the family room. Her mother was on the couch looking at *The New York Times* and her father held a novel on the recliner. They were not reading.

"So," her father said.

"Thank God she's home," her mother said.

"Are the children asleep?" Rina said.

Her mother nodded. Her father stared.

"There's Red Bull in the fridge," her mother said.

"It's nine o'clock at night, Mom."

"I picked some up today because I know you like it. I just didn't want to forget to say. I got diet."

"You're sleeping in Joshua's room," her father said.

"Thank you," Rina said, and then, "Sorry."

She waited a moment to see if there was going to be more talking. To see if her mother patted the couch or her father gestured toward his library, just off the family room. All of the light bulbs had been changed from incandescent to compact fluorescents just in the week since she'd last been in their house. David had been trying to get them to switch for years and she wondered now if this was some sort of a gesture, if she had already been judged. If, via ambient light, her parents had sided against her. The house was paler, the air almost blue.

Rina carried her luggage upstairs to her brother's old room, sweating and refraining from cursing as the bags hit her ankles. She made almost no noise as she passed her old room, where her two children lay asleep. Their door was closed all the way because her parents' two cats made Shosh sneezy. She didn't open it to check on them. Her brother's bed still had dinosaur sheets on the twin mattress, the primary colors faded. They'd been his sheets in grade school and then again in his last year of high school, as an act of irony their mother took for nostalgia. Rina went to bed without washing her hands or face, without brushing her teeth, without calling Will, without putting on pajamas. She felt guilty for falling asleep mostly naked because she was sure her children would be in first thing in the morning to wake her with their doughy breath. David didn't like for the children to see them naked.

No one woke her in the morning.

She first opened her eyes at nine, then again a little after ten, and then finally just before noon. She read books with the children after school. She did not call Will, couldn't bear to tell him that she hadn't taken the chance when she had it, hadn't admitted the fact of him, her love for him. She ate dinner with her parents and children, pushing her father's chicken paprikash around her plate with a monogrammed fork. She helped the children brush their teeth and say the Shema and went to bed herself as soon as they were asleep. Will wasn't calling or texting her, either. The next day she didn't wake until after noon, and only then because the wind jangled the row of wind chimes on the citrus trees in the yard. She looked out the corner of the window she could see from the bed, watched the battered brass Magen Davids—the six-pointed stars—twisting against their chains, the bells hitting all six corners, then covered her head with a pillow. The bells grew louder. She got up.

Her mother was home and they said their good mornings, and Rina appreciated that her mother didn't say "Good afternoon," as she did when Rina or her brother slept in as teens. To avoid discussion, she took a broom from the closet and stepped out onto the porch to sweep the grass clippings and dirt brought overnight by the wind.

"You don't have to do that," her mother said from the door. Rina shrugged. "You'll sweep in your pajamas?"

"It's fine," Rina said.

Her pajamas covered her knees and elbows and collar bone, nothing improper about it other than sloth.

With every stroke of the broom the wind brought more grass, more sticks, more flower petals. She didn't mind. At sleepaway camp, sweeping was her favorite chore. Sometimes she manipulated the paper plate-and-brass brad chore chart so she could skip trash removal or sink scrubbing in order to sweep. She was the best at getting the dust from each corner and delighted in making myriad piles around the bunk, then sweeping them all out to the concrete porch, where she could while away another fifteen minutes with the broom—her mind on fire with fantasy—until not a single cloud of dust was raised when she moved it against the floor. At her summer camp they prayed three times a day, more on Shabbos. Oh, she spoke savagely about other, so-called Jewish camps. Camps such as the one her cousin Dafna attended, where they played guitars on Shabbos and girls often wore kippot over their long hair and tallisim over their thin shoulders, commandments reserved for men.

Then in college Rina went through a phase of rejecting the idea that women can't wear the prayer garments, rejecting the standard Orthodox defense that women were automatically holier because their bodies could bear children and therefore god didn't require them to wear prayer garments. She called Dafna and apologized for speaking ill of her summer camp, for literally being holier-than-thou. Dafna said it was no big deal, but to Rina it was.

Now Rina no longer cared. She didn't want to wear a tallis, or be in a room full of men wearing tallisim, or set herself apart from the gentiles by the things she wore. The things her husband wore. God required nothing of any human, required nothing because god was a figment of the human imagination, designed to explain away shadows and seasons and natural catastrophes, designed to bolster the patriarchy and relegate women to the kitchen and the birthing bed. She flushed and swept harder. She tried to push from her mind the vision of Will in a tallis—maybe a thick, woven one like her grandfather wore, or an oversize silk shawl in the burnt-umber color of his eyes, such a thing could be special ordered—she no longer wanted to want him to be a Jew. But as she moved down the walkway with the broom, she imagined Will davening under a huge, fringed shawl, bending his knees deeply at the *modim anachnu lach*—"we thank you god"—knowing when to bend without being told, knowing the hoary choreography as well as any born Jew.

She didn't even put the broom away before returning to her room, just leaned it in a corner of the porch. From a prone position in bed, a small corner of one window was visible, and lemon branches cast complex patterns of light on the leaves as the tree bent with the wind. What was bright green one moment was gray the next and then so lustrous in the midday sun that she had to look away. She read books to the children after school, fed them yogurt and steamed broccoli, picked a bay leaf out of a leftover container of her mother's vegetarian chili, dished up a few spoonfuls for herself, went to bed just after the children.

On Thursday Will started texting again and she had even more reason to stay in her room, squirreled away, her fingers moving furiously over the letters as she typed out her news. She told him most of it, that David knew about Anshel and that she'd decamped to her parents'. After all that talk of babies and a library, his first thought—profoundly unhelpful— was whether his wife also suspected. He recovered himself quickly and became supportive, but also texted Rina endless questions that exhausted her. The fourth day was Friday, and her mother made her get out of bed to help prepare for Shabbos. Rina drove around the neighborhood with her mother, wearing her slippers to the market, to the fish monger, to the bakery, and to the school to pick up the children. Rina always drove through the car pool line but her mother preferred to park and go in to pick them up. This would have been a huge hassle for Rina, who wasn't a good parallel parker and could never find a spot in the afternoon, but her mother's handicap placard—a remnant from a knee replacement a few years back—earned them a spot in the school's tiny garage.

Since most of the school events were in the shul or event hall, she didn't often get to roam the halls, particularly the preschool halls, where she had also gone to school as a child. They seemed so small now. Many of the murals had been repainted but there was still a portion of wall between two classrooms painted with a Jonah and the Whale mural in which she, Rina, had painted the buildings of Nineveh on the distant horizon. She ran her finger along the painted cement blocks and thought that even the doors looked shorter, the teachers smaller, the ceilings oppressively low. Once she wet her pants in the four-year-old class when she got lost on the way to the bathroom—lost in this tiny hallway!—and then couldn't get her pink overalls down in time once she found it. The sounds of the bead toy she'd been playing with just before the accident still rattled in her head, the faded veneer of the green and blue beads passing through different-size holes when she turned a plastic cylinder in her mind.

The children, thrilled to see Rina at their classroom doors, jumped up and down and screamed, "Ima, Ima, Ima, Ima, Ima." She hugged them; a headache bloomed. It stayed with her all through the challah baking and bath time and gefilte fish and chicken soup and brisket and mandelbrot. She went to bed at the same time as the children.

In the morning her mother woke her again and she dressed for shul and came downstairs, but the children were gone—away to a different shul with David—and Rina's parents wanted to talk. Growing up they weren't allowed to handle family business on Shabbos, or talk politics, or even excuse themselves from the table early. She never saw it coming on Shabbos; they must have wanted to catch her off guard.

They sat in the living room. This time neither of them read or pretended to read, but her father did say, "So . . ." And that's how it started.

Her mother did most of the talking. They were afraid they'd raised her in too secular a setting. They blamed themselves. They shouldn't have sent her to a summer camp where children played kissing games and listened to hip-hop behind the backs of the counselors. They shouldn't have let her go to those Phish concerts in high school. Should have made her go on a nice, Orthodox youth trip to Israel instead of the March of the Living and Paris. They shouldn't have gone to non-kosher restaurants on vacation, even if they didn't ever order meat.

"There's nothing wrong with me," Rina said.

"You sleep all day and your marriage is ending." Her mother said this succinctly and with weight, as if nothing greater could possibly be wrong with her.

"It's not your fault," Rina said. "It's David's."

"That's the father of your children," her mother said.

Her dad made a gruff sound by which he meant, I have something important to say. The women looked at him.

"David is an asshole," he said. "I've always known it."

"He is not," her mother said, but her dad continued.

"He raises his voice, he's distant, he works too much, and the work he does, I don't like. You and I agreeing he's an asshole excuses neither you committing adultery nor moping about the house like a sixteen-year-old while your mother raises your children."

Rina's face got hot and tears threatened, but she kept her voice steady.

"It's been a week."

"It's a shande."

"So David told you everything?" Rina said.

"Yes," her mother said. "But not until we asked."

"And he told you who it was?" Her parents shook their heads. So David spared Anshel that humiliation. As a child, all the way through early adulthood, the simplest disagreement with her parents made her cry. This time, she would not.

"So that you know," Rina said. "He's a nice, religious Jew. Frum from birth. Isn't that what matters to you? You didn't care what I studied in college, if I studied in college, if I became a doctor or a lawyer, if anyone ever took my painting seriously."

"That won't help your reputation," her mother said. "People won't stop talking."

Rina got up and walked to the front door, plenty visible from the living room, and picked up her purse and keys, idle since Tuesday. She was careful not to look at her parents' faces.

"My reputation. All you cared is that when the time came for me to make a Jewish home, I should make a Jewish home with a real Jew. Oh, you were so disappointed with David at first. Barely a BT, practically a sheygetz. Chol. What would you say now? This one's too religious? A zealot, even? I made a Jewish home. You eat in it with your Jewish grandchildren on the Jewish holidays. Isn't that koydesh? Isn't that enough? Who cares what people say?"

She closed the door behind her gently, not wanting to give the satisfaction of a slam, and started the car. Not until she passed a group of women hurrying to shul did she even think about the fact that she'd broken Shabbos for the first time in her life.

She broke the Sabbath. That would really give them something to talk about.

She texted Will without slowing down or pulling over. *See me today?* Turned right on Olympic, toward Koreatown and the women's bath houses, gripping her phone, glad to be rid of a day where she couldn't be in touch with Will, although it hadn't ever bothered her before that she couldn't use her phone on Shabbos. There were Orthodox Jews who smoked. It had never occurred to her before, how difficult it must be to make it through each Shabbos without cigarettes. And why, if they could make it through twenty-five hours each week, couldn't they quit for good?

Shabbos, her phone buzzed back. Then, *Rina, is this you?*

Call, she texted.

David? her phone buzzed back.

She dialed Will.

"David?" she said.

"Why are you texting on Shabbos?" Will said. "I thought maybe it was him. I thought maybe he was going to. I don't know . . ."

"Phone fight you? Tell your wife?"

"Don't be mean," he said. "What's wrong, cariño? What are you doing?"

"I'm in the car. Meet me."

"You broke Shabbos," Will said. Rina hated when people

stated the obvious, hated the phrase *needless to say* above all others.

"It doesn't feel like breaking."

"I'm worried."

"I'm taking myself for a massage or something," Rina said. "Meet me after."

"I will. Because I'm worried."

"You will because you want to," she said.

"I won't have much time. Where will you be?"

"Koreatown," she said. She'd been to an all-women's spa there once or twice before, many years ago, before children.

"I can't leave now but I'll come as soon as I can."

"I will be fresh and warm and pliant." Rina shivered a bit as she said this, flashed forward to the backseat in an underused parking lot. On Shabbos. In a car. Maybe she'd leave it running, play music. NPR, even. News seemed more defiant.

"Hey," Will said. She could hear the disquiet in his voice. "Letters."

There were plenty of spots on the street in front of the spa, but she wanted to sin again by handling money. She valeted and handed the driver a bill. He was surprised by the pre-tip but took it. Behind the building a bank of washers and dryers were tumbling white towels from the heavy client load. She walked into the marble-tiled lobby, paid for a one-and-a-half-hour milk-and-honey treatment, changed, showered, forwent the squat-and-scrub ritual that the old Korean ladies practiced by the little stream that ran through the center of the spa, and dipped herself into a scalding pool of mugwort tea.

She'd avoided the mugwort pool in her previous visits. It was hotter by far than the Jacuzzi and she preferred the stone-walled sauna, the steam room, and even the heated jade floor where women lay around on woven reed mats, reading books, eating sour kimchi, and smoking cigarettes. But she relaxed into the hot tea this time, acclimating to the temperature and watching her breasts bob at the surface. If only they looked as good every day as they did in the dense, hot water. She drank absinthe once in college, brought illegally from a friend who had studied abroad in the Czech Republic, and someone said mugwort was another name for wormwood. Although she knew now that wormwood didn't have the hallucinogenic properties of its rumor, she leaned back in the pool, closed her eyes, and imagined it could wipe her brain free of reality.

"Rina?"

She looked around. A Korean mameh in a black bikini was motioning toward the service area. There were ten massage beds, all out in the open, each with its own shower head and shelves full of washes and tinctures. Ablution was a matter of course.

Before her wedding, before each child, once she stopped bleeding after each child, and monthly on the twelfth day after her period started, she immersed herself in the ritual waters of the mikveh. For a while she and David observed the laws of niddah, of purity, and never had sex other than the days between mikveh and her next period, although he often asked for blow jobs in between. During the last three years of their marriage, after they stopped practicing niddah, she'd walked monthly down the seven steps into the water—makeup free, nails trimmed, toe polish removed, hair washed—and wondered if she didn't go to the mikveh, would he not touch her? She immersed fully three times, holding her breath as long as she could, at peace in the warm, natal waters that demanded nothing of her, no price of her body. The waters buoyed her up and held her in her oneness, her aloneness. In the waters of the mikveh women tried to bring themselves closer to a godly purity, but for Rina, alone in the water, it was when she felt most fully realized, almost redeemed. She displaced the water and the weight of her mattered; the water knew the curves of her body and the depths of her mind and held her without reproach: *la'da'at*, to know.

She knew this place, even if its waters contained mug-wort instead of rainwater. Women didn't have to remove their nail polish to enter, but they had to shower before going in the baths just the same. Women weren't coming at a specific point in their cycle but any time they needed to be held, held up, stripped down, recognized in their womanness. Her scrub would be a great shedding of the prescriptive Orthodox life that bound her to carry the weight of marital purification on her own. Broke. She broke Shabbos. She broke her vows. She broke the system. It was broken.

Rina walked, naked, to her table, then lay cold and face down. She remembered this part well. The mameh would wash her in milk, scrub her body with mitts until she thought she'd bleed, scrub as if the mameh thought Rina's belly but-ton or moles or nipples might be cleansed away with enough effort. The mameh would even hold open her ass and scrub right down the middle. After each delicious douse of warm water Rina would freeze again while the mameh shampooed her hair, massaged her muscles, rubbed her with honey oil, washed her face with pineapple cream and cucumber pulp, put rose petals over her eyes, and washed her body with a bottle labeled MEADOW FOAM followed by a slather of shea butter. Hot, cold, bled, buttered.

But as the mameh, who wore rubber gloves, brushed by Rina's face as she shampooed her hair, the smell of the rubber and the honey overwhelmed Rina. The smell of condoms and jelly and slick bodies, of Brandon's wide, wet mouth and the daisy with two browning petals. The rotting-fruit smell of the whisky glasses that Brandon's wife, Anat, had been crooked over the sink scrubbing as she and David left that night. She'd thought then that Anat looked tired—everyone was tired—but perhaps she was confidence drained, pale in the glow of having been traded. The slump.

Rina jumped off the table, sticky with honey and meadow foam. The mameh protested in quick Korean but Rina motioned to her with frantic hands and made her way to the showers.

When she'd dressed and tipped 40%—money that might not clear her checking account—she'd missed a call. Will, not knowing her exact location, was waiting for her on some corner in Koreatown, and he was anxious. She left her car at the valet and headed east on foot.

In front of a strip mall, between a tiny Korean church and a piñata store, he wrapped his long arms around her and didn't let go for over a minute, even after she began to wiggle, tried to pry her way to his face for a kiss. He was not in the mood for tongues or wandering hands, and he took her face in his hands, investigated her.

"Stop," he said. "Not now. Why'd you do that?"

"David told my parents. About Anshel. Not by name, but the crux of it."

"I'm sorry, Rina. Did you defend yourself?"

"A little," she said. "Then I left, I didn't even think about it."

"And it feels good to you? Not doing . . . not keeping Shabbos?" he said.

"It felt good at first because it didn't feel strange at all. So freeing. But now I'm exhausted."

"I'll bet," he said, then kissed her on each eyelid. "You need to go home."

"Another man telling me what to do."

"Then let's walk."

They walked, his arm around her, for many blocks. She wasn't wearing the right shoes for it, but she wanted to keep moving.

"A botánica," Will said, pointing across the street at a compact storefront that said BOTÁNICA NAVOJOA. An A-frame sign on the sidewalk read AMARRES Y DESAMARRES / AMULETOS / AGUAS ESPIRITUALES / FARMACIA / AMOR / GOT LICE? "Like I was telling you my brother goes to, for my dad."

"Doesn't *amarres* mean to tie?" she said. "I wonder what it means in context."

"Probably to rope someone in. It's all witchcraft."

"Jews have stuff, too," she said. "Every place has brujas."

"But these are curanderas, mi corazón. Healers. Not witches."

They stopped there, on the sidewalk, collapsed into each other.

"Should we, then?" he said, nodding across the street.

"I don't think so," she said. But then: "How much does it cost?"

"No idea. Would it cheer you up?"

They crossed at the light and when Rina saw the dusty woman sitting on a stool in front of her shop and counting the rosary, she wished they hadn't. The woman's long brown braids reached past her waist and up close she was younger than Rina had thought.

"Ten dollars, two palm reads," she said, grabbing Rina's hand. Rina's impulse was to wrench it away, but she just smiled and tried to loosen her fingers. The woman had many necklaces around her neck, including a Magen David.

A younger woman appeared from behind a curtain, long

white-tipped fingernails preceding her. She looked hard at Will.

"Palm readings are for gringos. You know that, right?" she said to Will, with a trace of an accent, a trace of a smile. She took a step forward and sets of large hoop earrings clinked against each other. Neither woman wore any makeup, but their eyes, their striking, matching eyes, commanded attention. "We'll do the cards, real stuff. We can protect you."

The older woman continued moving the rosary in her left hand and opened her right hand and held it in the air; Will had a darkness about him, she said, a slowness, yes, but also a rage; Rina glowed like gold, but her soul was in chains; the two of them had troubles that required spiritual intervention. Revelation. Redemption.

"Fun," Will said, looking at Rina. He pulled out his wallet. The old woman got off the stool.

"My mamá will read the lady in the back," the younger one said, motioning Rina to open the curtain.

Rina hesitated. She didn't want to go inside or leave Will or let the woman touch her skin again, but this was not her element, so she did as told, splitting the bead curtain with her shoulder and following the woman through a small shop with shelves so packed they sagged in the middle. Herbs and spices, candles and oils, rows and rows of Vicks VapoRub, waters, plants, amulets, dark dolls that looked like racist relics, Satan heads, Jesus statuettes with dollar bills affixed, and everywhere there were skulls. Not spooky, though. It was bright, clearly signed in Spanish, and the air was burly with cinnamon and the garlic that hung in ropes from the ceiling. In a back room Rina sat, where indicated, in a plastic folding chair. To her left was a curio cabinet full of what looked like Catholic saints, but also some that looked like the Grim

Reaper or ancient Mayan gods; there were more Magen Davids. To her right, a shelf with a toaster, two junked coffee makers, different-size brass bowls lined up in a row, a microwave, a Tarot chart, a white dove hopping from foot to foot inside a wooden cage.

"Why did you come?" the woman asked. She drew chalk symbols on the floor around Rina's chair.

"He wanted to." Rina pulled her feet in closer.

"What's your trouble? Why do you come here?"

"No trouble," Rina said.

"Sure you do. Married?" The woman lit an incense stick and waved it over Rina's head, then her own. The movement was familiar. She'd seen incense at a Catholic funeral for a college friend's dad, but this was more like the four species Jews shook at Sukkot: three tree branches bound and held together with a citron, stem facing up, shaken in all directions, stem turned down, this in the right hand, this in the left, everything choreographed to bring the rains and the harvest. Or, to the religious, to indicate that god is everywhere.

"Married," Rina said.

"Very handsome," the woman said. For a moment Rina was confused, but of course she and Will both wore wedding rings; they came together; yes, he was handsome.

"Babies?" she said.

Rina nodded.

The woman took Rina's hand, more gently, but didn't examine it. She dropped it, then rolled over a small wooden desk with an attached chair. From her pocket she pulled a deck of cards. "Mexican Tarot," she said. She pointed out various things to Rina, strong life, an abundance of love, a certain number of children, weak health (but not too weak), moon spirit. "A very strong moon *conexión*," she said. "A moon

person. *Extraordinariamente* moon strong." Then she pulled
a series of three cards, arranged them, rearranged them. "A
baby," she said. "A baby in your future. And *liberación*, a *liberación* story. For certain." She paused, bit her lip, seemed to
want to say something and then stopped herself. Finally, she
added, "Yes, that is what I see."

Rina looked at the floor. Did they tell everyone about babies and liberation? Probably.

"Does he want more babies?"

"Yes," Rina said. Then added, "Of course."

The woman looked at Rina a long time, drew an uncertain breath. "Healthy baby," the woman said, and Rina tuned
out, lost in the idea of carrying Will's baby. This was Will's
culture, even if it was foreign to him; this was the ancient
spiritual practice of his people before colonization. The noble
Aztecs, the humble farmers, the women who—like Rebecca in
the Torah, like Hannah, tormented, throwing herself on the
floor of the Temple—came, childless, begging the curanderas
for help. And it was the job of these women to heal. To make
the corn and beans and chile and bread, of course, but not
just to make the corn and beans and chile and bread. Not just
to raise the children and wash the floor and wash their hands
and wash the floor again. To heal. What could Rina even have
been? Not a healer. The modern Orthodox women she knew
who had trained as doctors and dentists no longer practiced
once they had children. Same with the lawyers. A restaurant
owner, maybe, but most of the kosher restaurants and all the
bakeries were owned by men. Besides, just more floor washing. She knew one woman who considered herself an artist and
spent a few hours each Sunday making Judaic jewelry in her
converted garage. A preschool teacher she could have been,
certainly, although they were looked down upon for having to

work. A rabbi, never. When her faith was still strong it was a thing unheard, and even now, with rumors that a school in the Bronx was going to make Orthodox women rabbis, even now her parents' shul was appalled by the idea, terrified of the title *rabbanit* and all that it implied. She was what she was. A set of weathered hands, a back that ached, a lush womb, her name.

She was called back to attention when the woman, who had been talking for minutes, handed her a large black candle. Rina took it, but almost dropped it in embarrassment when she realized it was shaped like a penis.

"A little every night. Believe me, you need it. I don't give lots of black candles, but you need protection. Burn it?"

Rina nodded. Motioning with her head, the woman showed Rina the way out.

"What'd she tell you?" Will asked when they were out of earshot of the shop, walking toward his car. He was carrying a plant with roots wrapped in a wet paper towel, a plant Rina didn't recognize, with almond-shaped leaves the size and shade of key limes. The air smelled of citrus blossoms, sweet and grassy, the smell of something familiar, like the inside of her parents' linen closet or the way the air tasted when she waited on the front steps for her car pool to arrive in elementary school.

Rina took the candle out of a paper bag and waved it in front of his face. She giggled.

"Holy shit, you bought that?"

"She gave it to me," Rina said. "Told me to burn it every night."

"This is why I hate this stuff. A wax dick. It's fraud to tell people they can heal."

"It's no different than god or prayer or lighting Shabbos candles each week," Rina said. "I don't believe it, so it offers no protection." She threw the candle in an overflowing city trash bin. "But the people who believe it works, for them, it works."

"So what did she tell you?" Will said.

"It doesn't matter. I don't believe. What did she tell you?"

"We'll be very happy," Will said. "But I didn't need to part with ten bucks to know that."

She smiled. "When can I see you again? I want you."

"Not this week," he said. "We can talk on the phone. We can do it over the phone. Next weekend. Next weekend maybe. But I need you to be in touch all the time. I need to know where you're living and how you are. We have to start making plans."

"We can't even make a plan to fuck," Rina said. "But you want to know everything at every moment?"

Will took her in his arms and whispered "Patience" into her ear.

"I'm not feeling patient," she said, pulling away a little. "But I'll make you a deal."

"Anything," he said.

She pulled him in close again.

"Promise not to sleep with your wife again."

"I don't think it's going to be an issue," he said.

"It's important to me. And it's a hard thing to ask. Promise not to sleep with her again, ever, and I'll answer all your texts and leave my phone on all the time and tell you everything you think you need to know."

"I won't," he said.

"Won't what?"

"Sleep with the person I married," he said. "But you, too."

"Of course, me too," she said.

After that, there was no more to say.

She was a robot behind the wheel of her car on the way to her parents', turning from memory, lost in her own scent, which was milk and honey, cigarette smoke and incense. Will was her mind's only refrain: the next time they could be together, the next time he'd text, the next time they'd get inside each other, when he'd be ready to have her every day, have her forever, have her have his baby.

A few blocks from her parents' house she turned at the same time a large group of Haredim stepped off the curb to cross. The mass of black jackets and hats slipped into her periphery just in time to slam the brakes. No screech, but her chassis bounced forward and settled back. She looked up on impulse, although she did not want to see their faces. An old man in front held his hand out like a stop sign and shook his head at her. Two mothers recovered from the scare and took up again singing for Moshiach, swinging the clasped hands of their laughing young children. To avoid their gazes, she looked away and . . . Oh god, oh god, she met the stare of Anshel, pushing two of his daughters in a hooded double stroller. She'd given him the first blow job of his life in the back of this very minivan, months into the affair, when he finally got brave enough to consent to it. He didn't recognize her until their eyes met. She watched him comprehend her sins and his eyes didn't widen so much as darken. His jaw hardened and his beard stood on end, the wiry, red tail of an angry cat. She closed her eyes and for the first time since she broke the commandment of Shabbos, she had the feeling she'd be struck down. Struck by lightning, she'd heard Christians say of god's wrath. It wasn't that she feared god, or even karma. But under the hard, righteous stare of Anshel she became Lot's wife; her desperate, glancing stab at happiness had turned her life to salt, and future generations would point at the frowning mass of Rina in old photographs and say, Of this woman, god made an example.

No one was home when she returned to her parents'. At a neighbor's for the third meal of Shabbos, seudah shlishit. She locked her door, lay in bed, and looked out her corner of window.

If it had been misery keeping her down, she'd have started a revolution. But it was loveliness that pinned her to the bed. It was not the misery of the world crushing her but the overwhelming beauty. She could not get up from under the weight of the hope and joy that flowed off people, even when everything—*everything*—was broken. She was undone by the shocking yellows and greens of the young lemon tree beyond the window of the bedroom, heavy with the last season's fruit and the next season's flowers; the thin lip of milky light where the ocean met the horizon on an otherwise black night on the bluffs overlooking Santa Monica; the tiny, perfect proportions of a child, the conch spiral of a baby's ear; the way the air of 5:00 a.m. filled her lungs until it seemed the bracing taste, the very breath of possibility. It was the ceaseless trying of humanity that pinned her to the bed. She stayed in bed and watched time pass in light and shadows through the slice of view out the window. When Will said her name it was as if she contained all the ingredients of a new star, fully Rina. Until he called her name freely—called her his own—she had no place in the beauty of the world; she was salt under the feet of the people who revel in earth's glory. The god she no longer accepted had made of her an example.

PART II

14.

S unday evening. The sun set over the Sepulveda Pass. The Santa Monica Mountains shone, the taut, mottled skin of a Japanese eggplant. The cloudless sky behind the mountains as opaque as a tequila sour, the sun a carmine cherry sinking toward the horizon. Rina knew he'd signed up for classes but didn't know Will was actually here at the Jewish university, actually working toward conversion. A little bit he wanted to surprise her. A little bit he was embarrassed. A little bit he knew that the pluralist class Google churned up wasn't how she would want him to convert.

He loved the class. He did. But his thoughts often drifted from the teacher's words. To the frothy, cloudless sky. The cherried sunset.

In his imagination, Will whispered "Rina" as she circled him seven times in the tradition of Jewish weddings. Most Orthodox Jews wore a thick veil, but he imagined Rina's was light. Lace gusset cut from his abuela's wedding dress and pinned to a tortoiseshell comb at the crown of her chamomile head.

A three-piece band was playing, an East L.A. garage band he'd loved in high school. Rina indulged him. She circled an

eighth time. A twist on convention, devised to honor his late
mother after he'd tried to describe to Rina how it felt to live
in a world without one.

"The Sheva Brachot," the rabbi who taught the class said.
"The seven wedding blessings."

The rabbi was slight and beardless, with masses of creamy,
fist-size curls and a very large kippah, almost the exact apricot
color of his hair. He was about Will's age; he'd dated himself
with comments many times in class, but he had a baby face.
Youthful and fleshy. The remnants of once copious freckles.

"The first is simply the kiddush over the wine, which by
now you all already know," the rabbi said. "Then we thank
God for creating everything. And then it gets more specific:
thank you for creating humans, for creating people in your
image, for granting joy to the bride and groom."

Will pushed away memories from his two actual weddings. In his mind, he looked at Rina under a chuppah and
she became shy.

The ad online said the class was for those considering
conversion, those already married to Jews, those wanting to
learn more about the Jewish religion. Even Jews who wanted
to bone up on their own heritage. Will had every intention of
converting at its culmination, and each of the four weeks in
class so far had been a new way to daydream about his future
life. This week was particularly ripe.

Shrugging off the colonial crown. Choosing something his
own, his selfhood. It felt almost like a homecoming. Maybe
that's why he kept it a secret from Rina, back when he registered over winter break, before he knew if he'd convert. Why
he kept it a secret still.

He daydreamed frequently of the ritual bath, the mikveh,
in which he'd immerse himself to make it official. Rina went

monthly after her period but was ambivalent about the mikveh in her neighborhood. The air thick as lichen, she said. She went because she'd always gone, because it was expected. But in class Will toured a newly tiled mikveh, its terra-cotta air warm from the buoyant waters. He would dip himself in and float, underwater, each scrap of his flesh submerged. Not like the aspersion of his baptismal font. Not immersed in the holy spirit. Alone. Unadulterated. Maybe from behind a screen, the muffled sounds of the rabbi giving a blessing. He would come out pure.

Mikvehs were a certain percentage rainwater, and it smelled of rain. Like the tiny jade creosote leaves he crushed in his hands the time he and his brother were caught in a monsoon on a trip to Tijuana. The creosote plant recorded the scent of rain during the bountiful monsoons, recorded the scent the way he might record the sight. It stored the impression of rain like nectar in its cottony buds. The mikveh smelled of crushed creosote. Smelled of the muddy riverbed where his people had sprung into being. A sidewalk dried after a spring shower. Wet dirt through a ravine.

He would go under three times, every strand of hair fully submerged on each count, into the water that would make him a Jew. Because of Rina. But also not because of Rina. Because nearly orphaned, he longed to be reborn, the son of words and ideas. Because he belonged. Because of the scent of Persian cucumbers and the idea of Shabbos, an idea unlike any he'd ever known. In the mikveh he would be naked because the law required it. But he would not be ashamed.

Men and women could not attend mikveh at the same time, but he liked to imagine Rina there, too. Standing naked on the slippery deck. Waiting to cleanse herself. He often held this thought in holy reverie, as if they'd both be suspended there in the ritualistic stop and start of time as Will went below and came above the amniotic surface.

Sometimes, between the warmth and wetness and peace of these waking dreams, Rina's form was too much to resist. Her curves and divots. The puckered flesh of her thighs. The thin stretch marks that reminded him of her strength. The dip at the base of her spine. The slight imbalance of her pale, heavy breasts. The tiny lick of pink from her perfect brown cunt. He grew hard as he imagined the rabbi seeing her like that.

For one thing, it would never happen that way. For another, they would never accept someone who had these thoughts. If they knew, they would bar the way to Zion. But Will couldn't stop the thoughts from coming.

In his imaginings the rabbi would also be aroused. Will thought of Rina walking to the rabbi, taking off his coat, hooking one leg over his hip and moving against him while Will watched. He imagined Rina on her knees on the shallow stairs of the mikveh, putting her mouth on Will's cock while the rabbi pressed her from behind. He backed up the scene and it was just the two of them again. He and Rina. Floating in the middle of the bath, her legs wrapped around his. Him holding them both above water. They hallowed the water.

Jesus, was nothing holy?

Embarrassing, all these erections in class. At two of the four classes he'd excused himself at the break to beat off in a second-floor bathroom, something he'd only done once or twice even in college. Both times he looked at a picture Rina had texted. She was holding one of her cutoff T-shirts in her mouth to show him her naked chest. God, the humiliation. The exhilaration. He vowed to stop doing it during conversion class.

Sometimes at home he would beat off while thinking about beating off at class to his mikveh fantasies. Ironic, since he'd read that Orthodox men went to the mikveh to cleanse from emissions. All the more humiliating. Exhilarating. Once he beat off in bed with his back to Holly, trying to imagine it was Rina behind him and that she was also touching herself. A game.

When he and Rina had talked about conversion classes, she'd wanted him to wait. That made him nervous. But it wasn't for her anymore. Finally, there were ideas and stories and colors swirling across the blank expanse of his personal identity. There was a there there, as the rabbi liked to say. For five thousand years, Jews had been wrestling with god. Will recognized in himself a wrestler. Jacob had been anointed, and when Will touched his own hair, he felt the belonging so strongly that it was as oil running down his face.

Sometimes there was guilt as he made the drive over Mulholland, perched between the city and the Valley. He spoke to Rina by phone during the drives but told her he'd picked up a class at a community college in the Valley. On the way home, if she wasn't available, he listened to a cantorial CD he'd purchased at the campus bookshop. The music wasn't the kind Orthodox Jews listened to, at least he suspected it wasn't, but he liked the sound of it. It made his breathing slower, the melodies otherworldly. Between the classes and the Hebrew-learning software he downloaded on his work computer, he could pick out certain words. *Adonai* for god. *Baruch* was blessed. *Chai* was life. *Yodeah*, of course, was "I know," from the verb "to know."

After the wedding class he had a good ride home, still daydreaming, talking on the phone to Rina in real life about where they would live. She wanted his Topanga home, but he needed to start fresh. Anyway, giving Holly the house would speed things along.

"No Topanga at all?" she said.

"It only seems romantic," he said.

"I want to change everything."

"So do I."

"Malibu?" she said.

"Is there a shul?"

"Let's not pick that way," she said. He heard the sandy apprehension in her voice.

She would miss her birthright rituals more than she anticipated if she left Orthodoxy. Over time she would miss them. He would not bear the brunt of her nostalgia when it came. It could ruin them. They would live near a shul.

"The neighborhood might have to pick us," he said. "We'll have to give things up."

He drove around and around a half-mile circle of dirt road in Topanga to stay on the phone with her longer. She loved to talk dirty as he approached home. He adored the filthy talk, but it was born of her insecurity and that frightened him. She always started haltingly. Nothing dumb. No "What are you wearing?" Her voice became timid, and she'd say something sweet. "I kiss your neck," maybe. Then she'd exhale with a specific ache, and he'd know to pull over and cut the lights.

She'd just asked him to come on his stomach and send her a photo when her line went muffled. "Yoni's up. I love you. I'm so sorry," she said and hung up. The phone was hot in his right hand, his dick in his left. This made twice in two weeks. He slammed his palm against the steering wheel and the cell phone clunked to the floor of the car. He pumped the brake hard a few times. His neck pulsed at the jugular. He zipped up and made for home and did not pick up the phone when she called him back ten minutes later. He wanted her to feel his frustration from the flats across the city. He turned off the ringer.

At home Dylan was still awake even though it was after nine. Holly was doing his physical therapy exercises with him.

"A little late?" Will said.

"He has so much energy," Holly said.

Dylan was squeezing a turquoise rubber balloon filled with silicone sand. He looked from his mother to his father. He stopped squeezing and his mom gave him a harsh look. Will put his hand on Holly's shoulder.

"The pediatrician said it's better if he's asleep by seven. We agreed."

Holly threw her hands up and headed for the bedroom, leaving Dylan on the carpet with the balloon. Will picked up a plastic bowl of SpaghettiOs with a film across the top.

"Did you and Mommy eat dinner on the floor?" he asked.

"Just me," Dylan said.

Will nodded and stretched out his arms toward the boy.

"Time for bed," he said.

Dylan held out the balloon. "Done?"

"Yup," Will said, then squeezed the boy's arm above the elbow. "Your muscles are stronger today than yesterday."

"Yeah," Dylan said. Will nodded and kissed him on the nose. His son's biceps felt like wet spaghetti.

Dylan was supposed to do the exercises for five minutes in each hand daily, along with certain core strength exercises, seven reps of each per side. Will guessed Holly had handed him the balloon when she heard his car in the driveway.

When Will was ten he had his appendix removed. On his second day in the hospital, his dad worked a full day in surgery and then came upstairs to sit with Will so Will's mom

could go home and fix dinner for his brother, Frank. His dad
sat next to Will's bed and held his hand and stroked his thumb
along Will's palm and asked if he wanted anything. Will's
drug-induced dreams were all Wild West phantasmagoria,
full of images he'd seen on TV. He wanted cowboy boots.

"Do you think Mama would be mad if I left the hospital
for a while?" his dad said. "I'll have one of my residents come
sit with you."

Will shrugged. His mother would be livid. Will hadn't
spent a moment alone since he entered the hospital. But he
was glad for a stretch of quiet.

His dad returned with a huge shopping bag. It could have
been hours later, or minutes. He lined up five boxes on the
bench under the window.

"Boots," his father said. "Cowboy boots."

"How many?" Will asked and sat up halfway.

"I didn't know what size you wore," his father said.

His father had underestimated the size of his feet and only
the largest pair fit. A sunburned leather, with a burnished
pattern at the toe and a one-inch heel. Will thought cowboy
boots came with spurs but was embarrassed to ask his dad
why there were none. He played in them, sometimes, but it
was uncomfortable to sit cross-legged. His mother never let
him wear the pair that fit to school. Her children weren't
gauchos, she said. He outgrew them quickly, angry that his
own father didn't know his shoe size. Angry with himself for
being an ungrateful little shit. As he started to outgrow the
boots, he would stand on them, naked, in front of his full-
length mirror. They were sturdy enough to support him even
though his feet couldn't fit all the way down. They gave him
loft. He turned side to side and imagined himself grown up.
Tall. Taller than his dad, who was almost six feet. He flexed

his dick and tried to make it look bigger. Someday he would have a son and know his son's shoe size. And how to say the words in the stories like they mattered. And how his son liked his toast. At age ten, these were the longings of his heart.

"Can I skip bath tonight, Papa?" Dylan asked.

It was three hours past his bedtime and Will did not intend to run one.

"Well, we took one last night, right?" Will asked. Dylan nodded. Will picked up Dylan's spaghetti arm, sniffed under his armpit and fell over on the floor, gripped his own throat. Made choking sounds. Dylan giggled, stuck his cat nose into his father's armpit. Threw himself down on top of Will, choking and laughing.

Once the game exhausted itself, Will picked the boy up and took him to his room. He brushed his body all over with the therapy brush that was supposed to wake up Dylan's senses. Then he got out a fresh pair of pajamas.

"Already wearing jammies," Dylan said.

"Yes," Will said. "But there are SpaghettiOs here," Will poked him in the softness of his tummy, "and here," under the left arm, "and here," under the right arm, "and everywhere," he said, tickling Dylan while he pulled off his faded dinosaur shirt.

It was nearly ten by the time Will finished brushing Dylan's teeth. Reading *The Tale of Custard the Dragon*, Will laid on the floor next to Dylan's carved pine bed. Dylan's thumb rubbed circles into the palm of Will's hand as the boy fell asleep. Will himself usually fell asleep for a few minutes during this routine. But tonight he lay awake on the rough carpet, lonely now that his boy was asleep. He pushed the limp arm back through a slat. Dylan drew the covers around himself and turned his back to Will with a tiny snore.

Rarely alone, always lonely. A nameless feeling.

There was a specific moment in his life when Will first realized that lonely was how he moved through the world. He'd been at his friend Diego's place. Diego's parents were college professors with an earthy-smelling house full of film canisters packed with stale marijuana. Will always found them when he went looking for toothpaste. A glass for water.

Diego was never made to play outside or to clean his room or to turn down his music. He read books and practiced cruelty on those around him. His parents believed it was better for kids to experiment with substances under supervision, and so, nearly every weekend for two years, Will, Diego, and their friend Tommy got drunk in the two-story guesthouse at the edge of Diego's yard. Usually they drank beer secured by Diego's older sister. Sometimes they drank cheap vodka that Diego's parents kept in the guesthouse. Once in a while, Will or Tommy filched from their own folks, some liqueur certain not to be missed. Tuaca. Rompope. These produced the worst hangovers. The least conclusive results in the jacking-off contests orchestrated by Diego. Somehow Will didn't feel shame when he recalled the contests. Who could come the fastest. Last the longest. Come after reading some horrible excerpt about genocide from a discarded college textbook. The effects of Tapatío, applied topically.

The night he put a name to his loneliness, Tommy had already gone home. Diego was in the bedroom with a girl named Tasha, whom they'd all thought about plenty of times. Tasha with the Sun-In hair. She lived up the street from Diego and came over to sit in the hot tub with his sister sometimes. She drank their beer. Laughed loudly at their jokes. Got close in the hot tub, in her bright-white, one-piece bathing suit.

Will was drunk that night. He could hear Diego and Tasha talking behind the closed bedroom door. He picked up a can of beer and a box of Marlboro Reds from the glass-topped coffee table. The box was always there, even though none of them smoked. There were seven cigarettes left and a book of matches from the gas station where Diego's sister bought their beer. Will went to the bathroom and pushed open a window. He sat on the floor in front of a mirror-covered wall and left the door open so he could continue to listen to Diego and Tasha. It took two matches for him to light a cigarette. He inhaled the first breath and it burned. After that, he only took the smoke into his mouth before exhaling. On his knees, he got as close to the mirror as he could without touching his nose to the glass. He took off his glasses. He tried exhaling different ways. Blew the smoke out the right corner of his mouth. He tried making smoke rings but gagged. He took a sip of beer and slurped it through his teeth. Tried to make the roiling sound his mother made when she was tasting a new bottle of wine. The beer fizzed in his mouth, and he burped.

In the bedroom, Diego was trying to get into Tasha's pants, literally. He spoke urgently. "Just unzip them for me." "Come on, just your pants. You can leave your underthings on." Underthings. Diego said *underthings*. Will couldn't hear Tasha as clearly, but he could hear dissent. Diego kept asking. "See? That feels good, right?"

Will looked at himself hard. He dragged on the cigarette and exhaled. The smoke made a screen in front of his face. His eyes were a funny color. Not green or blue or brown or hazel. Not a mutation like violet. They were bronze. Almost orange. The only person in the world with almost-orange eyes.

That's what the feeling has always been. Loneliness.

Will heard Tasha's muffled dissent again.

Tasha wasn't nice to Will. He tried to talk to her like a person. About real things. About ideas and art and especially poetry. Diego, who was better-read than anyone, would say, "She doesn't want to talk about that shit, she just wants to blow off a little steam." And that's who she went to the bedroom with. The asshole who read Pynchon and pronounced Nabokov nah-*bow*-cough.

His best friend was a dick. His brother was at college. His parents, in the absence of his brother, retreated back into their own love for each other. He lit another cigarette and didn't inhale at all but just held it in front of his face and watched the smoke obscure the view. Heard the voices in the next room.

He had to take action. To stop Diego.

He dropped the butt into his beer can and got up. Just as he got to the bedroom door, Tasha came out of the room, clothed and unruffled. All he managed was a shrug before she pushed past him, grabbed her purse, and let herself out. Diego came slinking out.

"Man, I could not even get past her belt," Diego said.

Will shook his head and went to sleep off the drunk. He barely saw Diego after that and was shocked to receive an invitation to Diego's wedding not long after his own first wedding.

Holly poked her head in Dylan's door.

"You sleeping?" she said.

"Just lonely memories," he said.

She came to him, stretched out her hands. Lent him her balance as he hefted himself off the floor. She moved her hand over the skin on his arm where Dylan's carpet left a patterned imprint. He shuddered, followed her through the Jack-and-Jill bathroom to their bedroom.

He lay down next to her and she was kissing him for the first time in months. Since before he met Rina. Rina. Rina. He tried to think about Rina. The way her mouth was hot, not slick. The way her hands slid under his clothes with confidence instead of the small, questioning gestures of his wife's hands. The way Rina was either drenched or bone-dry, never anything in between.

These thoughts had the opposite effect of what he intended.

Holly climbed on top of him, and he didn't know he was inside her, didn't know he'd broken his vow to Rina, until her specific Holly grunts brought him out of his reverie. Out of the tangle of Rina's golden hair. Out of the mess of her wet-dry insides and all their immense, clenching pleasures. He didn't even realize he was about to come until Holly pulled back on his hair, rolled her eyes, and bounced a few last times before collapsing.

"What's wrong?" she said, looking at him. At his face. He laughed, an inescapable laugh of horror. A tiny, perilous chuckle.

Holly laughed, too. Nervous at first, and then with wide relief. She went into hysterics, rocking naked on the bed. Tears rolled from the outer corners of her eyes. She hadn't laughed much since Dylan's accident, and now one fuck had unclasped her anxiety. Months of suppressed mirth was gurgling up, copious and pointless as confetti. He watched her, a smile of horror wide across his face. He did not enjoy her company. Did not enjoy her being the mother of his son. He hadn't even enjoyed the sex, and he was disappointed in his body.

Just like any other man. A flawed leftover of evolution.

Holly thought they were sharing a moment. The corners of his smile began to relax, and his lips caught on his dry teeth as his face went slack. He looked down at the body that betrayed him. The parts complicit in breaking his promise to Rina. His cock was flaccid and shriveled. White flakes of drying sex crackled on its surface, gathered at its base.

Will vomited on the bed. Right on top of the fitted sheet, in a tidy pile that missed Holly but splattered his left hand, on which he'd been leaning his prone body. He heaved again. The pool spread, grew high, then starting seeping into the mattress.

"Jesus," Holly said and rolled off the bed. "Jesus, are you okay?"

Will didn't say anything but heaved again. Vomit spilled down his chin and chest.

"Should I call 911?" Holly asked. Will shook his head. "Can you get to the bathroom?" Will shook his head again. Got in a few breaths.

"It's over," Will said after a moment. "Get dressed. I'll clean it up."

He shook a pillow out of its case and used the pillowcase to wipe off his chin, his chest, his arm.

Will hadn't intended this. Hadn't intended this to be the night. Hadn't thought through the conversation or what would happen next. Hadn't taken any time to consider how it would feel to pack a suitcase and check into a seventy-nine-dollar-per-night motel while his son slept unaware. But the opening was there. He couldn't hesitate. He loved Rina. His soul had stood at Sinai. He could not save Holly from those truths.

"The marriage," Will said. "Our marriage is over."

"What are you talking about?"

"Crumbs and bathwater and what's best for Dylan and my stupid job and whether there's god and what art means."

Holly took a few steps closer to the bed and put her palm

on his forehead. He took her hand off his forehead, softly. Turned her wrist and put the back of her hand to his head.

"That's how you check for fever," he said.

"We're fine," she said.

"I'm in love with someone else and she checks for fevers with the back of her hand. I'm going to make a life with her."

Holly sat down on the floor and pulled her knees to her uncovered chest. Will stripped the bed of all but the bottom sheet, then gathered that one up carefully and took it to the bathroom, sidestepping Holly. Emptied as much as he could into the toilet. Started a load of laundry. Hot. Bleach in the dispenser. Holly said nothing. He brushed his teeth. Rinsed himself in the shower stall. Sprinkled sal de uvas on his tongue and let the hot shower water turn it to bubbles in his mouth, swallowed down the antacid. He left the door open in case she decided to talk.

He dried off. The towel smelled like gym underwear. He wanted so much to throw a towel over Holly. Cover her nakedness. Make her see that they were in new territory. They were angry and naked and scared. But also free and full of knowledge. In his conversion class they studied Bereshit, the book of Genesis. It was as if he'd never known the Adam and Eve story before. In Judaism there was no particular afterlife. The idea of original sin was something different from what he'd known. God said do not eat. But they had. And then they knew they were naked. The result was pathos and knowledge. Roasted chicken and procreation. Humanity and culture and art. Who cared if god was real? The ancients gave voice to fears. The same fears people still faced. Humanity, the story said, started with knowledge. And the challenge of absolute power. The stories were about creation and revolution. He was creating. He was about to break free. He'd eaten and his eyes were open. He did not fear looking back at the terrible fire. His way back was blocked, but his very being was warmed by the fire. By his self-awareness. Rina was the mother of all the living. The first love. They were forged of the same osseous material. Their naked bodies were warmed by the flames of sin, and they would go forth, he and she. They would be a nation unto themselves. They would live in peace with the idea that they were insignificant flecks of matter in an incomprehensibly vast universe. All they could do was create and love and make the most of their limited, inconsequential days.

He looked at himself in the vanity, shower fog clouding the mirror. He got up close and looked at his face. The face of a free man. The face of a man who for once wasn't afraid to say what needed to be said. Stop what needed to be stopped. Adam, staring into the wilderness, armed with his Eve against the wildness of the world.

"Get out," Holly said. Her voice was quiet but firm. He looked away from the mirror. The sight of her on the floor opened a pit of guilt in him. A leaden stone in his solar plexus.

"Pack some things, fast," she said. "Get out of my house."

"It's my house, too."

"You forfeit this house."

"I don't believe in that," Will said. "And that will feel foreign to you because I always acquiesce. I will leave, but I'm not leaving yet. Because I owe you an explanation."

"Why?" Holly's face was blotches; veins surged in her neck. "To make yourself feel better?"

"It's selfish," he said. "But I'm going to tell you some things you need to know. So we are clear."

He went to the closet and pulled down her favorite nightshirt. A ratty old shirt they bought at a gift shop in a beach town many years ago. It had a big silk screen of Betty Boop on the front and was stretched and lopsided from her pregnancy. He handed it to her.

She balled it up and threw it at him.

"I'm alright to get your dick wet but can't sit naked in my own bedroom?" she said.

Then she stood up, picked up the nightshirt, and began tearing it. It was threadbare, so her work was easy. It made a thick sound. She held it in front of his face, tore it again and again. Then she locked herself in the bathroom.

"Say whatever you have to say from out there. Then leave."

He'd expected her to be more relieved. He sat down on the other side of the bathroom door and put his hand to the particleboard.

"It's Rina," he said. Holly had heard the name enough. They couldn't see each other so often and be complete secrets. He'd called her a colleague, not a student.

"I know who it is," Holly said. "If that's all you wanted to say."

"It's a long time now, since before the accident," Will said. It was important to clear that up right away. "And I love her. We are in love."

Will wanted to say more. Wanted to drive home to Holly how complete his love for Rina was, how impossible it would be to resurrect their marriage. But it would be unkind.

"Does she know this is your second marriage?" Holly asked. "Does she know you digest the love of your wives, then shit it out?"

This was his biggest anxiety, just as it had been when he married Holly. She knew it. Serial monogamy. It sounded like a disease.

"She knows everything," he said.

"Oh really, she knows about—"

"Yes," Will said, cutting her off. "And many other things neither of my wives have known."

"You must feel better now," Holly said. "Pack and get out."

"There's more. I'm converting."

At this there was another long pause and Will realized how little Holly knew about Rina, about who she was. About who Will had been for many months now.

"To what?" she asked.

"I'm going to be Jewish."

There was silence again, but Will could almost hear Holly's hands moving, see her frenetic, angry response to this information.

"I doubt it," she said at last. "I can remember fifty-two other things you were going to be. A children's book illustrator. A farmer. But mazel tov, Will. Mazel tov to you."

Even though the words were acidic, Will couldn't suppress a flicker of pride. *Mazel tov* was for him now.

"What about Dylan?" Will asked.

"You may not proselytize my son," she said, shrieking.

"No, I mean . . . I'll leave tonight. But what about Dylan?"

"Don't talk about my son."

"Our son," Will said. "I can't stand the idea of being without him and you're not equipped to care for him full-time." He dumped the gym clothes, athletic shoes, and wrist wraps out of his gym bag. Packed two pairs of boxer briefs, his ripped jeans, and his dark jeans. White T-shirts, two flannel shirts, two light jackets. Some socks. He took five boxes of cigarettes out of the case Holly kept under her side of the bed. "I will have split custody and I will not be away very many nights before we need to come to an interim agreement."

"Oh Christ, your platitudes," said Holly. "Aren't you going to quote any poetry on your way out?"

He went to the kitchen to grab a corkscrew and a box of matchbooks. Returning to the bedroom, he went for his toothbrush and contact case, but she wouldn't let him into the bathroom. Instead, he took one large mother pothos in a wicker basket and a bowlful of money plant cuttings growing in wine corks. He could get a new toothbrush.

He remembered everything he usually forgot: glasses case, keys, folder of schoolwork, laptop, the book on the coffee table he'd been sort-of reading for months. All this, other than the plants, he shoved into the gym bag, then set it by the door and went to his son's room. He did not cry. It wouldn't be long. It could not be long. Not even with Rina by his side, not for anything. He would cry when it came time to tell Dylan what was happening. His chest heaved just thinking of it. But now his boy was calm. Will bent down and kissed his sweaty cheek, whispered, "See you tomorrow, mijo." He would. Tomorrow. Like always. Will grabbed a plastic dinosaur off the floor and shoved it in his pocket. A Therizinosaurus. He knew because Dylan had told him.

He walked out of his own front door, clicked it behind him, and locked up. It was his house. His house more than hers. He had painted the pansies and nailed the wood into the walls and burnished the walls. But he didn't care about it anymore. Anywhere he had Dylan and Rina and her kids, that would be home. Anywhere Rina wasn't a secret. He sat down in his car and lit a cigarette. When he pulled out of his driveway, he didn't know if it would ever really be his again.

He called Rina five times before the service got spotty. She didn't answer. 10:50 p.m. She should be able to answer. Even if she was asleep, she would answer. Unless she was with people. Her parents. Or. Ugly possibilities coursed through his mind. David. Anshel.

Without pulling over he sent her a text: *Left Holly, told everything. Have to talk. Letters.* He typed while doing sixty down Topanga, taking curves with one hand and racing to get low enough down the mountain that spotty cell service wouldn't keep Rina from him.

He still signed "letters" even though she stayed with her parents now, even though the threat of her husband reading her texts was scarce, even though he openly wrote *I love you* in other messages.

His phone glowed. *Give me ten. I will call.*

It took less than ten minutes. He'd already reached the base of the mountain and turned onto the Pacific Coast Highway. They were on the phone as he made an illegal left turn into an overpriced liquor store, bought two bottles of the cheapest red, made an illegal left back onto PCH, and headed toward Pico-Robertson. He opened a bottle of wine, a screw top, took several swigs, and told her everything. How he'd fucked his wife. More vomit welled as he tried to explain it, wiped tears from his eyes. He drank more wine.

"Did you like it?" Rina asked.

"I didn't even know I was doing it."

"Bullshit."

"I'm so sorry. I was thinking about you and then . . . I already told you how it happened."

"But you came."

"What?"

"You came."

"Will you see me?"

"Did you come?"

"Don't do this. Yes, I came. Then I puked all over our bed. It's not an excuse, I just—"

"Do you still love her?"

"No."

"Do you think she's beautiful?"

"What?" Will unscrewed the second wine cap with a single hand and tossed the lid on the floor of the passenger seat. He drank deeply, wine splashing down his chin and onto his shirt. He jammed the bottle into the cupholder on the dashboard.

"Is she sexy, Will? You broke a promise. Is she sexy to you?"

"No."

"She must be."

"You fucked David plenty of times after he repulsed you. Palm Springs, for starters. As a bartering tool."

"To see *you*."

"Will you see me now?" he said.

"So you can fuck us both in one night?"

"Because I love you. Because I want to make a life with you. I want to start now. I'm sorry. God, I'm so sorry. But I told her. I told her I love you."

"I'm worried," she said.

"We'll get through this."

"I'm worried you're not attracted to me."

"That's crazy. I told her I love you. I told her I'm converting. I told her she couldn't just have the house or—"

"You're what?" Rina said.

He was baffled by Rina's lack of self-confidence, her inability to know how much he wanted her. Only her. Confident, smart Rina wondering if he was more attracted to Holly. Holly!

"You're actually converting?" Rina said.

"Yes, I'm studying. Our family is going to be . . . there aren't going to be . . ." He drank again. Rina could hear it, he knew. "I think I stood at Sinai."

"Alright," she said.

"Alright you'll see me?"

"Stop drinking. Where are you?"

He wasn't quite sure where her parents' house was, but he thought he was almost there. He made a left off Robertson, disappeared behind twenty-foot shrubs.

"Near you," he said. "Can I pick you up?"

"No. Park where it's dark. I don't know if I can come out. You can't just summon me."

Will parked on a dark block in front of an empty, fenced-off lot between a salmon-colored mansion and a Tudor-style cottage. He told Rina where he was. She told him to calm down.

"I need a plan. Where am I going to sleep?"

"Was Dylan asleep?" Rina asked.

"I put him down when I got home. Seems like days ago."

"Will you see him tomorrow?"

"I hope so," Will said. "I need your help."

"First thing, let's finish what we started."

"What?"

"Take it out," Rina said.

"I can't," Will said, and he started to cry. Really cry.

"You can. And you'll get hard if you love me."

"Please . . ."

"I want to hear your hand. I want to hear it."

Will did as he was told. He was drunk. His teeth were filmy with wine; his cock was soap-soft and out of his hand poured all of the anger, all the confusion. He rubbed until it burned but nothing happened.

"I can't, mi corazón. I'm not tapped out, I just . . ."

"Try again," she said, her voice soft.

There were three raps on his window and there she was, sharp against the dark, wearing that boho skirt she'd worn the first day they met outside of class. That same cutoff shirt. Her unwashed hair fell around her face. She did not smile. She looked more beautiful than in all their months. Round in the elegant slope of her shoulders under the shirt. So soft. So his. He was an idiot, sitting with his limp dick. Just the sight of her there, though. He grew so much that he pushed uncomfortably against the bottom of his open fly. He was rabid for her. Ashamed. Worried for her. She climbed in the driver's side. Reached down and slid his seat back, closed and locked the door behind her. Lifted her skirt to reveal she was naked underneath. Even as she climbed on top of him and he kissed her and kissed her and cried right into her face, he was worried. Even as she smoothed his hair and kissed him back, unfazed by the sour wine. Even as she rocked faster and in one bright moment they came together, he worried for her. Worried for the broken psyche of a girl who shed the funk of depression long enough to choose with profound knowing the two pieces of clothing that would work. Worried for his poor, broken Rina. His love. The only love of the rest of his life, who didn't know and couldn't fathom that it was her face, her presence, the promise of her smell, her voice, her hard-won laugh, access to her thoughts that made him excited.

PART III

15.

Rina helped him find the nearest, cheapest hotel in Pico-Robertson. At least he'll be close, she thought. She dropped off the kids in the mornings and then stayed out most of the days, which her parents took as a good sign, saying little but making approving clucks when she appeared dressed in the morning or packed a sack lunch. She went to Will after drop-off and stayed until he had to teach, or waited until he was done teaching. For the first few days there was no planning, no future talk. They would fuck, shower together, talk about poetry and museums and their children, lie back down, hold each other until one of them had to be somewhere.

In the afternoons of the first week, she sometimes went with him to pick up Dylan and then the three of them would go pick up Yoni and Shosh and take them to a park with a duck pond before going their separate ways. She, to cook dinner with her mother, and he, to feed Dylan a dinner cooked in an Extended Stay America kitchenette before dropping him in Topanga by 7:00 p.m.

She didn't explain the afternoon outings to the children; they already knew Will. If they reported back to David maybe she'd hear about it, or maybe it would sound too ridiculous to be true. Some nights she feigned excuses, book club or committee meetings, that took her out of the house after the children were sleeping, and she went back to Will for an hour or two. She would lie with his cock in her hand—before and after, hard and yielding—and just look, look at the contrast of his body against hers. At times she felt the sheer power of their togetherness could stave off the danger of the choices they'd yet to make.

All Thursday afternoon he had meetings and obligations after he taught. She asked her mother to pick up the children and went near dusk to walk along the Palisades, to be alone with her thoughts of him until she next went to him. Her new closeness with Will was overpowering, their ability to see each other. At first she thought the pier rides weren't going, but then she heard the ebbing screams of jubilant coaster riders, caught the lazy movement of the Ferris wheel loading. She imagined herself in the topmost gondola with Will, looking not at the eastern view of city lights unfolding like the rings of a tree trunk, but west over the quantity of the Pacific. They could go up to the top of the Ferris wheel together and stay there, the two of them starving and wasting in a time-lapsed sequence of sunups and sundowns, shivering against each other, finally evaporating into the gauzy breath of the other, never coming down to face the conspiratorial world of identities and choices, the certainty of hurting others. The sun emerged from low clouds and spilled its orange light over the water like an upended bucket of paint, the tangerine refractions stippling the ocean in an inverse V. The horizon was round and lithium-ripe, the sun lowering so fast that she could almost perceive the earth in its rotation. She caught herself against the rail, felt gravity's heavy, gratifying pull.

The ocean smelled primitive against the mild air of an early budding spring, strong and saline, like the great, salty gush of the planet's spinning birth. Over it she smelled the crisp new leaves of the eucalyptus trees and herself, went saline and wet remembering the scent on his hands after he'd gathered firewood in Big Sur, the sappy taste of them, the astringent burn of them filling her up. The moon had been hanging, fertile, in the daytime sky, and turned milky and bright in the absence of the sun. It looked close enough to lean a ladder against, to throw her arms around. Its reflected light caused the bank of seafront homes below her to glow cozily, and she imagined a fireplace in each, young families playing board games, couples pouring glasses of wine for each other, making love on the couches, the kitchen counters, right on the floor. The breeze picked up and she shuddered against it, and then she was taken with warmth remembering his arms around her, his hands in her pockets, the fact of his existence. For a few minutes—for almost an hour, maybe, before she went home for dinner—she let herself believe that she was happy.

David took the children the first Shabbos after Will left his wife, and Rina ate with her parents, went to shul with her parents, snuck out of the house after sundown when they were making Havdalah with friends, and rode with Will to campus. She stayed for the Saturday evening class he taught.

On his eighth night at the Extended Stay he stopped paying with his checking account—afraid to cut into Holly's monthly needs—and began taking from his savings, so they had to talk about what choices needed to be made, and in what order. There were too many to wrangle. Rina committed to making a list, full of parentheticals and colossal tasks. It took her four days just to make the list, that's how impossible it all seemed.

Leave David (officially)
File for divorce (both)
Assess finances (including divorce fees, likely alimony
    and child support dollars going both ways; establish
    rent budget)
Make a new household budget
Find an apartment together
Tell parents and kids
Find family therapist
Possibly switch Dylan to a more convenient day care
    (lawyer thing?)
Move
Rina finds job?

She finished the list on Valentine's Day, cruel and fitting. Will wanted to celebrate in some way, but she wasn't comfortable with gift giving, or even romance, in the name of a saint. She knew he'd have something for her, though, and her gift to him was to bring order to the chaos of their path forward. It wasn't until she finished the list, sitting in her brother's dinosaur bed in her childhood home, that the immensity of it walloped her. From even thinking about addressing the tasks on the lists, she was paralyzed. It was only 9:30 a.m. and Will was teaching. She had the day in front of her but couldn't be still with the list occupying her mind. She gathered her keys, wallet, and sunglasses and headed to Jewish Family Services. She texted Will, *Going to volunteer today. Letters*, and entered through the front door, not the alley door she used with An-shel. She hoped he wasn't there, but she needed what to do. The volunteer coordinator—today a gray-haired man with bloated jowls and a very small kippah—was glad to have another set of hands and sent her next door to the kosher soup kitchen. For two hours the only task was to boil kosher hot dogs, slice them into coins, stir them into a pot of cholent. There often wasn't brisket to make the bean-and-barley stew, so the kitchen used hot dogs when they could get them. Her fingers pruned from steam, from grabbing the hot dogs out of the giant vat with short metal tongs, until the man with the small kippah had her stop making cholent for Saturday and start making soup for Friday night. She funneled her anxiety into chopping, mixing, and the soothing roll-drop of matzah balls into soup that made her hands ache under the muscle memory of generations of women with wheat dust in their hair and oil slicks on their knotty fingers. Condensation gathered on her eyelashes. The celery bobbed.

"Every mitzvah helps perfect the world," Anshel said from behind her, his breath full of mint, a cup of sugared tea drunk after lunch.

She dropped the matzah ball too quickly and the hot soup splashed back onto her face.

"You are thin," he said.

"I am happy."

Anshel opened his mouth, then shut it again. He wiped a smudge of matzah meal from Rina's temple, looked around to see that no one had noticed him touching the face of a woman in public, a woman who did not belong to him.

"Three times a day I thank Hashem for the blessings of this world, including the blessing of forgiveness between people," Anshel said. "I hope forgiveness can find you. What I deserve is a matter between Him and me, and we shall see how soon it will be settled."

"Do you practice these speeches in your head?" Rina asked.

Anshel took a step back. "You didn't used to be unkind."

"I'm sorry," Rina said. "I'm tired."

"I'll pray for you to sleep."

"Don't pray for me. Why have you gone back to that?"

"I wish we could help each other," Anshel said. He walked out of the kitchen but then turned at the door and said, "I pray because it's easier."

She saw Will Friday morning, and he gave her a red card in which he'd written the e. e. cummings poem "i carry your heart with me," along with a small painting he'd made of their cabin in Big Sur. She gave him the list. It was her Shabbos with the children, although David would have them for a few hours on Sunday. All afternoon Friday she shopped and cooked and cleaned with her mother. All Friday evening she read books, first to the children, and then curled up in a corner of the living room with a novel. Saturday she went to shul, played with the children, longed for Will until they could speak after his Saturday evening class.

As the third week of Will's hotel stay dragged forward, they began looking at apartment listings online. Will insisted they'd be able to afford three bedrooms. Yoni and Dylan would share a room and Shosh would get her own.

"And we'll hope the next one is a girl," Rina said.

Will leaned sideways in the rolling chair and looked at her, sitting on the edge of the glass-topped hotel desk. His mouth was pressed thin, but his eyes were lively.

"Only if you want the next one, mi amor," he said.

"Don't you?"

"Want to put a baby in you?" Will said, reaching over to touch her soft belly with his right hand. "So much. But for the first time, you get to choose."

"I could have five more babies with you. I could be the frum baby factory I've always detested."

Will pulled her off the desk and into his wide lap, laying her out left to right. He lifted her shirt and kissed her belly, one, two, three times.

"Right here," Will said, pointing to a spot below her belly button. "Right here is where baby Ochoa-Kirsch will have its genesis."

Rina wanted to stay and let him do it right then, but she had to work an evening shift at the opening night of the book-fair at the kids' school. She hated leaving Will any time, but especially on nights when he didn't have Dylan. She stood up and smoothed her skirt.

"I'm sorry I can't come back after," she said.

"You have to start a more normal schedule. We have to begin to settle."

"I know," Rina said.

"Call me after?"

Rina nodded. They liked to put each other to sleep on the phone, speaking slowly as they drifted off. They woke to a hot, still-connected phone in the morning, or sometimes to the sound of the others' alarm clock or, most often, to a cold phone that had been disconnected by a turned cheek in the night. She'd switched the phone bill to paperless; she handled the bills anyway. David didn't even have the password.

Her mother brought the kids to the bookfair and let them pick out chazerai, even though Rina's rule was just books. While they were playing with the cash register Yoni said something about Will. He'd been teaching the boy math.

Instead of saying, Who's Will?, or asking a dozen questions, her mother said something ominous. "They learn so many interesting things from Will."

Rina rolled her eyes and began to ring up the transaction.

"He has a little boy; they play," Rina said.

"I know," her mother said. And then, without lowering her voice for the children's sake, she added, "Your father and I think it's good to have a friend. Outside the community. Do we also worry? Of course."

If only Rina believed in a soul. The sharp pain inside of her—needling her chest, her lower abdomen, her sternum—felt very much like its shattering upon hearing even one sweet word from her mother about Will. The immediate future would bring so much rage against him, so much misunderstanding.

The children picked out lollipops and went home with her mother to bathe. Rina's shift went another forty minutes, but the bookfair was dead and the president of the PTA—a tall woman who was one of the few ladies in the school to cover her hair with a wig—told Rina to go ahead home, adding, with a pejorative cant of her head, that they'd all missed her at the Hanukkah craft fair.

"Everyone is davening for you, of course," she said, not unkindly. "That your troubles should end."

Rina, who did not want their prayers, thought, If they missed me at Hanukkah, wait until they find out the Kirsch family will not be delivering mishloach manot for Purim this year.

Rina was hungry and knew she shouldn't go back to Will's; she drove toward Pico, stopping not at Eilat Market or Little Jerusalem or Glatt Mart or even the giant supermarket on Beverwil, but at the grocery store on the east end of the Pico-Robertson neighborhood. Although both supermarkets bordered the modern Orthodox enclave, the neighborhood's segregation was neatly distilled by the supermarkets. The easternmost store did not carry Israeli goat cheese or kosher soup croutons but was full of products that befuddled kosher shoppers (pickled eggs, pork cracklings, a whole refrigerator full of gelatin cups laid out like jewels). The store to the west had no tripe at its butcher stand, but four different types of fish salad.

Rina grabbed a shopping basket. A project was taking shape in her head. An experiment. If she ran into someone, they would probably be checking to see if she was wearing a wedding ring, which she was, rather than what was in her basket. And if they did look in the cart it would confirm everything they were all saying about her anyway. Still, she moved fast. She went straight for the SpaghettiOs.

SpaghettiOs, the great regret of her childhood. Rina had been convinced that SpaghettiOs were the best food on the planet and that she was denied a great pleasure of the world because SpaghettiOs lacked a kosher hechsher, although they contained no treif. Sunday-morning television taught her about the foreign concept of dinner from a can, and she wanted into that Eden. In fourth grade, she wrote about SpaghettiOs endlessly in her classroom journal. Her teacher's responses, written in tight red letters in the margins, began as sympathetic, then went through stages of reasoning, reverse psychology, and rebuke. She and her parents were invited to a teacher conference on the great blessing of kashrut. They bought her a can of kosher stars-in-sauce, which tasted awful.

She put three cans of SpaghettiOs into her basket and a tin can of Chef Boyardee cheese tortellini. What next? As a child she couldn't eat Oreos. The original formula contained lard, so instead Jewish kids ate barely sweet Hydrox cookies, which crumbled into greasy dirt at the bottom of lunch bags. Oreos had long since changed their formula. Gatorade had stopped using a grape base—subject to much stricter kosher laws about the fruit of the vine—and was now also kosher.

What was still forbidden? She shifted the basket from hand to hand, standing in the middle of the soup aisle.

Cheese. Real cheese, made with rennet; salad from the deli counter that had come into contact with treif; lunch meat sliced fresh from the hock.

She picked a white cheddar—white cheddar!—a round cardboard package of Brie, and something she'd never heard of, selected on the merits of high price. As she touched the cold, soft slabs, her stomach jolted and clinched and she had to clutch her side: a new kind of hunger, something salty and unknown. She wanted Velveeta and got waylaid trying to find it, until she finally had to ask a clerk, who took her to a whole section of cheese foods. She bought one of everything except the bacon-flavored spray cheese; it was too cruel to bring it into her parents' home.

Her whole life she'd heard friends and neighbors talking about how actually you could get fine kosher wines, which gave her the untested impression that kosher wines must be shit. In college it was all vodka and beer and these days it was a sip of kiddush on Shabbos, a glass of Scotch late at night, a nip of slivovitz to make sure the flavor was right. She didn't know wine and usually just picked the most beautiful labels on the kosher bottles. Will told her how wines were named for the grapes from which they were made. She picked a non-kosher bottle made from malbec grapes, a bottle made from pinot grigio, and a bottle made from zinfandel, which seemed to be the most popular type. Her basket grew heavy, so she went to the front of the store to transfer her contraband to a rolling cart.

By the time she was standing in line she had over two hundred dollars' worth of non-kosher foods, including a small tub of chicken salad, Boar's Head honey-roasted turkey slices, Oscar Mayer beef wieners, plum-flavored baby food (what possible difference could exist between the kosher and non-kosher jarred baby foods?), a loaf of Wonder Bread (she'd heard it was kosher on the East Coast but it wasn't in California), a can of Campbell's condensed tomato soup, and a small carton of generic-brand cookie-dough ice cream that lacked a hechsher.

Once she'd snuck the bags up to her room, she realized she had no way to keep it cold. She shoved it all into a large tote bag and put it on the bench below her open window. Then she put her children to bed, answering the call for one more story with two more stories and singing three lullabies plus the Oscar Mayer wiener song from the commercials of her childhood, to the children's delight. "Does everybody really want to eat Oscar Mayer wieners?" said Yoni slowly, from beneath the covers. "No, darling, that's just what the commercial wants you to believe." She kissed him on both eyelids and backed out of the room, singing the song again in a whisper.

The ice cream melted while she popped open a can of SpaghettiOs with a key chain. She had no spoon and would not defile her parents' flatware, so she tipped the can toward her mouth and gulped her first mushy taste of non-kosher food in the home. It tasted just like the kosher stars-in-sauce. Will called and she ignored it. She didn't yet know what she would say about her little revolution. She sprayed jalapeño-flavored cheese food onto a piece of Wonder Bread and ate it in one folded bite. She carved up Velveeta with her fingers. She had no corkscrew, but the zinfandel had a screw top. She drank directly from the bottle. She liked the wine. She loved the white cheddar and the chicken salad, which she ate together, doubling the laws broken. She saw "fully cooked" on the hot dog package and ate one cold. She returned to the disgusting can of SpaghettiOs, fulfilling an obligation to her ten-year-old self, sucking it from the can. She cut her tongue trying to reach the last mouthfuls and it bled like crazy. In kindergarten she'd bitten her tongue on the playground and spit mouthfuls of blood onto the concrete bike path until a teacher brought her a raw egg and made her stick her tongue into the white to stop the bleeding. She had no egg, but she wrapped a slice of cold turkey around the tip of her tongue like a compress.

Sleepiness came on fast. She washed well, shoved all the food under her bed, and went to sleep, barely able to speak to Will, drooling onto the pillow next to the glowing phone that connected them. She did not tell him about her debauchery.

She woke at two in the morning, from a dream in which nothing went right. She'd been standing over a well that looked like it was in the ancient Near East, although in the dream it was Los Angeles. She'd been filling a bucket and trying to pass it to Will over the well, but she was never able to get the water to him. Once the bucket tipped; once all the water slipped out of rust holes that formed as she passed it. When she finally got a full bucket to the other side, Will refused it.

"You're thirsty," she said. But he was hungry.

David was there in the dream, behind her. Not thirty-two-year-old David, but David as he had been when they met. She panicked and began spewing excuses about why she was with Will. David just shook his head and beckoned her. Sweat needled her armpits and between her legs. There was a sharp, familiar sensation in her stomach, and she looked down to find that she was pregnant—terribly pregnant—her skin rippling where the baby pounded to get out. She could hear its voice, muffled by liquid and shadow. "Mommy." Her children did not call her mommy. Sweat began to come off her body in sheets, splashing to the ground.

She woke to drenched sheets, bunched around her abdomen. Two corners of the fitted sheet had popped off the mattress and the bedding gathered around her, sticking.

It was so hot. Without sitting, she reached under the bed, feeling around for the carton of ice cream, a pool of melt. Oh, her throat, the thirst. She flipped the lid off with her thumb, lifted her neck and drank it—all of it—the chunks of chocolate and dough catching in her throat, then collapsed back into the pillow.

When she woke next, she knew immediately that she wouldn't make it to the bathroom and grabbed the wastebasket, dumping its receipts and cotton balls and used Kleenex onto her floor just in time to fill it with a profane mess. Mucus ran from her nose, tears spilled from her eyes, the sweat kept coming.

At her first possible breath, she muttered the Shema, a frum impulse, a panic prayer, and she said it over and over again until her breathing was steady, until she could close her eyes and drift toward slumber.

The next time she woke, the light was bright and high through her window, the house was silent, and the smell was dense in the air. A sparse but steady stream of small, brown ants was colonizing the open package of turkey. The punishment was all the bitterer from a god she'd scorned.

Nausea overtook her when she stood, but this time, she made it to the bathroom. Her insides scoured, and she felt a little better. She worked fast while her mother was out, bagging the food and the trash scattered on her floor. This went in the dumpster in the alley behind her parents' house. She tipped her wastebasket into the toilet, then washed it with water and vinegar in the bathtub. Her mother kept half a dozen old sheet sets in the upstairs linen closet. The flat sheets were folded and stacked neatly, but the fitted sheets were rolled and piled into lumpy masses. She risked her mother's reproach at mismatched sheets and pulled down a blue, bleach-stained flat sheet and a flower-printed fitted sheet because they were easiest to reach. After changing the linens, she took her toothbrush into the shower and emerged clean and more alkaline. She put an inch of water in the bottom of her wastebasket, set it next to her bed, and laid back down. Dizziness took hold and though all traces of cheese were gone, she smelled it everywhere.

She opened her eyes to steady herself and realized it was late. The light had shifted to the left half of her window. A small breeze moved the lemon tree and purple bougainvillea blossoms scraped against the pane. Her head throbbed. She shivered and pulled the sheet around her, then pulled a blanket over her head. Holding her knees to her chest, she listened to the voices of her children. Silverware clinked and oh god, why supper? The dirty sheets had been cleared from her floor, a glass of water placed on her nightstand. Her reading lamp was on. In its light she saw a thin layer of dust motes floating on top of the water. The nausea returned. She leaned out of bed and buried her face in the wastebasket, then wiped her mouth with a tissue and drifted back to sleep with it bunched in her hand. Before she fell asleep, she thought, I hope Will comes to find me.

She woke up to Yoni's nose buried in her neck and the sound of her mother shooing him away.

"She's sick, she's sick," her mother said. "You don't want those germs."

She smelled Lysol and knew that her mother was walking around with a can of it—as she always did when there was illness in the house—spraying doorknobs, thresholds, and furniture as she passed. Rina gagged a little.

"Ima!" Yoni said. "Abba is taking us to see Bubbe and Zayde and we can stay until Purim and we are bringing our bathing suits."

He bounced up and down on the bed, sending shocks the length of Rina's body. Her neck was immobile. A sensation branched out from the back of her neck: intense pain, unlike anything she'd experienced before.

Rina's mother lifted the boy up and off the bed with a *tsk*.

"Wait," Rina said. It hurt her throat to talk, and her lips were papery. They stuck together in the corners.

She reached her arms out and Yoni catapulted into them. It was difficult to hug him, and this made Rina feel weak, but she put her dry lips into his hair and kissed him.

"Love you, Yo-Yo Ma," she said, quietly.

"Love you, Ima," he said. "Will you be better when we get back?"

"I hope so," she said and nuzzled him. His smell of sweat and baby shampoo was much better than the overpowering Lysol. She looked at her mom. "What do I have?"

Her mother shrugged. "The flu maybe. You'll go to the doctor."

"Yoni, go get your sister. I want to see her." The boy went running.

"It's food poisoning," Rina said to her mother. "I got the flu shot."

"I meant the stomach flu. But you'll definitely go to the doctor. Your fever is very high and now you have a rash. You didn't eat one bite yesterday, so you're dehydrated. Daddy will take you today, but we didn't know which doctor you see now. Neither did David."

"David knows," Rina said. Her mother shrugged again. "The kids are going to San Diego?"

"For a week," her mother said. "David is taking them out of school. I don't think it's a good idea, especially the month before Pesach break, but what do I know?"

Any other time, news of a week without husband or children would have made Rina think of being with Will. But she could barely conjure a wispy image of his face.

"They're just little. It will be nice for them," Rina said. She turned her head to lie back down and winced. "And a break for you."

"I suppose," her mother said.

"I'll go home," Rina said. "You'll have a complete break. I want to be at home."

"Like an animal, you'll be by yourself when you're sick?"

"I'll be more comfortable. I can take care of myself," Rina said.

"Let's see what the doctor says."

Shosh came into the room. She looked ready to pounce on her mother as Yoni had, but stopped before she reached the bed.

"You're very sick, Ima," Shosh said. "You smell funny."

"Not so sick," Rina said. "How are you, Shoshi?"

"Did you know we're going to Bubbe and Zayde's and they said they were going to take us to SeaWorld and Abba said we couldn't go because of cruelty to the animals. I don't even want to miss school if we can't go to SeaWorld."

Rina reached out her arms and hugged Shosh, who hugged back cautiously.

"Maybe he'll change his mind," Rina said.

"Do you care about the cruelty?" Shosh said.

"If Abba cares about it, I probably do, too," she said.

"Do you care about Abba?" Shosh said.

It was difficult to keep her eyes open, but she didn't want to qualify her answer by closing them.

"Of course," she said. "Are you bringing your bathing suit?"

Shosh nodded. Rina felt safe closing her eyes. She turned her head away from her daughter and a spasm of nausea roiled her body.

"It's Doctor Falkow on Pico," Rina said to her mother. "You can Google it."

At Dr. Falkow's office with her father, Rina charged her phone in the lobby. She'd picked it up on the way out the door. How worried must Will be? What could he be thinking?

Her name was called. Her father stayed in the lobby reading his *Economist* but gave her an awkward pat on her elbow as she dragged herself toward the nurse. She turned around and gave his hand a little squeeze, grateful for his quiet company.

There was another wait in the exam room, so she plugged in her phone and called Will. He picked up before she even heard a ring. She explained, briefly. She didn't feel coherent but understood that he was angry, then wilted, then worried.

Nurses bustled, her vitals were noted, Dr. Falkow walked in with a smile and a tablet. He took one look at her, upturned a heavy glass jar full of Q-tips, and pressed the open end of the jar to her arm, peering through the glass bottom.

"It's just food poisoning," Rina said.

"Things will happen very fast," Dr. Falkow said. "Could you be pregnant?"

Rina thought of the curandera's prophecy, but then of her copper IUD. She shook her head. "But I promise you, it's just food poisoning."

She remembered holding her arm out for a needle and

walking around the corner into an X-ray room. She was barely conscious during the ride to the hospital, the spinal tap, and the first IV drip of antibiotics. She did not remember calling or texting Will, but when a doctor woke her it was bright, afternoon maybe, and Will was the only other person in the room besides the doctor. He sat in a battered armchair next to her bed, biting his nails.

The doctor had a clipboard and also a computer on a rolling stand.

"Sorry to wake you, Ms. Kirsch," the doctor said, typing as she spoke. "But what you contracted could be a public health risk. I'm from the county. I need you to help me figure out the source."

Rina tried to shake her head.

"It's listeria," Will said. His voice was matter-of-fact, angry maybe. He didn't stop biting his nails. "You were not contagious to the children, but we have to know if they ate the same contaminated food."

The way he said *we* fortified her. The doctor stopped typing and looked at Will. "Is this your husband?"

"Yes," Rina said. Will took his finger out of his mouth, reached out, and squeezed her hand.

"Did you eat anything atypical in the days leading up to the onset of your illness?"

"Yes," said Rina. "But the children are safe."

The story came out. It was slow at first, hard to form words. Will gave her a few ice chips. Once she got past the SpaghettiOs, the rest came out in a hurry. Will's face was hard to read.

"What brand of lunch meat?" the doctor asked.

Rina told the brand, and then about cutting her mouth

on the SpaghettiOs can and holding turkey to it to stop the bleeding.

"And did that work?" the doctor said.

She's mocking me, Rina thought, and looked to Will for confirmation. He just stared at her, mouth slack.

"How long after eating the . . . well . . . everything, did you start to feel sick?"

It was difficult to think back. Maybe a couple hours, Rina said. The doctor shook her head and scanned the computer screen.

"Before that night . . . before that night," the doctor said. "Had you prepared or eaten any hot dogs recently?"

Rina told her about the single, cold Oscar Mayer wiener. "It said fully cooked."

She looked to Will again to see if he was mad, but he was engrossed in his phone.

"Any other hot dogs? It would take a couple days to set in, minimum. Maybe kosher hot dogs?"

"No," Rina said.

"Yes," Will said and held out his phone toward Rina. "You texted me from the soup kitchen. 'Already chopped five packages of hot dogs and cut up three watermelons, going to make the soup. Letters.'"

That's what the doctor was looking for. She connected Rina's illness to a listeria outbreak among people who'd come in contact with the packaged liquid in a certain brand of kosher hot dog.

"Most healthy people can consume it without any problems . . ." said the doctor.

"I didn't consume it," Rina said.

"We've had seven reported cases of illness from pregnant

women and the elderly. You're the eighth. You're not pregnant; we checked. I'm sending in the report right now."

"They thought you had meningitis from it, Rina," Will said, in a quiet voice. "They thought it might be life-threatening."

"But we ruled that out," said the doctor. "Just a bad case of listeriosis."

Her fingers clicked over the keyboard a while longer, then she left.

"You look terrible," Will said.

"Are you angry?"

He brushed hair back from her face. "I'm confused. I'm worried you thought I wouldn't understand," he said.

"Do you?" she said.

"Not really. But I haven't lived my whole life as an atheist who keeps kosher."

"Not my whole life," Rina said.

Will was quiet for a moment. He nodded his head and stared at a whiteboard pegged to the hospital wall.

"I'm jealous," he said.

"You told me you were never jealous."

"I'm jealous of that whole other life of yours that I wasn't a part of. I'm worried it will call you back."

She sat up and it neither hurt nor brought a wave of nausea. "Never. I've heard the siren call of SpaghettiOs."

Will laughed, and then Rina, and they both laughed hard when the room's door opened, but it wasn't a doctor or a nurse.

Anshel took his hat in his hand, looked from Rina to Will. He was unable to hide the hurt in his face, although he shifted his jaw as if he was trying hard to cover it. "I'm interrupting," he said.

Neither Will nor Rina said otherwise.

"Of course, we were contacted at the office yesterday,"

Anshel continued. "Because of the listeria. They thought the soup kitchen might be the source. I guessed that's what happened to you; word is out in the community that you're in the hospital."

"You must be Anshel." Will stood up, introduced himself, and shook Anshel's hand. Anshel, confused, offered a strong and long shake, not at all like his usual soft, two-handed gesture.

"I've come to bring you an early Purim gift," Anshel said. He used the word *gift* instead of *mishloach manot* so Will would understand, Rina thought. How strange it sounded.

"A gift?" she said, then thought of something and asked Will, "How did *you* know I was here?"

"You know my name," Anshel said to Will, before Will could answer Rina. "I know only her husband's name."

Rina closed her eyes. If she had never given him a taste of herself—never leaned in to clean his cock with her mouth after sex—he'd have gone on living his good life with Nechama forever. He wouldn't be standing in the doorway of her hospital room thinking he loved a woman because she let him come on her tits. She'd ruined his ability to be as he was. Honesty would be cruel, but also it would be the most effective.

"Will and I have been seeing each other since the chagim. I love him. I'm going to marry him. I've been living at my parents', David knows we are separating. But he doesn't know about Will. Not that you'd speak with him, but . . . I just have to find the right way to tell David," Rina added, in a louder voice, to stop the protest Anshel began: "When we were involved, you knew I was miserable, you loved me then, and . . ."

"I love you still," Anshel said.

Rina could feel Will tense up.

"Well, now I'm happy."

The men said nothing. Rina didn't dare look for the reaction in Will's face.

"You may think I'm selfish . . ." Rina began.

"Not primarily," Anshel said.

". . . but only Will and I have to live with the choices we make."

"And the children," Anshel said.

"We are very much aware of our children," Will said, his voice cracking on *children*.

"Will," Anshel said, turning the name over in his mouth. Rina knew what he was thinking and wanted so much to tell him that Will would be a Jew. But that, too, would be cruel. How could Anshel understand how a woman who scorned god could help create a new Jew?

"You're being kind," Will said. "I'm sure we haven't repaid your kindness. I hope the next time we meet there won't be so much—"

"Exposition?" Anshel interrupted.

"Thank you," Rina said.

Anshel pulled a small book out of his jacket pocket.

"I got it for you," he said to Rina as he shoved the object toward Will. Rina was struck by this, as if she and all her possessions now belonged to Will in the ceaseless paternal march of her people. "For Purim. I wasn't sure if you could eat yet. I wanted to bring you a shalach manos that would matter."

Will passed it to Rina and she saw that it was a book of poetry, Wallace Stevens.

"It is not Torah," Anshel said. "It was sacrilegious of me, possibly. But it does contain a sort of Torah. Anyway, I was reading it at a bookstore and I thought of you."

He left, placing his hat back on his head as he exited the room, leaving the door open. Will closed it. Rina thumbed through the book and saw that a poem called "The Man with the Blue Guitar" was dog-eared.

"I love that poem," Will said, looking over her shoulder.

"I don't know it," Rina said.

"I'll read it to you, but then I have to go. We're pushing our luck."

He didn't read it, he recited it, pausing between cantos and taking care not to overemphasize the rhymes. Rina closed her eyes and let herself be surrounded by his voice, the constant, rolling flux of the sea spray in Big Sur, immersive, thrilling, full of succor.

Will came to the hospital again the following morning, full of anxiety.

He pulled up a chair to her bedside and sat hunched over. Her hospital room faced east, and the light pushed through, revealing the large shallow pores on his cheeks, the greasy fingerprints and charcoal dust on his glasses. He hadn't shaved, maybe hadn't washed; a torn and faded Dodgers cap cast a shadow over his eyes. The light and the circumstance brought to the surface the man he would become. The everyman. Exhausted and defeated, waning ambitions and growing hunger, flaking skin, a shirt half untucked, yard work on the to-do list, a sublime Sunday spaghetti sauce recipe. It was the first time he'd ever fully looked his age.

He was picking flecks of brown from his nails, she saw.

"You're painting? At the hotel?"

"At work," he said. "A little bit. It feels like a curse."

"Painting?"

"All this bad shit. My mom, my dad, Dylan, you. This isn't normal. Living our lives in hospitals. And all the barf. Remember when Yoni had the stomach flu? Before we'd ever . . . before we took the drive to my old house?"

"You puked on your bed with Holly," she said.

Will narrowed his eyes. "And that," he said.

"It is normal."

"I keep thinking that thing everyone says: why do bad things happen to good people? But maybe we're not good people. I keep waiting for sin to come up in my conversion classes. We didn't go to church a bunch growing up, but the threat of sin was around our necks like a chain. Dress this way, don't dress that way, don't talk to her, don't eat that, don't say that word. It appeals to me so much about Judaism that you don't really have that. But we fucked up. You don't have to believe in god to be haunted by karma. And you don't even seem to feel guilty."

"I don't feel guilty?"

"Do you? Two affairs like that? One after the other?"

"So this *is* about Anshel." She wanted to show that now she was angry, but the hospital bed made hostile gestures artless. She tried to shift her body away from him but settled for crossing her arms across her chest, tugging taut the IV line in her hand.

"I'm sorry. I'm sorry, mi corazón. It's just. Our life together hasn't even started yet, and already it's mired in barf."

"Our life together has started," she said. "You're in my hospital room at a quarter to six in the morning. And this is nothing compared to the shitstorm to come. And then it will be over. And there will still be sickness and hospitals and there will be death. It's literally written into goyishe wedding vows."

"More death," he said.

"Some people live their whole lives, their kid never breaks a bone, their parents never have malignant moles, they never get . . . what do I have?"

"Listeriosis," he said, and he picked up her left hand, stroked it with his thumb.

"And their parents die one of old age, the other of heartbreak, and they never lose all their hair to radiation in their thirties, never have a double mastectomy in their forties, never have a baby with violent asthma or a toddler get run over by a car or a kid who steps on a rusty nail or a teenager who takes pills one night at a party and then wastes away because he can't stop. And some people have all those things, and they didn't bring it on themselves."

Will was quiet, in his Will way, and then he smiled. She uncrossed her arms, massaged the top of her right hand. They hadn't changed the IV, and the yellow bruising spread up into her knuckles, the color of a citron left rotting on a windowsill after Sukkot.

"I feel a little better," he said. "But you might have to give your speech again tomorrow."

"I understand you, though. I thought god was striking me down for eating SpaghettiOs," she said, and he laughed a little.

"I have to go," he said. "They're going to release you, I think. Be in touch. If you go to your house, I will come to you."

"You never said how you found out I was here."

"I worked up my courage and called your home. I spoke to your father. Told him I was your professor and you missed class," he said. Rina still used art class as an excuse to get out of the house even though she no longer attended. "He knew who I was. He thanked me for my kindness and told me you'd be missing more class. I got the hospital out of him, no problem."

A couple hours after Will left, a nurse brought her discharge paperwork and street clothes. Her father arrived not long after to gather her while her mother waited in the car.

Her father helped her pack up her belongings, as well as plastic puke buckets, sponge toothbrushes, tissue boxes. "I'm not sick to my stomach, Daddy," she said, "what do I want with this?" But her father insisted Rina would pay for it anyway, and he stuffed a flimsy pink pitcher into her duffel. David called while they were waiting for an escort to take them downstairs.

"Your parents told me not to come back, too scary for the kids," he said. "We are coming home a day early, though. The children are worried. We'll go to a Purim carnival with my parents Sunday morning and then drive back to L.A."

"Can I go home while you're gone?" she said.

It was a long pause; David took quick, dry breaths, a thing he did when he was trying to make known his discontent. She picked up the book of poetry from a small side table her father had not cleared and shoved it into the large kangaroo pocket on her hoodie.

"Yes," he said at last, then hung up.

Her mother pulled the car to the front of the hospital, and her parents made small talk during the short drive. Rina said nothing but was grateful when her father told her mother, "Rina's going to recuperate in her own home," and then answered her mother's many protestations.

At the townhouse, her father brought her bags up while her mother made sure she was steady as she got out of the car. They walked her in; her mother went up and fluffed the bed, set out a glass of water.

"Don't worry about the community," her mother said, her own taut face full of worry. "They'll forget, all of them. And even if they don't, they'll never speak of it now that you're home. Don't worry about anything."

And then they left.

She locked up. Gratitude and loneliness came in waves, one after the other.

Her home was clean but not tidy. The air smelled vaguely of citrus, but the general order was missing. Many things were put away where they didn't belong and many more weren't put away at all. The coatrack was lopsided, weighed down on one side with Yoni's peewee soccer bag, Shosh's karate uniform, three dirty sweatshirts. She dragged her duffel into the bedroom, texted Will, and then, overwhelmed, sat in the rocking chair in the corner of her room and waited for him to arrive.

He did not have Dylan with him, and by late afternoon the house was put back to rights. Will did most of the work, taking direction from her, but Rina felt good working side by side with him and appreciated that he didn't order her to bed as she gathered and reshelved children's books, arranging them in sections (Jewish, seasonal, picture books, the whole Judy Blume shelf they were too young to read, but pulled down just the same . . .). He told her that he'd hired an attorney and made progress in the divorce proceedings. His attorney advised that Rina use a different lawyer, and he had a list of names for her. They discussed what to do about dinner but came to no conclusions and Rina was sitting on a beanbag chair sorting Legos into drawers, weighing kosher Chinese delivery against a supermarket run, when Will came in holding the Wallace Stevens book.

"Want some more?" he asked. He stretched out his hands and she pulled herself from the floor. "We'll need fruit. Pears and pineapples and watermelon. Stevens adores fruit. Fruit and Florida are his muses. I can go to the store."

"Everything packaged has to have a kosher marking," she said.

"I know. I also know it's called a hechsher. What do you want, mi corazón? Other than fruit?"

"Something garlicky," she said. "Are we cooking?"

"Of course."

"May I take a shower while you're gone?"

"Are you lightheaded?" She shook her head. "Then I think you get to decide for yourself."

Later—after Rina was clean and full of sopa de ajo, home-griddled flour tortillas, and pineapple—she climbed into her marital bed and Will climbed in beside her, with the book of poetry. It was the first time he'd been under the covers of her bed, the bed in which she'd slept for almost ten years, with its mattress corners marked A, B, C, D, its plain particleboard frame, its pillowtop mattress pad, the bamboo sheets that were supposed to absorb David's nighttime sweats and were scratchy on her feet. The mattress with milk stains from nursing and a scarlet dribble from the time Shosh came running in, panicked, after cracking her chin on the bunk bed. The bed that received clean linens each Friday before Shabbos, rinsed in vinegar, sprayed with lavender water, made up with military precision, as fresh and white as the Sabbath bride herself. Rina expected it to feel foreign when Will climbed into it. But as he set a small plate on the nightstand with the green crown of the eaten pineapple, her body let go of tension in a luxurious flood of serotonin.

"Do 'The Man With the Blue Guitar' again," she said, settling into the crease where his arm met his torso. He was naked and had not showered; he smelled of himself, linseed oil, sandalwood soap, and sweat, plus lemon and vinegar from cleaning the kitchen after supper.

He kissed the top of her head. "And again, and again," he said.

Sometime around the eighth stanza she adjusted her position and her arm brushed over him. He was hard. She climbed on top of him. He kept reciting, although he held the book in his hand. She knew she shouldn't, knew he would think it was too soon and she was too weak. He tried to put the book down, but she raised it in front of his eyes. She took off her T-shirt and underwear and slid up and down over him, but didn't let him in. Her body was weak and sore, her arms mottled with anemia, and her skin sagging. He breathed between the lyrics, moved his hips, tried to be in her. Finally, he could speak no more.

She pulled the book out of his hand, pushed down on his chest, and kissed his mouth.

"Like a guitar," she said, moving her hips over him. His stomach was dewy with her.

He made a thick noise that reverberated through her weary nerves, rolled her over, and held her wrists lightly above the bed. They kissed and kissed and now she wanted him inside badly.

His phone rang, the stark, blaring triple beep of a digital alarm clock. It startled them and he slipped inside her and she cried out. The phone blared.

"Ignore it," he said. "Ignore it."

"And if it's about Dylan?" Rina said. "So answer." He reached toward the phone and she pushed down on his back. "Stay in me," she said.

Will stayed and she made slow circles with her hips while he asked if everything was alright. She could hear Holly's voice coming through, loud but calm. She could hear her say, "Dylan's fine." She kissed the dip in the center of Will's chest. She could hear Holly say, "I need to tell you something." She clenched inadvertently all around him when, at the same time, Will and Rina both found out Holly was pregnant.

This is all a dream, Rina thought.

But she knew. Even as she held on to Will's tremulous body, pushed him out of her, she knew.

It was the end of a dream.

16.

FEBRUARY 2013

Rina was a cypress when they got the news. Tenacious. Yielding. During the phone call with Holly, she managed to stay close to Will and he'd held the phone a little away from his ear so that they could both hear everything. She sat next to him with her hand held over her mouth as Holly asked him to come to a doctor's appointment the day after next. As Holly said, in a steady voice, "Whatever happens, we're facing quite an adventure."

Will was silent for a moment. "*We* are not having anything."

He laid the groundwork for how it would be with Holly, Rina thought. He didn't understand that it wouldn't matter.

"*We* are having a baby," Holly said.

"It's decided?"

"Well, no . . ."

After he hung up, he couldn't sit still.

He paced. He squatted on the floor and held his head low between his knees. He punched a hole through the drywall connecting Rina's bedroom and bathroom. He rummaged through his bag, found cigarettes, opened the bedroom window, and sat on the sill smoking. Between drags he bit the cuticles on his right hand. Two fingers bled. He put the cigarette out and paced again. Rina sat naked and cross-legged on the bed. She followed Will with her eyes. She did not cry. She did not shake. Will shook. He cried. Eventually she brought him a glass of water, set it next to him on the sill. He took a sip, reached his hand around her waist, and then slid to the floor. She slid down behind him, wrapped her bruised arms around his chest, and laid her head on his shoulder. She made soothing sounds. Told herself the hospital narcotics' slinky trail was clouding her mind, that Will was still Will.

"Is it crazy to ask you to come to the house with me?" he said to Rina the next day, after two of the Ativan she kept in the back of the medicine cabinet and nine hours of blackout sleep. He'd already apprised his divorce attorney, gotten her advice, done some reading on custody law. After lunch, he and Rina were going through potential scenarios of how the pregnancy might play out. He refused outright Holly's request for him to go to the next morning's doctor appointment. Whatever happened, he told Rina, he would not be dragged back into a semblance of couplehood. He agreed to meet Holly at the house in Topanga after the appointment. Dylan would be at day care.

Rina looked at him for a moment, head tilted.

"It would send a clear message to Holly about what can and cannot happen, if you come with me," he said.

"It would be an act of war," Rina said.

"At least come to Topanga? To be in the car with me? I'll drop you somewhere to wait."

Rina sunk her teeth into her lips and nodded. Just like in the lobby of the Children's Hospital, just like at the base of the hill under the cypress tree, she would wait for him. Will set Rina up in bed, tucked her in, left her with water and Tylenol, and let her sleep.

The drive to Topanga the following morning was a non-stop conversation. Rina rested her hand on top of his as he shifted. Yet nothing changed, she said to herself, over and over. A mantra, pushing against what she knew. But maybe it was true. Maybe nothing had changed. Maybe they'd been doomed from the first moment at the easel. Will hoped that Holly would end the pregnancy, he said, it was extremely early. Rina wasn't opposed to this. They agreed it would be the best possible outcome for Dylan. But Rina kept steering Will back to other what ifs.

⚘

There was an outdoor theater built into the shady slopes of Topanga's mountains, where the tree line met the creek. Rina knew she would be agitated while Will met with Holly; she told him she would be miserable sitting in a coffee shop. Will had volunteered to paint sets for the theater in the past. He didn't think it would be an imposition to drop Rina there while he met with Holly. The grounds were always open, anyway. It was the offseason and Rina was unlikely to run into anyone, maybe just the groundskeeper who lived in the adjacent cabin. She'd have space. The sound of cold creek water finding its way downhill. She could sit under a small bank of cypress trees.

By the time they arrived in the dirt parking lot at the theater grounds, Rina was frustrated.

"You don't get to decide," she said. "You have no idea what she wants."

He helped her out of the car and gave her his windbreaker and tissues. He leaned down to kiss her head.

"From the verb *lenashek*," he said. "'To kiss.'"

"A game," she said, and gave a smile full of effort.

"It won't last long," he said. "I've only learned the words that suit me. One verb per night. *Feel* and *touch* and *help* and *paint*, so far. And, of course, *know.*"

Would it be enough, to be known? To have been?

"I wish I could skip what's about to happen and just have the conclusion to report to you," Will said.

Rina waved him away.

She sat in the front row, watching the empty stage, knees clutched to her chest, her skirt gathered mid-calf. She ran through scenarios like plays, like all her future possibilities blocking on the boards. It didn't matter whether it started with a wedding at the Madonna Inn or a fight on the drive down the canyon, she could see only one last act, one way it ended. She and Will, Shosh and Yoni and Dylan, they were all already soiled by enmity and acrimony, love and strife. But a tiny new life, an unintended life, a life born into the ugliness of her sin. The weight of her community, her peoplehood, of the commandments themselves, of the seventh as heavy as the stone the stories had it carved on: *lo teenaf. Lo ne'aft, lo ne'afa, lo ana'ef, lo tena'afi, lo tena-ef, lo ne'afti*: from the verb *lena'ef,* "to commit adultery."

He was gone an hour.

"She'd planted silk flowers along the walk outside," he told Rina when he picked her up. "It was terrifying."

"Were you kind?" Rina said.

"I tried," he said. "Even when she threw things at me. I told the truth, but I tried to be kind. I told her it's not a good way to bring a child into the world."

"What else did you tell her?"

"I asked how she even knew so soon, if she had been planning it, if she had a stack of pregnancy tests hidden somewhere."

"Kind of mean. And?"

"She didn't answer. I told her she's unlikely to qualify for alimony from me. I will decline to accept alimony or child support from her. I'm going to have fifty-percent custody of both children and pay for fifty percent of the new baby's costs and fifty percent of her pregnancy-related medical bills. We will put the house up for sale. She'll have plenty of time to find a new place. That's what killed her."

"The house?" Rina said.

"The custody. She doesn't want to share the baby. So I told her she could terminate the pregnancy," he said.

"And so?" Rina said, disgusted by the still, small hope this brought her, even though it wouldn't come to pass, even though she didn't want it to, not really.

"She won't."

Rina thought and Will drove. He parked at a meter in front of a small café in Santa Monica, at the base of the hill.

"Yes?" he asked, and Rina nodded.

Their patio table had a view of the pier where they'd walked so many times. The Ferris wheel moved sluggishly, and they could feel the ocean. Rina cupped her hand over his, and they ordered a plate of vegetarian mezze. Rina moved tzatziki around a bowl with a spear of cucumber.

"I was going to tell you this when you first got out of the hospital, but . . ." he trailed off.

She didn't look up when he spoke.

"I don't think I'm going to eat meat anymore," Rina said.

"I wouldn't either, if I were you," he said.

"But you're not me."

"It will be easier to cook," he said.

"No cholent," Rina said.

"Vegetarian cholent," Will said.

"You already know cholent." If not for the pregnancy, it would be every condition she required.

"I got you a job. At least, I think I did."

"A job." She said the word *job* slowly. Her eyes were fixed.

Will took twenty dollars from his wallet and put it on the table.

"It's too soon for you to be out like this," he said. "You're too weak. It was selfish for me to bring you here, to leave you outside in the wind, to expect you to sit at a restaurant and have a conversation. I'm sorry."

She didn't ask any questions but let him help her up. The mezze uneaten, they walked, elbows linked, to the car. He helped her buckle in.

"Did you learn a verb last night? After . . . ?"

He got in the car from his side.

"'To laugh' was the last one I learned," he said. "The night before you got out of the hospital."

"I don't think I even know that one," she said. "Maybe I did once."

"*Litzhok.*"

"Was something funny?"

"Nothing. But we have to get back to laughing. We have to laugh today. And then we have to plan."

She was quiet again. In two days, David and the children would return home; she couldn't draw this out.

"What job did you get me?" she asked.

"At the college. In the art department. For the degree students, not the extension program. Teaching, even. It's part-time, but it's something. You'd be TA-ing for the Intro to Drawing teacher. It's usually a student job, but I've arranged it. We're just waiting for written departmental approval, a formality. I didn't want to do that until I talked to you."

"Why would they hire me?"

"I could tell you all the stuff about how talented and organized and intellectual you are," Will said. "But it's because I told them so. I had some latitude with my department chair and I used it."

"A favor."

"Are you mad?"

"No," she said and tried to make her face blank.

"It's nothing," he said, and she heard the note of panic in his voice.

"I can't take that job," Rina said, and he convulsed a little. So okay, he understood.

"I shouldn't have done it without talking to you. I was just getting so much done, with the attorney and custody schedules. And I was making so many lists. And you said you wanted to work, so I thought . . ."

"I said I would *have* to work."

"It can be any job. It doesn't have to be this job."

"Nobody would ever make me a professor. I only have my sad little BA."

"That's all I have," Will said. "I worked my way into being a professor."

"Two Professor Ochoas in the art department, that's your vision?" she said, then smiled at him, let a little bit of light back in.

Back at home, Rina slept; she was tired, yes, but also to delay.

When Rina woke it wasn't long until Shabbos came in and Will was sanding her wall.

"I was trying to be quiet," he said. "Only not that quiet, because I don't know how to make Shabbos without you, and I don't want to screw it up. It's our first Shabbos, not counting Big Sur."

"What are you doing?" Rina said. She was groggy.

"I'm sorry about the wall," he said. "I patched it. All I have to do is paint. Do you have this color stored somewhere?"

She was awake now, propped up on one arm.

"Please, don't paint it," she said.

"What are you going to tell David?"

"I don't know. That I punched it, I guess."

"And that you patched it?"

"I want it to stay like that. I want to be reminded."

Even before she started crying, he was already saying "No, no, no, no," and shaking his head, shaking everywhere.

"You're wrong, mi corazón," he said, and her tears turned to sobs. "You're wrong. Don't."

"I know I can't do it," she said. "I'm sorry, I'm so sorry."

"I will fight this. I will fight for myself," he said.

"Don't make it worse."

"We don't have to suffer," he said.

"You don't," she said. "You don't have to suffer."

"I'm suffering now!" the words exploded out of Will. He'd never spoken like this to her. She'd heard it only on the drive back from Big Sur when he accosted that motorist. "I will always suffer. I will always suffer."

"The neighbors will hear you," Rina said.

"They are nothing to us. They are your past. Rina, I will never not love you."

"I will never not love you," she said, shaking her head. "But you'll have the baby, you'll have . . ."

"I'm never going back to her."

"That won't be on account of me," Rina said.

"It's already on account of you."

"No." Now her voice was loud, too.

"This is not real," Will repeated, over and over again. Rina

shook with tears. "This is not real. Our life is together. We exist for each other. I changed my will. You inherit everything."
He sputtered. "I made Shabbos ready while you slept. Rina,
I made vegetarian cholent, I bought challah and ingredients
for a salad and a frittata, I turned lights on and off around the
house. I looked up the candle lighting time and found your
kiddush cup. Rina."

"You have to go. Don't do this Shabbos. It won't be real,"
she said.

"You can't take Yoni and Shosh away from me," he said.

"They're not yours."

"You said they were. You said they were ours. You can't do
this to Dylan. He loves you."

"I can't stand this," she said and covered her ears.

"You owe me an explanation."

"We'll talk. We'll talk tomorrow . . ."

"We'll talk tonight," Will said.

"Tomorrow," Rina said. Her words were low and studied,
as if she was talking to herself. "If I can't get through these
next nine hours without you, I can't get through anything."

"Tonight."

"You're the one that fucked her," Rina shouted. "You
promised me you wouldn't."

She got up and gathered a few of his things in a pile on the
bed, then slumped on the floor and buried her head under her
hands.

"I will fight this," he said, his voice rising again. "This is
all wrong."

But he left.

Dusk advanced on Pico-Robertson. Dozens of cars were
parking up and down the street, their drivers and passengers
hurrying inside for Shabbos, arms loaded with flowers and

shopping bags. The streetlights came on. Chanting started to drift from second- and third-story windows. Different households were singing the same song. She didn't even light the candles, didn't get up at all.

There was noise at the front door.

"Hello?" Rina called when he opened the door.

"I let myself back in," Will said. "With the spare key in the tzedakah box."

Rina came into the foyer. Her hair was pulled in every direction, as if a bird had picked at it for nesting. She was wearing an old kimono, holes on the sleeves and at the hem. She saw the candles on the table, almost burned to the nubs, smelled the wax in the air.

"You lit candles before?" she said.

"Is that okay?" Will said. Rina shrugged. "Is it okay that I came back? Do you want me here?"

Will closed the door and locked it, as if to settle the matter.

"Of course I want you here," Rina said. "Don't you understand anything?"

"No," Will said in a flat voice.

"You'll have to just believe me."

"You love me," Will said.

"That's what I keep saying. I love you. I love you, I love you, I love you."

"That's what matters."

"Not anymore," she said.

Will made a case for them. He talked and talked, and she said nothing but wept. For several minutes they stood in the hallway, then he led her to the dining room. She let him lead her. They sat at the table, he at the end, she on a corner, the candles between them; he never stopped talking. The candle-light flooded their faces.

"Your eyes," he said. "Your eyes like in the painting. The golden fleck near your iris is glowing hazel. It's the inverse of how the sun lit you from behind the first day we spent time alone together, the day I kissed you. Don't you see the significance? Of the light on that day? The light on this one?" He didn't stop talking, talking nothingness.

She took his left hand between both of hers and clasped it. He wove his fingers through hers and she squeezed a little.

"We are known," Will said, and then he was quiet.

Rina was also quiet. It could have been moments they sat like that, or an hour. They watched each other through the candlelight, with the sound of the prayer after meals echoing from neighboring townhomes. The floor vibrated with the force of other families pounding the table in the delight of Shabbos.

Rina got up and said a long, quiet blessing over the wine. She went to the kitchen to wash her hands and put away the groceries he'd left out for dinner hours ago. It was a tradition not to speak between the handwashing prayer and the prayer over bread, she knew he knew this. She found small tasks to give herself more time to think. Water bubbled and spit in the percolator; he'd turned on the percolator for Shabbos tea, and here she was torturing him, she knew she was torturing him, he would go mad if she didn't speak soon. She tried not to blink, tried not to breathe.

At length she returned to the table with a saltshaker, uncovered the bread, and said the blessing. He tried along with her; he'd been learning blessings from a CD. Rina handed him a small piece of salted challah before she ate one herself.

"I guess you'll never be Jewish," Rina said, her voice rounded with pain.

He opened and closed his mouth several times. "I've almost finished conversion classes, Rina. You don't need to be cruel. With or without you, it's too late. It's too beautiful."

"I meant, will you still be Jewish?" she said, more gently.

"In the ways that matter, I already am," he said, and then added, "Isaiah." Her face knitted inward. Whatever she was expecting him to say, it was not that. "I've been reading some of the prophets and at the core of their message is something I didn't get in church but is like what my brother, Frank, preached with his politics: 'Learn to do good.' 'Devote your-selves to justice.' 'Aid the wronged.' That's a higher power. And I need one. I cannot believe in god, but I can believe that the world has a higher power and that power is justice. And I can choose to be part of a people who have kept that idea alive for five thousand years. And I can choose to believe my soul stood at Sinai next to yours. None of it is in conflict with my birth culture. I finally understand what Frank was talking about."

She closed her eyes for a moment, but then straightened up. She couldn't let this change her resolve.

"The prophets are zealots," Rina said. "You're cherry-picking."

"I don't have to cherry-pick. The rabbis have done all that. The culture was sustained on justice. Not magic tricks and sacrifice."

"It also says, 'Your hands are stained with crime—wash yourselves clean, put your evil doings away from my sight.'"

"You truly believe we've done evil?" he said.

"You should go now," Rina said. "We have to try being apart."

"I don't want to drive," he said. "It's supposed to be Shabbos. I called in sick to my class tomorrow. It's only my first time keeping Shabbos; don't make me break it."

Rina nodded. She wrapped the challah in foil. She stirred the cholent he'd put up in the slow cooker and replaced the lid. The home filled with a rich smell, but they weren't hungry.

"Should we move the candles to the sink?" he said.

She shook her head. "You can't move Shabbos candles." How long would it take him to know all the things? Would he really? Would he ever?

She climbed the stairs and he followed. They prepared for bed side by side, not talking. They took turns using the water and spitting as they brushed their teeth. She peed with the door open for the first time, an intimacy she'd been excited to achieve, and now here it was, a defeat. They climbed into the bed on opposite sides; he didn't try to hold her.

"I love you," she said.

"My real name's Guillermo," he said. "You can't leave me without knowing that. They never called me that. Memo sometimes, when I was little. Mostly Will. But it's not my real name. I never think about it, but now it feels like I'll die if you don't know."

She didn't say anything, but made the name Guillermo with her mouth—soundlessly, over and over again, tears flowing—to see how it felt. She also thought she'd die.

"I love you, too," he said.

For hours she lay awake, craving to roll over and be close to him. Heat came off his body and she wanted to move into it, to bathe in his exhales. Twice she reached out and held a hand above the slope of him, no sense of whether he was sleeping. The sky grew light again, and she got up quietly, dressed, left him there.

17.

She decided to spend Shabbos morning at a Haredi shul within walking distance, Anshel's shul. No one at this shul was likely to know she hadn't been living at home. Not many people there knew her at all, and Anshel's wife, Nechama, was blessedly not in the women's section. She sat close to the mechitzah that divided the men from the women and peered through the wood lattice. Anshel was standing there, near the front, davening and rocking his body forward and back. His eyes were closed. She smiled an apology at a couple men who caught her gaze through the mechitzah, so they would think she was humble. She picked up a prayer book and opened it, instinctively finding the place in the text.

At her shul there was no English in the books, but this place did outreach work. What sounded moving in ancient Aramaic and Hebrew was absurd in English. God speaks, does, decrees, and fulfills; god is eternal; god rescues and redeems. How long had she pretended she did not know what it meant? How many others in her community were certain there was no god—whether merciful or vengeful—but didn't wish to unshackle themselves from the order of Shabbos and kashrut and the Torah cycle? Her mouth was moving with rote knowledge and she made an effort to stop. David chose all this, back when he started becoming more religious. It had been slightly baffling to her, but it fit within the world she knew. She'd wanted Will to choose it, just a few months ago; she wanted it so much that her wanting was almost like prayer. Now she couldn't fathom it, this choosing.

She tested Will's idea, transposing his words over the text on the page. Justice spoke and the world came to be. Justice speaks, does, decrees, and fulfills. Justice is merciful. Justice rescues and redeems. Blessed is justice. *Baruch she-amar.*

There was no justice in her labor, no authority other than the entrenched patriarchy in the way the lunar calendar bent her body into servitude of the never-ending holidays, crippled the inertia of her selfhood in the cycle of baking, cooking, cleaning, making, burying errant forks in soil. There was no redemption in the gray and stale meticulousness of keeping a kosher home, a kosher marriage, a string of kosher children, the frantic weekly rush of preparing Shabbos just so she could have a few hours to recover from the madness that was preparing for Shabbos. Women were for ushering in the joy of others and were judged harshly if they didn't experience the proper amounts of joy themselves, humming along with the men singing at the table, their hands immersed in the jaundiced sink water where they stood washing cholent out of china dishes week after week after week. There was a certain irony in the ache of her fingers as she struck matches to bring in Shabbos, invite the queen of peace into her immaculate home.

She still lit candles after she stopped believing because there was nothing else to do; it was comforting and beautiful; she liked the way it felt, liked the way her daughter's small hands covered her eyes for the prayer. Rina held the memory of her own mother lighting candles each week, and her grandmother, and back through the generations, the rings of a tree with the nexus—the woody pulp—in some village in the eastern Pale, beyond that, even, thousands of years, the flicker of lit tallow in the unswept, mythical homeland. Even David's mother lit candles sometimes and waved in the light of Shabbos. Will had no memories of Friday-night candles, no memory and no god, no Semitic tallow in his bones—and still he lit. But lighting candles did not serve justice, did it?

She wanted to serve Will; their love was the higher power that bent her, bowed her knees. The idea of him going back to Holly pulsed at her temple and twitched in her eye. But she made herself think on it. Into this world a new baby would come—that was almost certain—and it would not be on account of Rina that its father wasn't home at night. Leaving Will was an act of penance, perhaps, a worthless act of penance for every mistake she'd ever made as a mother, for the mistake of marrying an embittered man and having one child with him and then—worse—having another, even after she no longer loved her husband or his god. This new baby would come, and it would look like Will but also like Holly, and she would not be the foreign mother giving the baby foreign bottles and teaching the baby foreign words. Her reasons were irrational, but so was Isaiah chapter one, so was Will's higher power.

She felt a stare and looked through the lattice at Anshel, but his face was prayerful. She felt the warmth of someone on the pew next to her.

Aliza.

"Good Shabbos," Rina whispered. She couldn't keep the surprise from her voice.

"You daven here?" Aliza asked.

"You do?" Rina replied sourly.

"I heard you went back home," she said. "How is David?"

"I went home, but he's away. You would know better."

Aliza nodded and puckered her face. "He hasn't spoken to me in over a month."

Rina considered this while Aliza kept whispering. "That's why I've been coming here, different crowd."

If David hadn't spoken to her since he confronted Rina, was that an admission of some sort? Was it a peace offering?

"I was set up with someone in the Valley," Aliza continued. "And I think it might be a match. It is a match. So I'm moving. Not far, but I'm moving. And I wanted to tell him myself. I guess now you'll tell him."

"I'm so sorry," Rina said.

"I'm happy," Aliza said. "Don't be sorry for me."

"No. For being rude. I'm sorry. It's not about you."

Aliza nodded. "Even so, I'm leaving," she said. "But you should know something. He was so afraid you'd ask for a divorce. He would have given you a *get*, of course, but it would have ruined him."

For a moment it looked like Aliza was going to lean in for an air kiss, but then she slid down the bench and was gone.

After services Rina stayed for kiddush, for challah, sweet wine, pickled herring, and hard-boiled eggs. She greeted people, said "Gut Shabbos" to the old rabbi. Anshel didn't come to her immediately; he circled the room with a cookie in his hand, talking with people and drawing ever nearer to where she stood, partially hidden behind a plastic ficus tree.

"Shabbos," he said when he finally approached her. She nodded toward him but didn't speak. "I'm glad to see you out of the hospital. I was saying a refua shlema."

She nodded again, smiled weakly. He tried to hold a poker face, but she could see that he was worried and also relieved.

So this would be easier than she imagined, they all expected her to come back; they would be appeased.

"I can't go home right now," she said.

"So you'll come for lunch."

"Thank you."

"Nechama is at her cousin's in Long Beach for Shabbos with the children. I couldn't go because I teach Fridays. You remember."

Rina nodded.

"If you are uncomfortable coming to my house for Shabbos, you can go to my parents' house," he said.

"I'm fine," Rina said. "If you're fine."

"I understand," Anshel said, and he lowered his voice, "that you need pastoral care. You should understand that I am not the best person to care for you."

"Can we go?" Rina asked.

"Of course."

It was a long way. Even though she believed no one other than David knew about their affair, they walked as if they were not going to the same place, Anshel ahead of her. They both nodded to others as they passed, and Anshel made small talk. Once he came within three feet of her and made a joke. Rina laughed out of pity and guilt.

The jacarandas were in bloom. It seemed early to Rina, but then it always seemed early. Each year she expected them to bloom in June—as they had when she was a child—and each year they started flowering in March or April. In a month they would be crowned with tufts of violet blooms and greenery, but now the purple was intermittent, as if placed with care. She thought of how she used to envision god's eyelashes in a sun-striped sky, imagined Justice, a benevolent being, shaking blossoms onto the jacarandas like her grandmother had done paprika over a pot of bean soup. The trunks of the trees were gnarled and slate gray. Most of the year Angelenos took no notice of them, and then for three months no one could escape them. The blossoms weren't falling yet, but within weeks they would blanket the sidewalks with their paper-thin petals.

Anshel's home—the bottom floor of an old Spanish-style duplex—was heavy with the smell of cholent and spilled wine. She never would have guessed that Anshel was the type to put up cholent even when his family was away.

"I'm not hungry," Rina said, before he even offered lunch.

Anshel made up a murphy bed that pulled down from the wall of an alcove in the living room. Rina took off her shoes and slid under the blanket.

"Thank you," she said.

"Do you know what you're doing?" he said.

"Now I do."

"When you're ready, maybe we'll talk about it," Anshel said.

Anshel woke her after dark, with his voice. Rina knew it was a conscious choice not to touch her, not even on the shoulder. He was treating her as he'd treat any other woman; he'd even left the front door cracked all afternoon. Except, of course, he'd never be alone with any other woman. Especially on Shabbos.

"I'm driving to Long Beach," he said. "For Purim."

The fact that their affair had started on Purim hung in the air. Rina stretched awkwardly, took the scarf off her head, and pulled her hair into a ponytail using a band around her wrist.

"Make Havdalah with me, then, wherever you want, I'll drop you," he said.

She heard revelers in the street. Purim, the most joyous of all holidays.

"Is it late?" she said. She'd intended to go home before the end of Shabbos, to see if Will was still there.

"Shabbos has been out for an hour," he said. "Come."

She joined him at the kitchen table. He had a braided candle, a ceramic wine cup, a metal tray, and an enameled box that held clove and nutmeg. He lit the candle and poured vodka and a little wine into the cup. Then he began chanting the blessings that signified the end of Shabbos. He chanted quickly, in a deep voice. Rina grew up singing beautiful melodies to these prayers, haunting melodies that made it one of her favorite rituals. At sleepaway camp on Saturday nights, everyone would gather in a circle around the fire pit, arms around each other. Dozens of braided candles were handed around and lit and the stars in the sky became a reflection of the points of light gathered and cupped in the hands of her friends. In the city, light pollution caged the stars behind a scrim, but at camp Rina got lost in their perpetuity, their gasses burning cobalt and heliotrope, bittersweet and blinding.

Anshel passed her the spice box and she inhaled, even though this Shabbos held no sweetness to carry into the week ahead. A heretical thought, Shabbos not being sweet.

She held the backs of her hands toward the glow of the Havdalah candle, curving her ragged fingernails toward herself as Anshel chanted. There was a law that in order to make the blessing over the Havdalah candle it must be close enough and bright enough to distinguish different currencies by its light, so each person must therefore distinguish between nail and flesh. It was an action she'd taken without thinking nearly every week of her life, but this week it was a surrender, holding her hands up in the primal light. An old midrash said you didn't hold your hands up to distinguish currency, but because the first fire of earth emanated from Adam's fingernails. This would be the interpretation Will would find; he had a way of separating the bullion from the tarnish.

Anshel poured the vodka onto the metal tray and then touched the candle to its surface. The candle went out, but the vodka ignited, and sapphire flames rolled across the tray. Anshel prayed for Moshiach.

Will believed that a world perfected by humans was some sort of Moshiach, Messiah. If only she had as much conviction about anything as she had about Will. Her return to her old life was doubly fraudulent; it was the life of one who has seen the beauty of earth's original fire, seen it and turned away.

To be fourteen again, singing under the stars at camp, white blouse mottled with purple, mind ripening, body like new fruit. She wanted it so much she could smell the bitter, smoky scent of olive leaves on her hands, the sagebrush of the southern California foothills. She should have chosen Eli Fruchter, the boy she made out with three summers in a row. Now he had a nice, secular family in Boston; he and his wife traveled to Paris, New Zealand, India. She should have summoned him to the olive grove, let him wash the stains from her, married him, and painted in those places. She should have married him and never known the blood-deep humiliation of being swapped by her husband, tossed aside like a limp vegetable. She'd kept the olives to herself, selfishly, and now it was too late.

Oh, but then she wouldn't have known anything. She wouldn't have known the love of her children—her Shosh and her Yoni—never would have seen Shosh come out of a bathtub and run through the house doing the cancan and singing the naked dance. Never would have woken to the bliss of Yoni's thumb stroking her cheek at dawn. And she wouldn't have known all-consuming love, the kind that changes the color of an entire ocean, that holds above the muck of life, that gives a reason to wake up and think, Yes, this day. She could have married Eli Fruchter, but she would never have been known.

Anshel was done singing. The flames took a last lick at the vodka. The room was dark, and the only sounds were a grandfather clock in the living room and their slow, ruminant breathing.

"Am I taking you home?" Anshel said. Rina nodded.

The house was empty. Of course Will was gone. Why had she let herself think otherwise?

She prostrated herself on the Persian rug in the foyer and lay with her face in it, trying to imagine she could smell the leather of Will's boots on her floor. She lay there like that all night, face down on the deep pile of the rug, tracing the patterns with her index finger, listening to the drunk merry-makers outside, getting up once to go to the bathroom and get a charger for her phone so that it would be on and near if Will reached out.

On Sunday morning there was a key in the front door, and Rina, still on the floor, still not sleeping, jumped up and ran her hands over her hair and clothes. She was ready to have a conversation with Will. She owed him that and anyway, a conversation—a big one—meant several hours with him.

Her parents' cleaning lady walked through the door.

"Sorry, Rina," she said. "I thought the house was empty. David asked me to clean before they come back."

"It's okay, Gris. Thank you for coming."

Gris stood in the doorway, uncertain.

Rina spent most of the day tidying and cleaning. She tried to stay out of Gris's way but buried herself in the minutiae of the home. She reorganized each of the children's closets and dressers, bringing seasonal clothes forward and burying off-season clothes. She opened and filed all the mail that had piled up while she was at her parents' and in the hospital. She paid thirty-seven bills that David had neglected, including pink warning bills from the power and gas companies. She washed the linens on her bed, even the duvet cover and decorative pillowcases. She unpacked her suitcase and used the step stool to put it back away on the top shelf of a utility closet. All morning the doorbell rang, families delivering mishloach manot. She did not answer the door but let the baskets and boxes pile up outside. The children would like finding them all at once like that.

Gris asked what to do with the pot of food. Rina followed her to the kitchen, which now smelled like lemons and bleach, and saw the slow cooker, still on low, cholent sludgy and crusted to the edges. Rina labeled a freezer bag to store what was still good, and saw a divot in the corner of the cooker, a serving gone. She checked the dish-drying rack: one clean bowl, one clean spoon, one clean ladle. He had been here all Shabbos. How long had he stayed? By how much had she missed him?

She took the spoon from the drying rack and put it in her pocket.

"Throw it all away," she said to Gris, then went to lie down. There was a note taped to the wall, where he'd patched it, sloping letters and loops, his perfect handwriting. A line from "The Man with the Blue Guitar."

✳

David and the children were surprised and happy to see her. She sat on the floor of the family room with the children and read them story after story and let them eat cookies and candy from the mishloach manot, as many as they wanted. "I didn't know if you'd really be here," David said. She asked if he could make an omelet or something, a world apart from the Purim feasts she typically cooked for this day.

Shosh and Yoni asked if they could have a sleepover in their parents' bed and Rina looked to David, who shrugged. She saw the children notice this, her looking to David for an answer. That never happened in the past; she had been the arbiter of all things.

She got stronger. The days and nights began to pile up.

David didn't bring up the issue of where Rina would sleep, and so she slept in their bed. Only she didn't really sleep. She tried to exhaust herself during the day. As soon as the children were at school, she grabbed the ten-pound weights used as doorstops in their home and set out on a four-mile walk around the neighborhood. She took the same route every day, listened to the same songs over and over again, nodded hello to the same babies out with the same nannies; if she encountered someone she knew she waved, pointed to her headphones, and did not stop; she learned the schedule of the front yard sprinklers so she wouldn't get wet. She came home and cleaned. She scrubbed the kitchen grout with a toothbrush and baking soda. She recaulked both bathrooms. She balanced a chair on top of the dining room table and polished the tops of cabinets she couldn't reach with a step stool. She did the laundry every day, folded it—god she hated folding laundry—and put it away. A certain authority and comfort came from clothes that were clean and put away within hours of having been worn.

Sleepless nights passed and she tried melatonin, unsweetened cherry juice, Benadryl, and valerian root. One night she

tried all four at once and fell asleep quickly but woke before
1:00 a.m. and couldn't sleep again.

Shabbos came and went just as most every Shabbos of her
life had come and gone. She couldn't bring herself to make
the cholent, so David did it, something he often did anyway.
She asked him to make it vegetarian, but he did not. She cried
quietly during Havdalah, but her children could not detect
her tears in the candlelit room. Another Shabbos came and
went just the same.

She trashed the leftover goodies from Purim's mishloach
manot, filling two trash bags just with treats that had to be
gone before Pesach. What a wasteful thing, to have a holiday
where each household receives loads of snacks full of chametz
only one month before the house had to be rid of them. She
tossed homemade pastries and cakes, took the store-bought
boxes of cookies and candies to the Pico food pantry. None of
it was kosher for Pesach.

She hauled plastic storage boxes up from the garage, full
of Pesach dishes and utensils, cloth napkins, books, and toy
frogs. She bought foil, stove burner covers, liners for the
sink, dish soap, vinegar, and industrial-size boxes of baking
soda. She scrubbed the oven and the drawer underneath it
with baking soda paste, did the same for the toaster oven. She
heated them each at five hundred degrees for eight hours and
then taped them off with painter's tape. They wouldn't cook
in them again until Pesach. She took everything out of the refrigerator. Because of her absence, it was mostly condiments
and kosher takeout. How like a sitcom, she thought, how like
a story in a fucking magazine. Ketchup and Chinese food, orange juice and cold chicken. There were a few guavas that Will
must have purchased, bruised and rotting; she shoved them
to the back of the fridge. Unopened bottles were stored in a

high cabinet that sat empty most of the year. She took each
shelf and drawer out of the refrigerator, carried them down
the back stairs, unfolded a tarp, and washed them with a hose.
The tarp was communal, used by all the Jewish neighbors, and
she was pleased to be the first preparing for Pesach. It would
go a long way toward repairing her reputation. She carried
down kettle after kettle of boiling water—a special kettle used
only for Pesach and heated, today, over a foil-encased burner
on the stove she hadn't yet sanitized for the holiday—and
poured steaming water over every surface. She left it to dry
in the sun and went back upstairs, scrubbed the inside of the
refrigerator with white vinegar, rubbed it with peppermint
essential oil, ignored the putrefying guavas. She polished the
Shabbos candlesticks, kiddush cups, and handwashing basins. She wore gloves, but the metal polish seeped through
a crack and turned her finger a silky black. She sealed the
challah trays inside a vacuum-packed bag and put them in the
cabinet. She wiped the dining room table with vinegar, used
a laundry steam cleaner to sanitize the surface, then rubbed
it with wood oil. She got underneath the table and did the
same three-step process for each of the table legs, cleaning
up splatters of spaghetti sauce, grape juice, smeared snot. She
covered the whole table with a brand-new disposable plastic
tablecloth, then with a heavy oilcloth handed down from her
grandmother that she only used in the weeks leading up to
Pesach, when she needed to protect the table from the chametz her family would continue to consume until the holiday
began; they'd cook only on the stove until she kashered it the
day before Pesach began. They'd store their food on the single refrigerator shelf she hadn't lined. She tied old T-shirts
around her head to gather the sweat, an old robe tie under
her breasts to sop it up. She made shopping lists for Pesach.

Although they would have one seder at her folks' home and one at theirs, she volunteered much of the cooking for both meals. How would she prepare the twenty-four pounds of brisket she usually purchased now that she didn't eat meat? Hand-grind the whole fish for eight loaves of gefilte fish? How would she stand in line at the fish monger on Pico when Will had told her the story of how he'd stood in line there one rainy night, dreaming of their future?

She picked the children up on time each day, took them to the park, ran when they said, "Run," climbed when they said, "Climb," and slid when they said, "Slide." She made elaborate, meat-free dinners and cleaned the kitchen afterward. She mopped every night. She rode the exercise bike while David watched TV in the evenings. She climbed into bed without showering and balanced herself on the far edge of the bed, holding her body in a straight line so as not to accidentally touch her husband. She got up early so she could shower without being naked in front of him. She got the kids ready for school. She dropped them off. She walked and walked; she did not stop moving.

All day, every day, she tried to push Will from her mind and all day, every day, she did little but think of him.

Each night she slid the spoon out of her nightstand, the spoon Will had used to eat cholent, and held it near her face, sometimes sucking on it. She stared at the spot on the wall, the spot he had punched and patched (when David had asked, she said, "I was mad," and he just shrugged). Sometimes she reached out and touched the drywall patch, running her hand over it, over where Will had run his own hand to smooth it.

One morning she got up early while David was doing yoga on their bedroom floor, got the kids ready for school, then realized when she arrived that it was Sunday. She dropped them back with David, who was astonished by her mistake, and she said, standing just outside their front door, "I'm going to walk the Rose Bowl."

"The what?" David asked.

"The Rose Bowl."

"You're going to walk it?"

"There's a course around it, three miles. I need to be alone."

"I have an organizing meeting for the agunot," David said. "What am I supposed to do with the kids?"

"Shosh said they went with you many times when I stayed with my parents," she said. "She told me all about how backward our system is and how anti-woman her own mother is. She told me quite a lot, in fact. Quite a lot about your friend Aliza and how much of an example you'd like to make of Seth Hartman—"

David interrupted. "You don't think an example should be made?"

"—and how Aliza said to my daughter that I was living in the dark ages."

"This has nothing to do with her," David said with a nasty wave.

"For the record," Rina said. "I think Seth Hartman is a terrible human being and deserves everything that's coming to him. I just don't think I have a better solution than a whole convention full of rabbis."

"A woman who doesn't want to change the way things are, yet you have no problem turning upside down every life that comes in contact with yours," David said. He closed the front door with a swift clunk after she walked out. It was the most they'd spoken since she'd come home.

Rina got in her car, but she had no real intention of going to the Rose Bowl. She didn't even know what it looked like—she'd only been to the Rose Parade once as a very young child. It only came to mind because Will had spoken of it so often, but she didn't want her first visit to be without him. She considered the possibility that since it was Sunday maybe he was there walking the perimeter, talking to the mountains. As she drove east on Pico, she absently imagined running into him at the Rose Bowl.

She was nearly downtown when she made a U-turn under a freeway overpass and headed back west, hoping to find Anshel at his office. When he didn't have meetings, he often took off Fridays and worked Sundays, the way they did in Israel. As in the old days, she used the back door so that even the secular man at the building's information desk wouldn't know that Anshel was alone in a room with a woman.

"I hoped you would come sooner," he said without looking up from his desk.

"I couldn't."

Anshel nodded. His black hat, which he usually wore when he worked, sat on the credenza behind his desk; a bottle of single malt Scotch and a paper Dixie cup were on the desk.

"Drinking in the morning?" she asked.

"Not a new habit," he said. "You don't know everything."

From early in their relationship, she had thought she understood Anshel well, understood he lived a simple life. Perhaps Anshel was not as one-dimensional as it was comfortable for her to believe.

"You're back at home," Anshel said.

"Yes."

"And Will Ochoa?"

Rina jolted at hearing his name like that; she'd never heard anyone else speak his full name. How did Anshel even remember?

"It wasn't like you think. It wasn't just a joke," she said. She began pacing the far end of his office. It wasn't a natural movement for her; it was the way Will paced when he was agitated.

"So, what was it?" Anshel said, his voice measured and not quite gentle. "You didn't say anything when you stayed with me that Shabbos."

"His wife is pregnant."

"His wife," Anshel repeated. "A pattern."

"Oh Jesus," she said. But then she softened. "You don't know the half of it."

She slumped and landed cross-legged on his office floor and told him about the wife swap, about Brandon coming in her and on her, about how she didn't know or care—had never asked—who her own husband fucked that night, but she knew for sure that he harbored feelings for Aliza, the younger sister of Brandon—Brandon, whom her husband had allowed inside of Rina. Not just allowed, begged for it.

"I'm not just trying to draw some psychobabble line between it and you and Will," she said. "But nothing was the same for me after. I want to hate myself for what I've done. For sure I take responsibility for my own misery, for some of yours, some of his. But I don't hate myself. There's this part of me, one of the last sparks, and it's almost . . . it's almost proud of the things I've done."

Anshel had moved from his chair and was standing by a window, his back to Rina. He didn't immediately speak. She couldn't see his face, but his hands were gripping the sill.

"I wish there was still some piece of my faith left to surrender," he said.

"You'll never lose your faith," Rina said.

"Ah," he said, turning around. He sat on the floor, but far

enough from her that he could not touch her. "Secrets. The first day we were together, I lost my faith. I realized, alone with you, trembling, that I went my whole life thinking god had mandated that I was forbidden to be alone with you. When I kissed you, then I knew. There was no god who made such a mandate. A person decided it and I let myself believe— we all let ourselves believe—that it was god. Your husband let himself believe that above all god wants marriages that last, and so he devised complicated justifications for desire. He let it destroy your self-worth. No, I do not believe. As I comply with the laws, except my one major falter, I do it with the perfect understanding that people have mandated it and I am choosing to submit. Being at large in the world, being untethered, that is what I cannot face."

Rina tried to swallow. Her mouth had grown dry as he spoke. It was too warm in his office, with vents blowing heat from above and a small space heater in the corner. She'd read books on atheism in furtive corners of the library, even read scores of articles by Jewish atheists, written and torn up hundreds of her own thoughts on it, but she had never dared raise the subject in her own community. It was unfathomable to her that a Haredi rabbi could be a nonbeliever and continue living the life of a Haredi rabbi. In a sickening wave it came upon her how wrong she was on the issue of ritual divorces and Seth Hartman, how backward. If a rabbi could be a nonbeliever, if an authority—even one—could turn away from god, then no court of rabbis had the authority to destroy a woman's life over a technicality of obsolete law. How many agunot had her complacency helped destroy? She adjusted her sweater, wiped sweat from her hair.

"So his wife is pregnant," Anshel said, looking at her. "And he's going back to her?"

"He says he's not," Rina said. "He's converting, not an Orthodox conversion. He says he's still going to become Jewish. He'll have half custody of the baby; he'll pay his share."

This seemed to surprise Anshel. He was quiet for a moment, tapping the fingers of one hand against the fingers of the other.

"All impediments have been removed from your path," Anshel said. "When things are that easy, you're uncomfortable."

"It's wrong," Rina said. "Can't you just tell me that? Just agree that it's a sin? I can't have him with her pregnant. There's a baby."

"It's not enough to make your own choices, you are also making his?"

"Riddles," Rina said.

"You came to me for help. You, who don't believe in sin."

Rina picked at a loose fiber in the industrial carpet and began to unravel a small loop with her thumbnail.

"I know myself. I can't. I love him, but I can't," Rina said.

"And he loves you?"

"For now," she said. "He's had two wives already." She covered her own mouth after saying it. She'd never let herself think consciously of this before, but here she was saying it. She kept her hand clutched to her mouth. She had always been afraid, always suppressed her fear that if she married Will she wouldn't be the last wife.

Anshel reached out and touched her on the knee, a light touch, and left his hand there. "So, nu? Now that you've come back, what becomes of you?"

Rina felt a cry coming. She was so tired of crying. She looked away from him but didn't try to silence herself.

"What has become of you?" she said through broken breaths.

"What I'm afraid of?" he said. "That you should become like me. But for you, for a woman, it's so much worse."

Rina closed her eyes.

"Rina," he said. "You think you opened my eyes to things I can't name. But those things I always knew, those angry longings of a boy. What I never knew before is what your life is, what Nechama's life is. I assumed happiness. And maybe she is happy. Maybe, Rina, you're the only frum woman in the world who is miserable and invisible. But even for one soul, even for one . . . I can barely face the burden of what it is to be a wife, what it means to make everything just so. It's not for the affair that I can't look my wife in the eyes anymore; it's for shame over what our life requires of her while I sit here drinking Scotch and studying. To think you could become like me, resigned and hopeless, but without the option of becoming lost in a job and in study. Always with a kitchen and a baby and a patriarchal law to uphold. I don't want you to become like me."

"You're trying to reason with me," she said. "But you can't reason with a ghost."

"Don't say that," he said. "Please, you are loved, please don't say that."

"What should I say?"

"You'll need help," Anshel said. "I have needed help. Has it worked? I don't know. But here I am. My children have a father. My wife has a husband. You will need help and I will help you get it."

He reached down to pull her up. It was different, touching his hands now.

"Please," Anshel said, gripping her hands. "Don't leave me in this world alone. Don't leave your children."

She couldn't look at him.

"If that's what you're afraid of, I'm already a shadow," she said. "And a coward. I can do no further self-harm."

"I'm afraid of everything," Anshel said. She squeezed his hands back. "That's my last secret. Everything."

They stayed like that for a moment, trembling, until the bones of her hands felt like they would break, until she had stopped crying. They stood in the interminable expanse of the life still in front of them, saying nothing.

Then he put on his hat and Rina knew to leave.

18.

MARCH 2013

Rina spent the better part of an hour composing a text to Will, sitting in the swivel chair in the loft, under the judgement-free gaze of the Captain. The day had been full of making and freezing Pesach desserts and breakfast cakes, fifteen types. The children were asleep, and David was working on his laptop in bed. For weeks she'd been so consumed with mourning Will that her corporeal needs had been all but imperceptible. She was never hungry, her muscles didn't ache after her walks, showers were just another thing she had to accomplish. She and David barely spoke, let alone touched, and she was glad he hadn't tried. She would have shuddered and shrunk away, making the space between them—the space she would wrangle for the rest of her life—a war zone.

The children were the only stimuli that affected her. Their hands on her face were cotton, their lips on her cheeks were supple; when they hugged her, she grasped for more nearness. It was too much pressure for the children. It's what *she* was supposed to be for them. She let them see her cry but not much, she tried to be upbeat but was not overly cheery, she made pots of slow-cooked pudding but did not indulge their impulse desires at the grocery checkout. She wanted to buy them every candy bar and ice cream confection they reached for, wanted to buy their kisses with sugar and tears in order to feel their hands on her arms and their faces on her face.

But in the last few days her body had begun to wake. First it was hunger. One day she wanted kettle-cooked potato chips and went through two family-size bags in her car. Two days later she made a forty-minute drive to a kosher restaurant in the San Fernando Valley for their red lentil soup, then ate it—with the bread that came on the side—standing outside her car because it had already been vacuumed and scrubbed for Pesach. She was so ravaged by want for more soup that she drove back to the restaurant with the kids in the car after school pickup the very same day to get a gallon of it for family dinner—hold the bread—and they ate it out of paper bowls.

Despite the drought, she'd taken two long showers, sitting on the floor of the stall and letting the steam shroud her until the water heater ran dry and cold water brought her out of her reverie of Will.

And then, one daybreak, all the parts of her body revived. Her body woke her with a dream so vivid that as soon as David got up, she stripped the bed to wash the smell of her off it before he got any ideas. All day she'd been consumed with a fervid need for Will that interfered with her ability to function. At pickup her children pointed out her mismatched shoes. In the kitchen after dinner, David gave her a look but said nothing when she threw a Tupperware container of left-over risotto in the trash and put a cutting board piled with vegetable scraps into the refrigerator. She only noticed what she'd done when David fished the leftovers out of the trash and transferred them to a clean container.

David used to sometimes work at the dining room table

after the children were asleep, but now he always worked from bed. His way of marking territory, maybe. So she'd climbed to the loft, tried to calm her inflamed nerve endings by scrolling through stock photos of Big Sur, but found she only became more agitated. She leaned back in the chair and replayed scenes with Will. His car, the supply closet, Big Sur, the first backseat blow job when he'd clumsily tapped her on the shoulder out of courtesy and she, misunderstanding, released him and looked up at his face and just then he came, lamely, on the waistband of his jeans. The cypress trees, the movie theater, his Topanga Canyon shower, the Madonna Inn.

Rina was touching herself, but she'd never been very good at it, and no place she put her hands brought her closer to unshackling herself from the loop of Will's body in her mind.

So she wrote to him. She deliberated over each word, precise in her need, telling him with total accuracy of her affliction, telling him just how her body flooded with a pent-up tide.

One text, in four parts.

> *I want you to spread me so wide my limbs revolt; want to be kissed till my lips bleed; fucked till I bleed everywhere else; I want a purple*

> *map of your mouth's wanderings over my body; want to open your skin with my teeth under cool sheets; memorize again the foreign shapes of*

> *your body; do things that make you gasp, shiver, smile; taste you; then I want to stay close so my heartbeat can take the rhythm of its*

downward lilt from the cues of your own in the
after. Letters.

She finished her thought and hit send in a single, habitual press of the thumb.

She meant it, of course, meant every syllable, none more than "Letters," none more than the single word that would tell him of her undiminished, consumptive love. But she would not see him. She would not let him spread her wide or bleed her lips. For forty minutes the only relief to her guilt was the fact that Will had not responded.

He had moved on, what she hoped and feared the most. Thinking of him not thinking of her caused a sharp twinge in her solar plexus, but it was also her only wish.

How are you, mi corazón? How are the children?
I love you.

She hated herself when his reply came, his perfect reply, full of grace. His beautiful, brief reply that told her he had not moved on, that he loved her, that everything he'd ever said had been true. It took her another hour to compose her reply.

I should not have texted. Forgive my weakness.
That's life, then: things as they are.

She would not text him again. Slumping down the stairs, she did not think she deserved to sleep, didn't deserve her home and her children and her risotto pot and her silver candlesticks. She did not deserve David's blind eye, or the way her parents hid their scorn. She would become worthy. She would fix herself, learn to control her own needs. In the morning, she would teach herself to masturbate. She fell asleep on the floor of the bathroom, arm between her legs, without washing her face or brushing her teeth.

After drop-off the next morning she didn't take her walk but began to approach the thing scientifically. She double-locked the doors and threw the chain on the front door. She was determined, but also full of shame. Shame at the idea of being caught and a more potent shame that she'd lived thirty-one years without knowing how to meet one of her own most basic needs.

In her whole life, she'd only gotten herself off with errant Jacuzzi jets and the shower hose in her parents' large bath-room. All the times on the phone with Will she'd tried, but had to be content with his contentedness. She and David had no sex toys. Her hands wouldn't work, not *just* her hands any-way, but she wasn't about to mine the produce bin.

She went to the loft and took off her skirt and her under-wear. She laid a hand towel over the seat of the swivel chair and glanced up at the Captain. If anyone would understand, it was him. She'd never looked for porn before, but it wasn't dif-ficult. She could see in the search results that several free sites had been accessed from the computer before. She watched the opening minute of many of the videos on the front page of the first site she found, without touching herself at all. It didn't disgust her, as she anticipated. Many of the titles made her laugh out loud. She figured out how to scroll through cat-egories, but she didn't have any idea where to start and won-dered if this was how David did this and which categories he chose.

She couldn't pick just one—there were so many prepos-terous options—and she opened six different windows, click-ing back and forth between them. She stuck a finger inside herself, but nothing happened. She put three fingers inside and still nothing. She looked around the desk, took a fat ballpoint pen from a cup, and tried that. Nothing. She used the pen on her clit, and it started. She needed something else. There was a smooth, oblong paperweight made of glass that fit nicely in the palm of her hand—a gift from David's sister, brought back from a college trip to Israel. Rina warmed it by putting it inside herself and then pressed it against the outside. She clicked to another screen. She opened her legs wider and pressed herself against the glass over and over again.

When it was done, she cleared the browser history, threw away the pen, wiped herself with the hand towel, got dressed, and washed the paperweight in the bathroom sink. She took the chain off the front door, but then put it back on. She went to her bedroom and got into her bed and pressed the paperweight down inside her underwear. She could do it without the computer.

The next day she skipped her walk again. She accomplished five climaxes before the kids' school day was over. In between she gathered all her sketches and paintings from college, everything she'd made in Will's class, all her half-used art supplies, and threw them into the dumpster in the alley. The unopened art supplies she put in the kids' craft bin. She went online and signed up to be in charge of the hot lunch program at the kids' school, something for which they were perpetually seeking volunteers. But she'd still need something else to do. She called Jewish Family Services and scheduled three shifts in three days. She called her shul and asked what committee was most in need of a new member. She joined the social action committee and scheduled the next meetings into her calendar.

She began researching healthy hot lunch options. It would

not be enough just to manage, she would improve: omega-3s and a rainbow of vegetables and complex, plant-based proteins.

Seth Hartman still hadn't given his wife a *get*. Rina knew what it was to be tied to the community, trussed into bondage by the invisible yoke of peoplehood, by laws, by swinging live chickens over your head, salting the corners of rooms, burying silverware in soil. Rina had been wrong; David had been right. And good for Mrs. Hartman, good for Batya. She shouldn't have to be Mrs. Hartman for one more week, one more day; she had stood at the foot of fire and stared it in the eye. Rina's skin blistered just thinking about it. She was a coward, in the face of the holy she had closed her eyes. But Batya, Batya Hartman was a vessel of liberation. Rina would fill her days with omega-3s and tofu kabobs, yes, but also with the plight of Batya Hartman. Rina would get Batya a *get*; she'd scream into the faces of those who would deny that woman freedom.

After all, that is what binds us as a people, each one to the other, the fact that once we had been slaves. Doesn't each of us, down to the wickedest child, doesn't each now deserve to be free?

Rina walked to pick up Shosh and Yoni. They complained about the walk home, but it ate up an hour of the afternoon. She slogged through the clot of oily, paper-thin jacaranda blossoms. They stuck to the bottoms of her sandals and her footsteps made grisly brown tracks, as though her presence pointed to a crime. On the sidewalk four blocks from her house there was a perfect oval, perhaps the size and shape of a surfboard, on the concrete. Not a single jacaranda blossom was in the oval, but the rest of the sidewalk was blanketed. Rina stopped and looked around, then up at the gnarled branches of the nearest tree, still awash in purple blooms.

Whatever had formed the blank space must have been there only moments ago. She set her purse in a patch of grass and laid down in the blank space, arms crossed over her chest. Eyes closed, she felt handfuls of falling flowers landing lightly on her body. The sidewalk was neither warm nor cold. The air was still, save for the bees buzzing in the mounds of purple. The blossoms were not fragrant. The children took little note but bickered with each other about whose turn it was to stand on a nearby tree stump. She boxed her hands over her ears and heard only static, not even the simmering of her own blood.

She alone would meet the demands of her body. And she would muffle her mind's recurring echo, lobotomize herself.

19.

The moon was high—a hole cut in the sky—the dull, gray nothingness of the universe showing through a dime-size puncture in the atmosphere. It was just after midnight, no one out but the Santa Monica bums, post-shift line cooks toking up behind brick walls, drunk couples across the street waiting in valet lines. The pier was dark, its boardwalk games shuttered, the rides quiet, static.

One especially glazed couple crossed to the Palisades side of the street and walked zigzag down the dirt path. The girl leaned into his leather jacket. He smoked a cigarette, his left hand down her pants. "I'm going to fuck you right here," the guy said, loopy and loud, his straight teeth glinting under a yellow streetlamp.

Rina turned her back to look at the wide pitch of the ocean and couldn't imagine that she—that she and Will—ever made such a spectacle of themselves. Had they?

Even night's chill couldn't cover the beachy stench: the entropy of washed-up seaweed, the rot of half-eaten salads and meat scraps filling trash bags behind the trendy eateries, the attendant rats, heavily pissed-on sidewalks, and the pungent eucalyptus sticking to her shirt, her hair.

The ground was springy, and she climbed over the low fence in the dark, held onto the center stalk of a century plant on the other side to steady herself. The lights were off in the homes below, in the homes of all the uber-rich who shelled out for ugly beachfront properties even though the traffic on the Pacific Coast Highway overpowered the sound of those expensive waves.

She thought of their cars shielded from the salt air in subterranean garages, of them sleeping miserably, next to spouses they regretted, under linens made of actual linen, under the meek whirr of ceiling fans.

She knew where the mountains were even if she couldn't see them: they were solid, unmovable, menacing, and ripe for mudslide season. She backed up, as if the mountains might charge her, and the century plant crumbled in her hand. It was dead, scorched by the drought, and she slid closer to the edge.

The cliff was just so jumpable. She could see herself there, a stain on PCH, guts running red out of her mouth like roadkill, bloated and broken and stuck to the asphalt like an upturned possum.

But she was a coward, as she'd told Anshel. If she were a jumper she would already be down there.

A wind picked up—a fat, tempest wind—and it bolstered her against a fall, whipped her hair into her face, and held her against the railing, pinned and limp, laundry hanging on the night.

The horizon was almost indistinguishable in the dark, but for the milky glow where the sea disappeared over the shoulder of the earth.

She let the wind blow her back against the fence, climbed over, and, arms wrapped around herself for warmth, started the walk to her car knowing she would never be happy again, not really.

20.

SEPTEMBER 2013

R ina stood in the back of the shul, her hair under a gray
scarf, her daughter by her side, her husband and son
on the other side of the mechitzah. It was early afternoon on Yom Kippur and the women around her were beginning to complain of hunger, beginning to thin out as they
went home to make preparations for the breaking of the fast.
It was not especially warm in the room, but Rina's cardigan
was heavy with sweat. She nudged her daughter.

"Walk home with Chana later," she said. "Tell Abba I'm
not feeling well and I went home."

Shosh nodded and leaned in to kiss her mother. Rina
walked out of the back of the shul and into the light of the
wide boulevard and turned west, away from home. She hadn't
planned it. It was a holiday, so she didn't have any money on
her to take a taxi or a bus. She had no idea how far in miles it
was to the community college, but she knew her shoes weren't
sensible enough to get her there in comfort. She walked west
and west, walked until she was sure her daughter would be
on her way to Chana's house to help set up. For the first time
in eight years, thank god, David and Rina were not hosting
break-fast.

On the outskirts of Santa Monica, she threw her cardigan into a trash bin at a bus stop.

It was past five when she arrived at the campus. A few students walked to the garages in small groups; the campus was quiet on a Saturday evening. Aware, suddenly, of how she must look, she removed the scarf from her head and pulled her hair out of its bun. Everything about her surely looked undone, everything but her nails. She'd had a manicure between Rosh Hashana and Yom Kippur; she'd picked a shimmering golden yellow, the color of pineapple flesh. She looked at her nails and they shone in the late-afternoon sun, her fingers swollen and ruddy from the walk, the heat. She'd had a male manicurist, the brother of the owner. Most of the frum women wouldn't sit with him and usually she tried to avoid him, too, but what did it matter anymore? When he'd lifted her right hand out of the water bowl and held it firm, she was overcome by how long it had been since she'd had physical touch and grasped his hand in hers, only for a moment. He'd been surprised, she had seen his eyes widen, but he dropped his head to focus on his work and brushed his thumb lightly along the top of her hand until she also dropped her head so that her tears could splash silently onto the neckline of her shirt.

She drew near to the classroom where Will taught. Her pulse was so rapid that she feared fainting.

Her ears rang as she came close enough to see the instructor.

The gray-haired woman at the front of the class didn't notice Rina, who stared in at the class through a window, from behind the bushes. Rina's first thought was that Will no longer used this classroom, but she could see his sample paintings clipped to the board behind the woman. Rina collapsed her forehead against the glass window.

It was Yom Kippur. Shabbos, too.

She hadn't wanted to believe that Will had done all he said he would do, hadn't wanted to believe he'd become a Jew. She sold herself the lie so thoroughly that she hadn't even considered, on any part of her unplanned trek across town, that he wouldn't be teaching class this day. Maybe he was in shul somewhere, swaying and rocking, sitting and standing, absolving himself of his own sins. And her standing in front of the window like an idiot. Then again, maybe he just had a different schedule.

There was a hand on her shoulder and Rina turned. The gray-haired professor cocked her head toward Rina and was kind enough not to say anything.

"I'm fine," Rina said to the woman, using the scarf to wipe her face. "I was just . . ."

"You don't need anything?" the woman asked gently.

Had she heard stories about this professor? Was it one of the colleagues Will talked about? Would this woman remember the interaction? Tell Will she'd seen a strange woman?

"Sorry," Rina said.

She walked out of the quad. She passed a bench every thirty feet but if she sat down pain would overtake her feet and she would not be able to get back up. She headed east and began to think of a lie to tell her husband when she arrived at the party late and a mess. There were two hours left until the breaking of the fast at least, but it would take her longer than that to get back. It had taken almost three hours to get to the college.

No lie was needed on her return. Not even an "I've been here the whole time."

David was in Chana's backyard, deep in conversation with Aliza and her fiancé from the Valley. As always. Yoni was asleep on a couch. Chana was in the kitchen with her mother-in-law, putting away platters. Shosh played in the backyard with the other children, the girls and boys mostly self-divided, even at so young an age. Rina drank glass after glass of orange juice, alone on a couch.

Four days later, the night Sukkot began, and with it an endless parade of guests and guesting and meals, Rina returned to the college, this time in her car.

"I'm not coming to dinner at the Melameds' tonight," she informed David before she left. "I already told Leeba I'm not feeling well." He took no note of her. She left, knowing that the drive back home—after sunset—would mean breaking chag for the second time in her life. The first two nights of the holiday were considered like Shabbos, no work, no cars, no cooking, no turning on lights.

Will was at the front of the classroom; if he was Jewish, he wasn't so religious that he took off work for Sukkot. Somehow that relieved a measure of her guilt. Like Rina, he looked thinner, but was otherwise the same. The same molten bronze eyes, the same paint-stained fingers. She obscured herself in the shadows. He was teaching an oil class and he'd given the water assignment. Most of the students were painting half-empty glasses of water at their easels. On the board behind Will was a black-and-white painting she recognized as a close-up of the secret spring at the schoolyard on Barrington, the roots of the giant cypress visible just behind the pool. And next to that, unrelated to the assignment, hung her green eye portrait. He'd never returned her portfolio to her, and she'd never asked for it back. She could see now how bitter she'd been when she painted it a year ago, how heartsick. When she'd dabbed in the imperfect foliage of her iris, she hadn't meant to bare her soul. He'd seen it, though. He'd seen it, and he'd seen her, and she had been known.

The middle of her body became heavy, as if her heart was recalling all the blood from her veins, as if she were one of those little pink flowers growing along the bluffs at Big Sur. Homogenous and unchanging on the surface maybe, but everything she had and had not done converged, heavy and pigmented, in her most broken places. Concentrated at the center. She'd been known, been fully known, and that weight at the center of her soul held the memory of having been known, of creating that divine knowingness, and she would keep it there like a secret, and it would have to be enough.

The last time they'd been together—that miserable Shabbos eve of their undoing—she'd sat across from him in the candlelight and taught him one final Hebrew word. *Lehakir.* Infinitive. From the verb "to realize."

Will began to move around the classroom, stopping at each easel to make corrections. Rina stood in the unlit quad without ambition or expectation, stood silent in that mysterious semicolon that briefly punctuated the endless list that was her life. She watched and watched.

Acknowledgments

This story is indebted to its earliest readers, including Alan Stewart Carl, Nikki Gordon, the indomitable Sarah Long, Talia Green, Evan Blackford, Jamey Davidsmeyer, Dr. Mark Benor, Rabbi Sharon Brous, Rabbi David Kasher, Bonnie Sedlmayr-Emerson, Laurie Sedlmayr, Joelle Emerson, and, of course, my beloved husband, Patrick. Thanks to the rest of my dear community of writers, especially Andrew Killmeier, Eric Steineger, the original Mentees-sans-Mentors, and all the Cobalts and other colors. Aimee Bender, Lisa See, and Cheryl Strayed helped shepherd me in this journey and I am grateful. In particular, the linguistic and cultural input from Dr. Curtis Acosta, Dr. Sarah Benor, and Chris Goldsmith had an invaluable impact on the manuscript. The book might not exist if not for Jeremy Mittman. The incredible team at Counterpoint literally made this book what it is: my gratitude to Laura Berry, Olenka Burgess, Nicole Caputo, Wah-Ming Chang, tracy danes, Rachel Fershleiser, Megan Fishmann, Brianna Lopez, Elana Rosenthal, Yukiko Tominaga, Kira Weiner, and Farjana Yasmin. It would not be on shelves if not for my extraordinary agents Carolyn Forde and Amanda Orozco at Transatlantic Agency, Dan Smetanka's vision and confidence, and the brilliant mind and careful hand of my editor Dan López.

My life is rich with teachers and mentors, and I would

never have written a book without the guidance of Lisa McCorkle, Mark Olbin, Chris Goldsmith, Brian Koppy, David Miller, the late Jack Langguth, the late Norman Corwin, Rob Roberge, Leonard Chang, Alistair McCartney, Steve Heller, Tod Goldberg, Rabbi Sharon Brous, Rabbi Ronit Tsadok, Rabbi Adam Greenwald, Melissa Balaban, David Boyle, and the tzaddik Curtis Acosta. Equally, I've learned from my students, most especially Elijah, Zach, Abigail, and Jordyn.

If Judy Blume didn't write her books, I wouldn't have written mine. If I didn't have the brilliance of Bob Dylan and Leonard Cohen ringing in my headphones, I wouldn't have gotten past page two. Without the generous people of Cambria, California, and the gorgeous ecosystem they tend so carefully, this book wouldn't be: I wrote and edited the bulk of it in three-day stretches in the most beautiful hamlet on California's coast, my favorite place on earth.

Gratitude to the libraries and librarians of the world, as well as the bookstores that helped form me: Bookmans, Antigone Books, and Stacks Book Club (Tucson), the bygone Haunted Bookshop at Tohono Chul (also Tucson), Magic City Books (Tulsa), the Elliot Bay Book Company (Seattle), the poetry room at City Lights (San Francisco), Politics and Prose (Washington, D.C.), and my favorite bookstores in Los Angeles: The Last Bookstore (where I was married), Children's Book World, Chevalier's, Vroman's, Skylight Books, Book Soup, and Sideshow Books.

More than anything, I am indebted to my family for the time they gifted me to write this book and the time they took away from its writing for the pursuits of family life: loving, eating, drinking, reading, arguing, playing, traveling, protesting, snuggling, and just being together at the end of a day. My parents, Bonnie and Randy, are my most formative mentors, and my siblings, Jordan and Joelle, were among my earliest teachers. My parents fostered a home where love of reading, the arts, and humanity were trumped only by love of one another, and I strive to create the same incubator for my children. Raising Noam, Phoenix, and Akiva is the truest work I'll ever do, and they have been my most benevolent and impactful teachers. The world is full of myriad kinds of families and I'm grateful to Uri, the co-parent of my two oldest children, for his collaboration.

The way my husband Patrick lives his life—moored in the values of his loving parents and siblings—inspires me to be diligent, generous, gentle, thoughtful, and, above all, willing to learn and evolve in the face of evidence and under the influence of empathy. I hope I become more like him each day. Certainly this book wouldn't exist if not for our love of each other, a love that takes my breath away every day. He also worked hard for this.

JESSICA ELISHEVA EMERSON is obsessed with cooking beans, growing food, eating pie, sleeping in on Shabbat, and working toward a better world. A Tucson native, Jessica spent twenty-two years in Los Angeles before returning to the Sonoran Desert, where she lives with her husband and children. Her stories and poems have been published in numerous journals, and she's a produced playwright. Find out more at elishevaemerson.com.